I've got you ♡

ALSO BY BECCA SEYMOUR

Zone Defense

No Take Backs | No More Secrets | No Wrong Moves

Fast Break

Rules, Schmules! | Facts, Smacts!

True–Blue

Let Me Show You | I've Got You | Becoming Us | Thinking It Over| Always For You | It's Not You | Our First & Last

Outback Boys

Stumble | Bounce | Wobble

Stand–Alone Contemporary

Not Used To Cute | High Alert | Realigned | Amalgamated

Urban Fantasy Romance

Thicker Than Water

For information, contact the author:
authorbeccaseymour@gmail.com

EDITING: HOT TREE EDITING

COVER DESIGNER: BOOKSMITH DESIGN

PUBLISHER: RAINBOW TREE PUBLISHING

E-BOOK ISBN: 978-1-925853-65-0

PAPERBACK ISBN: 978-1-925853-66-7

To Donna, my wifey,
(I don't care if Kevin disagrees—I'll fight him for you)
Your shit-talk makes me smile... sadistically. You're
totally a bad influence.

CHAPTER ONE

DAVIS

I CLOSED THE DOOR GENTLY BEHIND ME, HOPING LIKE hell it wouldn't make a loud noise and wake Libby. She was cutting two teeth, which made us both miserable. We'd continue to ride it out together, though. Her with lots of gum-numbing ointment and me with brain-numbing beer when she was sleeping peacefully.

A whoosh of breath hissed out of me when the door closed quietly. Baby monitor in hand, I turned and headed toward downstairs where the party was happening. Tanner, my best friend, and his boyfriend, Carter, were having a housewarming of sorts. I glanced around the space when I hit the foyer. Tanner had done a good job. Not that I was surprised; he was a talented bastard, so it was kinda kickass to see his craftsmanship hadn't gone to waste here in the hicksville town of Kirkby that we'd only called home for about a year or so.

"She go down okay?" Tanner asked, handing me a bottle of beer as I made my way into the kitchen.

I nodded and took the beer gratefully. "Thanks. Yeah, no problem at all." I took a swig and placed the baby monitor on the charger on the large sideboard.

During the final stages of refurbs, Carter, whose home it was prior to Tanner and he getting together and Tanner moving in, had set up one of the spare rooms as Libby's room. I'd been blown away by the gesture when Tanner had told me. While Tanner and I had known each other forever, he hadn't been with Carter for all that long. So for Carter to create a space for my baby girl in his home told me with absolute certainty, Tanner had got a good one.

What it also meant was Tanner and Carter supported me and my single-parenting gig even more by having Libby overnight on occasion. They'd had her a couple of nights already, my only nights without my daughter since she was born.

And what had I done on both nights? The first in almost a year with zero responsibility? Partied? Picked up? Neither. I'd had a few drinks without having to wait for Libby to fall asleep first, watched

Netflix, and stared at Libby's empty room a few times.

"What are your plans tomorrow?" Tanner stood next to me, both of us glancing around the room filled with a few faces I recognized from my coffee shop, while some were clearly out-of-towners, no doubt Carter's friends, since I was pretty much all Tanner had beyond a few other tradesmen in the area he'd got to know. There were also some of Carter's work colleagues, a bunch of vets, nurses, and such.

I shrugged. "Not much. Katie and Phil are working the morning shift, and Sandy and Craig are taking over so I have the day off." I took a pull of my beer before continuing. "If it stays sunny, I'll probably take Libby to the park and duck pond." I glanced at Carter heading our way, a bright smile on his face and his gaze intent on Tanner. "How about you?"

Tanner's shrug brushed against my arm lightly. "Tidy up, I suppose."

I snorted just as Carter reached us. Tanner's arm immediately went around his waist.

I glanced at Tanner and realized he was looking at me. "What?"

"What's the snort for?"

With a roll of my eyes, I took a large mouthful of beer. After swallowing the cool liquid, I said, "Just wondering when the fuck we got old and Sundays were filled with domestic shit."

"Who are you calling old, fucker?"

Carter laughed. "Well, the two of you are reaching your prime. *Ouch.*" Carter reached behind himself and rubbed his ass.

I chuckled. "See, your younger studmuffin knows it."

Tanner shook his head. "Studmuffin? For real? Who even uses that term anymore? Hell, did anyone ever?" He glanced over at said studmuffin, and his gaze softened before he turned back to me. "And I think you'll find it's you who's become the king of domestic duties since having that angel of yours. But hey, you know, if you want to go partying and spend the next day nursing a hangover, we can definitely have Libby for you."

Damn, he was right. That made me feel ancient, and I was so far from that shit it wasn't funny.

Carter nodded. "Absolutely, you know we love having Libby over. Though—" He paused and looked me up and down, his brows pulling together. *The hell?* "—I'm not sure you could handle it anymore."

I threw a look his way, not at all impressed with

his truths. Carter smiled and blinked innocently at me. So many blinks so damn close together was not natural, though I supposed he looked kinda cute doing it. *Asswipe.*

"For shit's sake, I'm only thirty-five."

Along with a shrug, Carter's smile turned into a grin. "So in that case, what are you waiting for? Live a little. You know, go and see if you can get a life beyond that sweet girl of yours."

"I've got a life," I grumbled. And I did, sort of. Admittedly it involved me juggling owning and running my business, keeping house, and most importantly being the best dad possible. That shit right there took time. Considering there was barely time to shit, sleep, or even jerk off, how in the hell could I handle more than I already had?

"I know you do." Carter reached out and placed his hand on my forearm, squeezing lightly. "You have a pretty amazing life, but you know—"

"You need to get laid."

"Tanner," Carter admonished at the same time that I groaned. "I was trying to be subtle. You know, go for tact, ease in gently?"

Tanner grinned, and I rolled my eyes at the pair of them. "Tact was never this dick's forte; you'll soon get used to it, Carter. And I'm fine." I was aiming for neutral, reassured, perhaps even as though I was in control. But fuck me, I did really need to get laid.

In all seriousness, it had been well before Libby's birth since the last time I'd got any. I had a serious case of blue balls and a constantly overworked hand.

When I'd discovered Libby's mom was pregnant, we hadn't been together. My beautiful baby girl was actually the product of a hot one-night stand. Mags had tracked me down when she'd been five months pregnant, and I'd shifted my life to Kirkby, where she'd lived at the time, to support her at the end of her pregnancy before taking sole custody of Libby.

"You know," Carter continued, "I could try to set you up."

I contemplated it for all of three seconds. A quick fuck was all that was on the cards for me, so being fixed up with someone who Carter knew didn't sit well. It screamed awkward. "Thanks, but I'll pass."

He raised his brow and made to speak, no doubt to argue his case. I stopped him with a slight flick of my raised hand. "Listen, Carter, I know you mean well, but honestly, I'm good."

From his dipped brows and the twist of his lips, I didn't think he bought it. But tough. Having my best friend happy with Carter was awesome, but it didn't mean I needed that or was chasing it.

Tanner, no doubt hearing the finality of my tone, intervened. "Hey, baby, you wanna help me a minute?"

With a smile, Carter angled toward Tanner. "Lead the way, handsome."

I threw Tanner a relieved smile. "I'm just gonna slip outside for a few. Will you listen out for Libby?"

Tanner nodded as he handed me an extra beer. "Yep, no worries." I took it, grateful, and headed outside.

As soon as I pulled the door closed behind me, the conversation and background music dulled. After a few steps away, heading further into the darkness toward the back of the yard, I was greeted by Rex. "Hey, boy." I rubbed one of his ears, holding the necks of my two beers with my other hand. Rex groaned and almost pushed me on my ass when he leaned against me. I chuckled. Rex was a Rhodesian Ridgeback and was pretty much pony size. He was also a big softie, though fiercely protective, especially of Libby. I bent and placed a kiss on his huge head. Tanner hadn't had him all that long, but there was no doubt Rex had found his home with his new family.

"Come on." I took more steps into the darkness, heading toward the faint outline of the patio.

It was pretty sad, I supposed, if I allowed myself to think about it too hard. At thirty-five, I was a single dad, used to spending my downtime with Libby or more usually myself, yet there I was, a rare night with actual adults beyond Carter and Tanner, a night to be social, and I was outside with the dog seeking solitude.

I snorted, the noise loud in the still night, as I sat, placing the unopened beer to my side before taking a pull of my already open bottle.

Rex harrumphed when he sat beside me, his head dropping heavily in my lap. I absently stroked his fur, wanting to focus on nothing but the dark starry night and the peace it provided.

Anything else beyond the here and now seemed too unattainable. I didn't even know if that was even the right word, but what I was sure about was my sleeping daughter, Rex's head in my lap, and the beer flowing down my throat as I took another drink. I didn't even dare to wish on any damn star.

CHAPTER TWO

SCOTT

I couldn't wait to get the hell out of there. From the get-go, I was uncomfortable… on edge… sure everyone in the room knew what a dick I was. Not only that, but there were too many people, and not enough space, enough air. I knew enough, could read into my surroundings enough—and the people filling the space—to know that there were many men like me, but not. They laughed, joked, smiled, patted the happy hosts on the shoulders and congratulated them on their newly renovated home. More than that, they were out in the open, whereas I just wanted to scurry back into the dark.

I eyed the kitchen door and edged toward it. Just four more steps and I'd reach freedom. There was nothing happy about living locked away, pretending to be something, someone I wasn't, but I'd used my brave card when I'd uttered those two words aloud for the first time. Not only to myself but to Carter, the guy I'd tried to screw over, who was now trying his hardest to be my friend.

I'm gay.

It had been a hell of a surprise to the both of us when the words had tumbled out of my mouth. I'd nearly passed out as nausea had swept through me, while Carter had looked like a startled rabbit. His face would have been comical if I hadn't been trying not to shit myself at the time.

I was thirty-three years old and still had no clue who I was.

Just two steps and I'd be able to breathe again.

One.

I clutched the handle and yanked the door open. Fresh air greeted me. I stepped into the darkness and pulled the door quietly closed behind me, then looked around the fenced backyard, only seeing the side panels and nothing beyond the darkness. My gaze settled on a couple of chairs. While it wasn't complete escape, it gave me time to catch my breath and get my head straight.

Easing into the wooden chair, I leaned back, stretching out my neck and glancing up at the star-filled sky. With no lights on in the yard and just the faint glow filtering out from the busy kitchen, I was able to focus on the tiny specks overhead. I released a heavy exhale, pulling the calmness of the outside into me. I shouldn't have come. Damn, I should have been at least two thousand miles away by now, away from this tiny town that threatened to split apart my whole world.

Claws on the wooden deck, a not-so-soft grunt and sigh, and I glanced to my right to see Carter and Tanner's monster dog, Rex, ambling over to me. The first couple of times I'd met Rex at the veterinary clinic, it was no surprise to Carter or me that the Ridgeback had taken an instant dislike to me. Hell, I didn't even like myself most of the time. But as he walked toward me, I no longer tensed in fear. This was the third visit I'd made to Carter's, and it seemed Rex had had a change of heart.

He huffed as he sat next to me, his large head immediately landing on my thighs. My first real smile of the night spread across my lips, and I reached out both hands and rubbed behind Rex's ears. "Hey there, mutt." I rubbed a bit harder, and he moaned happily. I snorted. "You like that, huh?" Rex tilted his head and leaned his right ear into my palm. "You know, bud, I think you've got the right idea."

He blew heavily out of his snout, and I laughed, the sound filling the quiet space. "Life's a hell of a lot easier if you've got no balls at all to lead you around and confuse the heck out of you."

A snort-laugh from out of the darkness had me tensing. I squinted, looking toward the end of the yard. After a moment, my eyes adjusted and I saw a man looming, his figure moving closer until he stepped into the faint light.

Damn. So much for alone.

Rex's head flipped to the side to look at the guy coming toward me. He grunted again and then thumped his head back down onto my thighs before nudging my hand for me to continue.

I started to rub, not as invested, nor as relaxed. With my jaw locked, I risked a glance at the guy. Light spilled onto the stranger's face, highlighting his strong jawline. While I couldn't see the color of his eyes, I did see the creases surrounding them. It immediately made him seem approachable and friendly. As he moved closer, a small smile lifted his mouth. My gaze landed on the slight curve of his lips before traveling back to his eyes. They were brown, but in the dull light, I couldn't tell the exact shade or depth.

Friendly, he most definitely was, if his smile and

the "Hey" he offered me were anything to go by. But he also looked tired as hell.

I cleared my throat, suddenly aware I'd stayed quiet for a few seconds too long. "Hey." My voice was gravelly and sounded unnaturally deep.

The guy paused in front of me, his hands dipping into his jeans pockets. He was quiet for a beat, seeming to contemplate what to say.

"You know Rex then?"

I nodded and then took a glance at the large head resting on my lap. With a small nod, I smiled. "Yeah. He finally likes me, so I'm taking it as a win that we're friends."

The brown-eyed man's head tilted slightly, his gaze scanning my face a moment before his eyes returned to mine. "So you're a friend of Carter's?"

A humorless snort burst free, not enough to startle Rex, but enough for the guy to raise his brows. I cleared my throat again, not especially liking the fact that it seemed to be closing up and becoming uncomfortably dry in front of this guy. "Well, sort of. We used to work together."

"Not anymore?"

I bit back the bitter retort dancing on my tongue, tempted to ask if that wasn't what "used to" explicitly meant. There was no need for me to be so defensive or any bigger of an asshole than I already had a reputation for being.

"Nope. Just trying to figure out my next move." I clamped my mouth shut, wondering why I'd shared so much. He sat on the lounger beside me, stopping my analysis. "Please, take a seat." Damn, I really needed to learn to keep my mouth shut and stop being a dickhead. "Sorry." I threw him a small grimace, noticing both of his perfectly arched brows were lifted, his attention solely on me. There was also a small smile on his lips. I was positive I saw it twitch.

"Hey, I can leave."

Though, he stayed put, making no indication he planned on moving. He didn't even shrug or twitch as he spoke.

While solitude had been what I'd craved, I was smart enough to recognize that just maybe not being alone was a good thing. Being alone, I was discovering, was not helpful at all. All it did was give me too much time with my thoughts. And that had a habit of screwing with my head. While I'd sought the quiet, especially since my blowout with Carter a while back, I recognized how dangerous isolation could be. Loneliness was a slippery slope.

I finally found my voice. "No need. I was just—"

His eyes widened, as though encouraging me to continue.

"—needing the quiet. It was all a bit much in there. But—" I released a heavy breath. "—perhaps it's better to have some company, a conversation, you know?"

Damn. I froze. Shit. Did he think I was flirting with him? Coming on to him? Asking him specifically for "company" in a whole different sense from plain conversation? Shit, was I? Was he gay? Fuck me dead—

"Shit, breathe."

His deep voice startled me, enough that my eyes shot to his. He was sitting close to me, concern in his eyes. His hands clamped onto my forearms.

"Breathe in." He bobbed his head with a silent beat. "And out."

With my eyes now on his mouth, I did as directed. I got my lungs to work again.

CHAPTER THREE

DAVIS

I HAD NO IDEA WHAT THE HELL HAD JUST HAPPENED, but I was sure the man beside me had been about to pass out. He'd turned white and seemed on the cusp of hyperventilating.

Still gripping his arms, I shook off the wayward thought of how strong they felt under my palms, instead concentrating on helping him breathe. Slowly, his color returned, yet I held on tightly, certain my touch was keeping him grounded.

His stare, which had been pointedly fixed on my mouth as I breathed with him, dropped down. Rex was no longer leaning on him, having shifted when I'd first reached out to him. I wasn't sure if his eyes remained open, but I felt his arms move, turn out slightly as his hands gripped my forearms so we were holding on to each other. I squeezed gently, not knowing what he needed, but hoping the gesture would continue to help him calm.

When I'd headed out this evening, this wasn't quite the position I'd expected to be in. Okay, hanging on to another man, or possibly a woman, wouldn't have been a shitty way to end the evening, but being someone's lifeline… definitely not my expectation.

His breaths started to even out, and his fingers flexed on my skin. I was quite happy to stay this way a while longer. Touching firm muscles, having his appealing scent wrap around me, was surprisingly familiar, and hell, kinda nice, despite the weird situation and the poor guy's meltdown.

Still holding on, I dipped my head a little, leaning closer. "You good?" I kept my voice low, quiet, not wanting to break the moment or startle him.

A slight, jerky nod was my answer.

"Okay. There's no rush." And there really wasn't. There was something about him, this random guy who was a sorta friend to Carter, that had made it easy to reach out and comfort him. He was attractive, sure, with short, dark brown hair that was a little messy, possibly from running his fingers through it one too many times, plus he had the prettiest eyes I'd ever seen on a man or woman. But there was something deeper there too. He seemed lost.

He'd mentioned being alone, and damn if I hadn't felt the sadness roll of him in waves. With the manic life I had, not only with my daughter but with my coffee shop, life was complicated enough. The last thing I needed was a lost soul complicating my shit even more. But still, I'd reached out to him and liked the feel of our connection.

That seemed all levels of screwed up and danger-ous. But *still*, I held on.

Smoothing my right thumb over his left arm, I rubbed soft circles on his skin. Goose bumps sprung up immediately, creating a new path for my thumb. I had no intention of releasing him yet. He took a deep breath before moving his head from side to side, as if stretching his neck. A couple of cracks followed. I considered releasing one arm to place on the back of his neck but thought better of it. The gesture seemed just a little too forward, too familiar.

"Better?" I dared to ask.

This time, he lifted his head, his eyes connecting with mine instantly. With my head still lowered, our faces were close, too close for strangers, but considering his near meltdown, it seemed we were beyond that level of formality.

"Yeah, thanks."

His face was now in line with mine, giving me the opportunity to search his features. His color seemed to have returned, which was tricky to tell in the poor light, but he no longer looked like a ghost. His eyes were wide though, almost frozen. Not quite sure if he was terrified, confused, or hell, for all I knew this could have been his usual expression, I smiled, trying to reassure him.

"You had me scar—"

He crushed his mouth to mine. While his eyes were now closed, mine were wide open as I oomphed in surprise. His kiss was rough, desperate, almost pleading as his lips worked mine, encouraging me to react. Warm lips and wet tongue, both tasting of beer and mint, continued their invasion. This guy was starving for contact, and damn if I didn't begin to reciprocate. I closed my eyes, our hands still gripping each other, and opened for him.

I allowed him to control the kiss for a few beats until I took over, needing to calm the pace and ease the desperation that clawed so close to the surface. Our lips came together with ease, moving together as though we'd practiced a hundred times. Darting my tongue out for a quick taste, I touched his and stroked gently, dragging a groan from the both of us. While we were no longer frantic, there was still urgency in our clash of lips and tongue, a fervor there I wasn't sure I'd ever experienced before.

Needing more, I loosened my left hand and reached for his face. The moment my fingers touched his cheek, he froze. Barely a second slipped by before he yanked himself back, almost falling off the chair. I reached out to him, but he was up and to the door without a backward glance.

Staring wide-eyed at the empty space before me, I could only blink as he bolted into the kitchen, and I imagined, straight out of the house.

What the hell just happened? I was still sitting in the same spot fifteen minutes later when Tanner found me. The kiss, his escape, his goddamn panic…. It all played through my head on a loop. The worst of it all: I still didn't know the guy's name.

"Hey," Tanner called.

I made to stand, asking, "Libby?"

"No." He shook his head. "She's fast asleep, not a peep."

I nodded my thanks and eased back onto the lounger.

Rex ambling over to Tanner had me smiling. He

was such a great, albeit huge dog. I'd been enjoying my quiet time with him earlier, but he'd abandoned me so he could get fussed over by the mystery guy—who I could still taste on my lips.

"Whatcha doing?" Tanner sat next to me, and I shrugged noncommittally.

"Just having a beer and some quiet time."

"Right." His tone held humor, enough to drag my attention to his amused face. He grinned over at me.

"What?" I lifted my beer.

"Don't what me. I saw you out here playing kissy with Dr. Dickwad."

Thankfully I'd not taken a drink from the beer bottle I held to my mouth. "What the fuck? Dr. Dickwad?" I asked in confusion. "And you were what, spying on me?"

He simply shrugged, not looking at all ashamed. Of course, I had no doubt I was completely overexaggerating and that his stealth-like skills were not being put to use on me, but still.

He remained silent, wearing that simple, annoying smirk of his that he got sometimes. Tanner and I had been friends forever, so I knew pretty much every look, smirk, and gesture. And at the moment, while he wanted to tease and laugh, there was something else lurking in his eyes.

"What?" I sighed the question this time, rather than spitting it out in frustration. Then it hit me. Dr. Dickwad. *Hell no.* I groaned, my shoulders dipping in defeat. "That was the closeted vet who did a number on Carter." It wasn't a question. "Doing a number" was the polite way of saying the asshole gave Carter hell and made his life a misery. He almost managed to drive him out of the practice before he came out —to Carter, of all people.

None of us had seen it coming, especially not Scott—that was the guy's name—from the looks of it.

"Oh shit."

"Uh-huh," Tanner added unhelpfully.

"Shit, do you think I was his first kiss with another man?" Out of all the things playing out in my head—remembering the brutal, sexy kiss, the smoothness of his cheekbones, the desperation in his eyes, let alone getting started on the crap he'd pulled with Carter—it surprised Tanner as much as me that I asked that question first.

"For real?"

"He was good, a natural," I said, trying to be as casual as possible.

"No."

"No?"

"Fuck no."

"What, are you the cockblock police, the closet patrol, out there to protect virgin asses from going public?" I quirked my brow, though I knew he wasn't fooled. The reality was I was affected. The short time with Scott had left its mark, and while I knew and had previously admitted to myself that was not a good thing, my interest was piqued. Knowing he was Dr. Dickwad should have changed all that for me. But it didn't.

Shaking his head in exasperation, Tanner swiped his hand through his hair. "That guy has issues to rival... fuck... whatever has big issues."

"Miley Cyrus?" I offered helpfully.

He tilted his head at me and rolled his eyes. "One, you're showing your damn age. Two, the last thing you need is to get entangled with his bullshit. And there's no way he's good enough to be anywhere near Libby."

I smiled at Tanner and the mention of my daughter. While I was the only blood relative in Libby's life, Tanner was her uncle in every way that mattered, and Carter too, now. His fierceness to protect was sappy sweet, and I'd call him out for it another time. Instead, I stood and patted him on the back. "Come on. It's all fine. You saw how quickly he hightailed it out of here. While the mini-make-out session was kinda nice"—lie, it was so goddamn hot that I would store it away for spank bank material—"it's not going to happen again. I know this town is small, but hell, I've never laid eyes on the dude before tonight"—and I would have remembered—"so I doubt we'll even cross paths again."

Tanner looked up at me. He appeared as uncertain as I was sure I sounded, but he let me have it and kept his mouth shut. That was until we got back in the house. "Carter, holy shit, you'll never guess who…."

CHAPTER FOUR

SCOTT

IT HAD BEEN THREE DAYS SINCE I'D LEFT MY HOUSE. I was too terrified to step outside. My fear was irrational, but it was steeped in such visceral anxiety and paranoia that I couldn't be anything but terrified. Rationally, I knew that even if anyone had seen me kiss another guy, it would have only been someone at Carter's house, who also was an openly gay man living with his boyfriend. And while there were women and straight couples at the party, there were also other gay men. It was unlikely anyone would take offense to seeing two men kissing, but still, fear was not always rational.

I was living just a few doors down from Carter's place, still staying at my godfather's while he was off exploring the world in his early retirement. I'd taken to hiding out since the major bullshit I'd caused Carter a couple or so months earlier. I'd quit the practice—well, as much as I could. My godfather, Denver, had officially rejected my resignation—it was his practice—so the position was mine if I still wanted it. I supposed I should have headed back east, back to my hometown, but after finally admitting to myself and out loud that I was gay, there was a pull to stay.

If I headed back, without a doubt I would have made up shit about why things hadn't worked out and gone back to living the same lie I had been since I was fourteen and realized that I'd wanted to kiss Mason, my sister's then-boyfriend. The thought of revisiting that life pushed me to not jump in my car.

But every day I had to ask myself what my plan was. The truth was, beyond getting up and feeding and watering myself, I had none. Carter, for all his interference and bizarre niceness, had both forgiven me and taken pity on me. That was still a head fuck. I still expected Tanner to kick my ass at any point. I was confident he was waiting for me to say one wrong thing, give one shitty look, and he'd be all over me and beat my sorry self.

Carter, though, was trying his hardest to take me

under his wing and get me to return to the veterinary clinic. I couldn't face it.

I'd just switched off the shower when I heard the doorbell ring. With a deep sigh, I took my time drying off, hoping Carter would leave. There was no one else it could be. Yanking on my clothes, I closed my eyes and waited for the bell to go again. It did. Carter was not a guy to give up easily. It made him painfully endearing. I wanted to hate the guy. Hell, I had for so long. He was everything I craved to be but was too terrified to become. When I looked at him, it was like a gut-wrenching taunt dangling in front of me, a version of what my life could have been. But despite his nagging and his interference, I liked the man. And who was I kidding? He was the only sorta friend I had. I would be a fool to push that away.

Once down the staircase, I pulled the door open just as Carter's finger pressed once more on the button. He jerked his head in my direction and smiled.

"Hey, stranger," he greeted.

"Hey." I backed away from the door and headed to the kitchen, leaving him to let himself in. "Coffee?" Despite my asshole ways, I could be civil when I wanted to be.

"Sounds good." He perched on a stool at the

kitchen counter. "I haven't seen much movement in the last couple of days."

"Stalker much," I grumbled.

"Your car hasn't even moved," he continued, completely ignoring me. "What's up?"

I placed a pod of the coffee he liked in the machine, then switched it on. "Nothing." I kept my back to him, my focus on the coffee machine.

"So nothing to do with Davis."

I froze, understanding what he was referring to. *Davis.* That was who the guy was? Shit, Tanner's best friend. *Just kill me now.* I kept silent, not trusting my voice.

"You know it's okay, right?"

His coffee finished, I picked up his mug and placed it in front of him. "It is? How'd you figure?" I backed away and leaned against the counter to face him. A ball of something I was all too familiar with rolled in my stomach. Dread. Despair. I pointedly ignored the sweat coating the palms of my hands as I gripped the edge of the counter.

Carter tilted his head as if studying me. I had no idea what he saw, but I could read pity pretty damn easily. My gut tightened at the thought. I didn't need anyone's pity. I was Scott fucking Anderson. I'd spent my life being on top of the game, partying hard, being the best in my field, so what if part of it was a lie?

"I don't need your pity, Carter. If that's all you're offering, you know where the door is." My jaw was tense, and I was certain I'd have jaw ache from grinding my teeth so damn hard.

"Hey." He raised his hands. "No pity here."

I raised my brows.

"Seriously." He sighed. "Tanner told me not to say anything to you."

I snorted. "And when do you ever listen to anything Tanner tells you to do?"

With a grin, Carter lifted his drink to his mouth and said, "Occasionally, I do, but it's good keeping him on his toes, and hell, he's even hotter when he gets mad at me," before taking a sip.

I was proud that I didn't blush. Over the past couple of months of Carter's frequent visits, I'd always been in awe of how open he was about his relationship with Tanner, which was ridiculous. Logically I was well aware he had every right to be open and himself, but in a world of forced repression, the concept still made me pause.

At first, I'd thought he was oversharing to get a reaction from me, pushing me to respond in some way by rubbing his relationship in my face. Yeah, I could be a self-absorbed dick when I wanted to be. It didn't take me long to realize he was a loved-up fool with no filter. He always gushed over Tanner. And while in the early days I blushed so hard that I had to escape the room quickly, I'd finally reached a place where talking about two guys together naturally and openly had become the norm. I didn't think I'd ever be as open and understanding about being in a gay relationship as Carter was, let alone have such awareness and compassion. The thought still threatened to blow my mind when I spent too much time letting it fill my head.

Quickly getting back on track—Carter, I'd discovered, liked to push my sorry ass—he continued. "Tanner said there was full-on open-mouthed action going on outside. Davis"—I gulped, my hands tensing at the mention of Davis's name—"won't tell me anything. But he does keep smiling."

My heart leaped, my stomach uncoiling and filling with something highly different.

"He didn't say anything?" I tried to sound casual but knew the slight pitch in my voice meant Carter wouldn't buy it.

"Nope. Not to me anyway, and Tanner's being annoyingly tight-lipped, but I have my ways of getting it out of him if you want me to find out." He wriggled his brows, and despite the tension thrumming through me, a laugh escaped me.

Carter grinned big and wide. Yeah, it was rare I laughed these days, and I knew Carter enjoyed it when he managed to break through the walls I'd erected around myself. He took it as a personal triumph. Of course, Carter being Carter had told me as much. It was as refreshing as it was annoying—his honesty and lack of filter.

"I'm good, but thanks." I had no plans to see Davis again. Hell, I still didn't know if I'd be staying in town, but that pull, that irritating niggle to stay put was still there, ruling me.

Carter shrugged. "Okay, but…." He trailed off, wide-eyed and amused, just waiting for me to take the bait.

It worked. Bastard. "But?"

"Well," he leaned in as though conspiring, placing his mug down, "he keeps doing this pause, eyes drifting off into the distance thing. Plus," he continued when I threw him a confused look, "in his daze, he keeps rubbing his bottom lip." He sat back, preening, as though totally satisfied with his weird observation.

I scrunched my brows. "That's your big buildup?"

A loud sigh escaped from his mouth. "This is huge."

"It is?" I was confused as hell.

He nodded. "Yep."

I stared at him dumbfounded.

Once again, Carter sighed loudly. "Yes, it's huge. Davis never gets that dreamy look. And that whole touching the lip thing is classic 'I'm thinking of a hot guy's tongue in my mouth' thing." He shook his head. "Are you really this naïve?"

Apparently, I was.

The clearing of his throat brought my attention back to him. "So…?"

"So?"

"Was that your first, you know, real kiss?"

I blanched, then tightened my jaw. This was far too gossipy, too personal for me.

"It's okay." Carter offered me a small smile. "I shouldn't have asked. But…" Yeah, he really couldn't help himself. "…you know, if you ever want to ask anything, chat about anything, you can… with me."

Wide-eyed, I stared at him, overwhelmed by his offer and the fact he was so nice to me. I didn't deserve nice. I didn't deserve understanding. Unable to answer, I nodded.

He smiled and took another sip of his coffee. The

whole time, his gaze remained on me, and I fought hard not to squirm under his scrutiny. I remembered back to a time when life was simpler. There was just me, friends I kept at a distance and who didn't know the real me, and a family whose rule was absolute. It wasn't perfect, but I'd trained myself from such an early age to know how to behave, how to act, how to hide. Fear had ruled me, similar to the driving emotion that did so today. It had been a miserable existence, but undoubtedly easier in day-to-day survival.

As I looked at Carter, I stifled a groan. My life was definitely no longer simple. "What?" I dared ask, knowing he was itching to carry on speaking.

"Have you spoken to Denver?"

I shook my head. "No." I didn't tell him that I hadn't returned any of his calls.

"But he's called you, right?" Carter continued. I gave him a reluctant nod. "Perhaps you need to pick up?"

I held back rolling my eyes and the slip of "No shit, Sherlock," that desperately wanted to escape. With his bright eager eyes still peering at me, I finally responded, "I will. Just figuring out my next move."

His lips pursed at that and his nose scrunched.

After a moment, he took a gulp of coffee and then seemed set for battle as he placed his mug firmly down and straightened up. "I think there's a lot here on offer for you, and leaving seems a little going backward considering everything that's happened." He paused a moment as if waiting for a reaction. When I didn't speak, he sighed. "Listen, I know you've been through so much, and to be honest, I have no idea what you're going through, but please don't make a decision just yet."

I huffed out a breath and leaned my head back. He was right, but I was so over thinking about this shit and overthinking everything.

"So stay, at least for a little while. Maybe give yourself another couple of months at least."

"I'll think about it." It was all I'd been doing anyway, so giving him this wasn't a big deal.

Carter smiled in victory. "And pick up the phone next time Denver calls. Okay?"

I gave him a noncommittal hum, not quite sure I was there yet. My godfather was actually a decent guy. It always surprised me how he'd managed to remain friends with my parents. They were so damn different.

I was lucky. I knew this. A position waited for me. But the thought of returning, especially to a job set up by my family, to a profession I'd been expected to take, made nausea sit in my gut. Before coming out, I'd played the game, bowed down and gone through the motions. And while I wasn't all the way out of the closet to the world at large—just to Carter and his inner circle—the idea of going back and living in the lie demanded of me was too much.

I couldn't do it anymore.

And that left me clueless.

CHAPTER FIVE

DAVIS

"Hey, Craig, can you unlock the door, please?"

Craig, one of my part-timers, dutifully nodded and did just that. I smiled my thanks and turned back to the kitchen. Yesterday we'd had a delivery, and I'd ordered the ingredients to bake mini chocolate and espresso Bundt cakes. They were a weakness of mine, which was the reason I rarely made them. Far too often I ate a good third of what I'd made to sell, which was a bitch on the minimal effort I made at keeping fit and healthy. But still, they were freakin' delicious and worth the time and energy to make. It also was apparent I wasn't the only addict of caffeine and chocolate in this town either. Combining the two meant there'd be a bigger line at the counter by midmorning, or earlier if news got around.

I cleaned the stainless steel counters after placing the rest of the cakes to cool. With the kitchen clean, I peered out of the large hatch into the filling shop front and smiled. This sleepy town was a far cry from where I'd imagined myself, but with how busy we were and the hours I managed to keep with the help of my staff, I wouldn't have it any other way. Libby was worth it all.

Watching Sandy at the coffee machine while Craig managed the till and juggled the orders, I considered it was probably time to extend my crew. Not only could we do with the extra help during peak times, but I wanted a few additional hours off. Every spare hour I had was dedicated to my girl. I loved every moment. Hell, just the thought of every new milestone made my heart clench with how fiercely I loved her. But, selfishly, it seemed opportune for some me time too.

The digs from Tanner and Carter, even though well meant, had hit their mark. I was lonely. I felt shit for admitting it to myself. As a dad, it almost seemed impossible I could feel such a way, but my feelings were real and try as I might, I couldn't ignore them anymore. While a casual hookup sounded great, 'cause hell, I needed to get my dick wet, my family life and "casual" just didn't have the right ring to it. I'd only just started coming to terms with the idea of meeting someone, largely because of seeing what Tanner had created with Carter. A part of me wanted that. Okay, it was a large part, but finding anyone good enough to be in Libby's life… shit, I couldn't even begin to fathom how that would work.

I headed out to the front to give the guys a hand to clear the morning rush. I greeted the many regulars and took over gathering the orders. Within an hour, the queue had died down, and I took the time to restock the front counter with fresh cakes and pastries. Sandy and Craig coped well for sure, and Phil was just as efficient, if not better. Between the four of us we managed, just, but looking at the chatting customers as they inhaled morning pastries, it was definitely time to advertise.

I told Craig and Sandy just that. "Don't suppose you know anyone who's looking?"

Craig scrunched his nose as if deep in thought. He was a good kid who had recently turned twenty. I knew I couldn't sweet-talk him into staying with me forever, but after he'd dropped out of college and returned home, I was lucky that he still had no idea what his plans were. He shook his head. "Not at the moment. I can ask around though. What sort of hours are you looking at?"

"Probably thirty or so. I need to come up with concrete plans and figure out shift changes with someone new on board."

"Sounds good," he said, before heading around the counter to clear a couple of tables.

I made my way back to the kitchen to start some prep for tomorrow's special. While we had a standard pastry and cake selection, I made an effort to ensure I mixed up the offerings with one or two different things on the menu. My customers seemed to like it. It also gave me an opportunity to be creative.

It didn't take me long to select a new recipe. I may have eaten a couple of chocolate and espresso Bundt cakes while making dough that I needed to set aside overnight for early morning prep. As I placed the dough in the refrigerator, I glanced into the shop's front just as Carter walked in. He looked in my direction and gave a little wave before stepping to the counter. I grinned, finished organizing the refrigerator, and then headed out to say hi.

I looked around. "By yourself?" It was unusual to

see Carter without Tanner these days. They were stuck at the hip.

"Just stopping for a coffee and meeting a friend, as it's my early day to finish. Tanner's out on a job."

"Cool. Have you already given your order?" I glanced over to see Sandy at the machine, wondering if the drink was for him.

"Yeah. I'm all sorted, thank you." He grinned. "If you're due a break, feel free to join us."

I twisted my mouth in confusion. "Okay." It seemed kind of odd he was inviting me for a break when he was meeting with someone. "Sure."

Carter's face lit up with pleasure. "That's great. What'll you have? My treat."

I rolled my eyes at him. "I'll take care of it. Just go sit your ass down."

"You sure?"

"'Course, now grab a table."

"Thanks." He turned and headed toward one of the small booths. He tended to always be happy, but sometimes he'd get a glint as though he was extra happy about something. It was one of those sorts of moments.

I shrugged and went to take over from Sandy. Carter had already ordered for his friend, so I finished them off and grabbed myself a black coffee.

I carried the tray over to the booth and sat, my back to the door. "So, how've you been?"

"Good. It was a quiet day, which was kind of nice. I'm relieved it's Friday tomorrow though."

"You on call this weekend?"

"Just Friday night," he said. "Then the weekend's free. How about you? You working this weekend?"

I shook my head. "Nope. I have a whole weekend to spend with my girl."

Carter smiled. "Awesome. What are you planning? You going to stop by?"

I nodded. "Probably. Libby needs some of her Uncle Tanner and Carter time."

Carter grinned. "Yeah, she does." It was the truth. Tanner had been supporting me with the care of Libby from when she was just a couple of months old. It was the reason why he'd relocated in the first place, to be my support. When Carter had joined our small family, it hadn't taken Libby long to win Carter over. Yeah, she had us all wrapped around her little finger. She also adored Carter and would immediately clamber to get to him whenever she saw him. "We can take her Saturday afternoon and night if you want?"

I raised my brows and smiled. "Yeah?"

"Sure we can. Take the night off. Perhaps go out."

I nodded, grateful for his suggestion, though I had no idea what I'd do with my time. "That would be great, thanks."

Carter seemed to read the barest hesitation I had. Not for the opportunity of a night off, but at the possibility of going out. "You know, it's okay to head out, have fun. I even think Lauren's heading out this weekend with some guys from work. She'll be here soon so we can ask her."

Lauren was cute. She was also a bit on the eager side and could chat my head off. I'd met her a couple of times and had happily flirted with her, but it had all been harmless. There was no pull there, no greater attraction. I'd never hid my sexuality. I was a proud bisexual man. At times my openness had been met with confusion and sometimes downright contempt. Confusion I could always handle, as long as people had brain cells so could get their heads around the concept. Bisexuality was not as confusing as some people made it.

What was confusing about being attracted to both men and women? I was attracted to people. It meant I could appreciate both sexes and love them equally. I'd yet to ever be in love. And when it happened, I had no idea who it would be with. But what I was 100 percent certain of was that for the right person, I would give my all.

Just as I was about to say I'd think about it, the door opened and Carter waved over my head at, I assumed, Lauren. A moment later, she sat beside Carter and placed a loud kiss on his cheek.

"Hey, good-looking."

He looked her way and grinned. "Hey, yourself. Good day?"

She nodded, just as she made eye contact with me. "Hey, Davis. You joining us?" Her grin was wide.

I smiled back. She really was cute, but cute was not what I was after. "I sure am. It's good to take a break."

"It is that," she replied. "And yes," she faced Carter once more, "no dramas from my end. Just busy catching up with paperwork. I haven't seen you all day."

Carter bobbed his head. "I know. Getting on top of things is good though."

"Yeah, I suppose. I just wish Denver would figure out what he was going to do about Scott's position."

I perked up at the mention of Scott.

Carter sighed. "I know. I get it though. I think he's just hoping like I am that Scott will get his head together and come back."

Lauren's face twisted.

"What?" I asked, curious. "You don't like the guy?"

She shot a look at Carter, and I followed her gaze.

"He knows everything," he responded, without her having to voice her question.

Ah, it all made sense. The whole "Scott is an asshole" debacle.

"I'm trying to give him the benefit of the doubt, but I'm not as forgiving as our friend over here," she said to me.

Carter rolled his eyes. "You need to move on. I've forgiven him, so that's all that should matter."

"Meh." Lauren shrugged, then laughed when Carter prodded her side. "I will, I will. And if he does come back, I'll be on my best behavior."

I glanced over at Carter, who didn't exactly look convinced.

Carter and Lauren continued to chat about work, Tanner, and a whole heap of stuff that I admittedly zoned out from. While I made the odd grunt of approval or acknowledgment where I thought one was needed, my mind kept drifting to Scott. As much of a prize asshole as he had been, I kinda felt sorry for the guy, especially based on what I'd learned about him from Carter, which to be honest, was very little. But still, from my brief encounter with Scott, on top of his history, as well as him being a hermit—according to Carter—it was obvious he was hurting. And while I'd already tried to talk myself down and lose interest in the guy, it seemed I was full of shit. Not only did I spend too much time thinking about our kiss, him, what his issues were, but also, whenever I heard his damn name, my ears perked up in interest.

Having completely lost all strands of their conversation, I was about to excuse myself and get back to work when I noticed their chatter had stopped and Carter was looking at me expectantly.

"Did I miss something?"

Carter rolled his eyes while Lauren snorted a laugh before she said, "I was inviting you to drinks Saturday night if you're interested. Nothing wild or fancy obviously, since we'll stay in town, but there's a group of us meeting up at Wild Oak. It's just been taken over and redone, I think."

"It has," Carter interrupted. "Tanner did some work on it. He said it's been done well and that the guys who own the place seem really nice."

"Cool," Lauren responded. "So what do you think?" She looked at me. "There are others going too, so it's not just guys from work. We won't bore you to death with work chatter." Lauren ended with a wide grin.

"I already said we'd have Libby, so this works perfectly." Carter's grin was almost the mirror image of Lauren's. I eyed them both, wondering why they were so wide-eyed. A more paranoid version of myself would have gone on red alert, but living in Kirkby didn't exactly leave a lot to the imagination of wild nights and evil plots. Plus, heading out and socializing sounded like a good plan.

"Sure," I agreed, "that sounds great."

Lauren actually clapped her hands. "Yay!"

I laughed. She was pretty damn cool, and I was kinda relieved I wasn't attracted to her. She truly was a handful and too much for me to handle. Hell, I didn't have the energy for her enthusiasm.

"Fabulous," she continued. "We'll be at Wild Oak at eight-ish on Saturday. We should be there for at least an hour before we decide if we're staying or moving on."

"Sounds good." I stood and picked up their empty cups. "You want another?"

"No thanks. I'm heading back. Tanner should be finishing soon."

I nodded and looked at Lauren.

"Not for me. For a short day, it's somehow been a

manic one, even though we haven't had a heap of patients. I'm heading home."

"Okay." I smiled. "Well, I'll see you on Saturday."

"Sounds like a plan," she said.

"And I'll sort out the details with you about Libby later if that's okay?" I said to Carter.

He bobbed his head. "No problem."

"Thanks. See you both later." I made my way to the kitchen and back to my day.

CHAPTER SIX

SCOTT

I TOOK A DEEP BREATH AND LOOKED IN THE MIRROR. I didn't dare look at my face though. Sometimes, I just couldn't stomach the sight. I was sure that was all levels of screwed up, but it was my truth. Instead, I focused on my T-shirt, wondering if it was too tight, wondering if anyone could tell from the way it clung to my toned body that I was... gay. I shook my head.

Gay.

I could totally do this. I had to get the hell over myself.

Maybe.

Possibly.

I sighed. I still had no idea if I *could* do this—accept this openness, something I'd spent pretty much my whole life ignoring—but being honest with myself, I was getting tired of my bullshit. Tired of my inner monologues. Tired of not stepping the fuck up and owning my sexuality once and for all.

But....

Yes, there was always a but, but this time, I clamped my jaw tight and stared at my face. I looked tense as all hell. It therefore made sense that a few beers would help. Getting out of my own company would help, surely to God it would.

Glancing away, I headed toward the front door, grabbing my wallet and keys on the way. Tonight I would stop the pity party and actually leave the damn house. As I stepped outside and pulled the door closed, I gave myself a moment to feel some of the tension disperse. Inhaling deeply, I savored the fresh air, the coolness in my lungs. This was good. I could do this. Even more, I was proud of myself for doing this alone. It would have been too easy to rely on Carter, my tentative friend who had implanted himself into my life. I could do this by myself. Pride felt a little alien as it settled in my head and on my chest. It was a strange sensation, and it had been a long time since I could honestly remember a time I felt honest-to-God proud of myself. Deception and self-loathing, plus a family who took every opportunity to drag me down and remind me I wasn't good enough, could do that to a guy.

With an exhale, I forced myself to smile, still staring at the door. Shit, damn tears filled my eyes. I blinked them away and swallowed the sentiment, hysterical emotion and laughter bubbling in my chest and making their way to my throat. It sprung free, a deep laugh, the action making the smile on my lips genuine. Shit, I was losing it. But still, I grinned and allowed myself the moment to feel lighter. I considered accepting the tears, knowing that, while spiked with fear, they were also coated with unfamiliar happiness and relief.

My lips still fixed with a smirk, I breathed out and closed my eyes before taking another breath. I had no idea what I was doing, where I was going (other than a local bar), and definitely no idea what tomorrow held, let alone the long-term future held, but still, I smiled.

I turned and headed down the street to the town center, the smile now lazily lifting my lips. As I walked past Carter's, I didn't hesitate or pause. He had become something of my safe haven. He knew who I was. Admittedly, while he didn't know my past, my history, he'd still given me the courage I needed to step out. I wouldn't falter and detour. Instead, I continued on.

Once at the Oak, I stepped in right away, forcing myself not to hesitate. While my heart rate picked up and my palms sweated just a little more than comfortable, I didn't experience the panic I'd half expected. In reality, I knew someone wasn't going to step out and call me a fag, wasn't going to reach out to my family and start gossiping and causing shit. A little voice in my head then pulled me short, almost making me stumble. *And so what if they do? Does it really matter?*

Weren't those a loaded couple of questions? Should I give a shit if people in this town knew I'd come out? Should I give a shit if my parents were told? Fuck, my dad already knew. It didn't matter how many times his leather belt had struck my skin. He was a prick to think he could beat it out of me.

I stood at the bar, eyes focused ahead and then skimming the length of the room. The bartender moved toward me.

"What'll it be?"

I glanced at the draft beers before making my selection. "Pale ale please."

"You got it." The guy nodded, grabbed a glass, and poured my drink.

I took the time to glance around the bar. I was out of my comfort zone. Majorly. I'd never done this, never needed to before. Back home, at college, and in the couple of other places I'd lived, I'd always had the safety of friends or colleagues. Yeah, I'd arrived at places ahead of time before so had ordered and started drinking by myself, but always with the knowledge I was waiting for someone.

The knowledge terrified me as well as shot a blast of courage through my veins. I was a grown-ass man. I could drink by myself. I could make small talk with locals if I wanted to. I felt kinda liberated by the idea as I paid for my drink and took a seat near the end of the bar. Tempted to pull my phone out and mess about with it rather than be so clearly alone, I tugged it out of my back pocket and instead, switched it off. As I did so, the bartender was back, this time putting a bowl of nuts in front of me.

"You're the vet, right?"

I glanced up, startled, my gaze landing on the guy's face. He was older than me by about ten years or so if I had to guess. He had deep brown eyes that were friendly. As I registered his words, I latched on to there being no accusation in his question. In a small town like this, it was always a possibility the rumor mill had started and venom could have spread.

"That's right." I nodded.

He smiled, and I mimicked the gesture. "Ted." He stuck out his hand. I took it with the barest of hesitation.

"Scott," I answered. "This your place?"

"Yeah, for better or worse." Ted rolled his eyes, though his small smile remained.

I glanced around the space. It was nicely decorated. It looked high-end and contemporary, with an edge of country charm. I'd heard the place had been purchased recently by out of towners, but since I was no longer in the position to be privy to gossip, I was out of the loop. "It's a nice place. You just moved here, right?"

He bobbed his head. "Yes, is it that obvious?" He laughed. He narrowed his eyes at me. "But saying that, you don't quite have the twang of the locals either." Ted picked up a cloth and wiped the side, eyes still on me.

"You got me." I took a small drink. "I haven't been in town for that long either, and I'm not sure I'm staying." I slammed my mouth closed. With no idea why I'd shared so much, I took another mouthful. I didn't want to give any locals anything to talk about at all when it came to me. "What about you?" I changed the subject. "Better or worse?"

He studied me for a beat but laughed. It was deeper than I expected. He was only five-ten, maybe, and had a slim frame and features. I expected something lighter, but still, his laugh was kind and put me at ease. "This place came as part of the package with the old ball and chain." He grinned. "Apparently, this is our 'great big adventure' of packing up, starting fresh in a small community, immersing ourselves in all that this great country has to offer, or something like that."

I couldn't help but laugh. "So this is your wif—"

"Husband's," he corrected.

My breath hitched before I regained my footing and continued. "Your husband's big plan?" Heat rose in my cheeks, and I wanted the ground to swallow me whole. I hated being embarrassed, being taken unaware. Karma was laughing her damn ass off as she continued to throw shit at me, or into situations, just to make it clear that my punishment wasn't over.

"Indeed. But what are you going to do when he's such a fine specimen of a man." He nudged his head to his right, and my eyes landed on a guy with a good six inches or so on Ted. He was fit and about my age. And yeah, he was a fine specimen. I almost got whiplash when I swung my head back to Ted quickly. I didn't want him to think I was checking his husband out, even though he'd drawn attention to him. And shit, why would he even do that? Did he know somehow that I was gay? Know I'd appreciate how hot his husband was? Heck, when I came out and finally admitted I was gay, did I start kicking off a new pheromone or some shit?

I stared at him wide-eyed, and I was sure with terror written all over my face.

"Hey there." Ted's amusement fled, and his voice softened with concern. His hand landed on my forearm, and I jolted. "You okay?"

I nodded abruptly, two sharp up-and-down movements.

"Okay." He patted my arm gently. "Don't move."

I watched dumbstruck as he turned away, reached for a bottle from the top shelf, and returned to stand before me. He then bent and placed two shot glasses in front of us. Once he poured in the brown liquid, he nudged one over to me. "Pick it up." I did so. My body buzzed, adrenaline pulsing through every nerve ending. I really needed to get my shit together. "Now"—he raised his glass—"here's to good liquor, kind words, and to good head."

I snorted. There was a small fracture in the irrational fear that had taken hold of me.

With a wink, he clinked his glass with mine and threw the shot back. I smiled then. It was real, still filled with nerves, but the tension loosened its steel grip. I lifted my own shot back and swallowed, wincing at the burn.

"I think one more's in order." He laughed and then looked hastily in the direction of his husband. "Quick, before Jason comes over and stops us."

His humor was infectious, and I smiled wider. "Better get to it then. But if I throw up, it's your fault."

"Ha! Sounds like a challenge to me." Warmth hit my back as I picked up the glass once more. I paused, my gaze landing on a wide-eyed Ted. His eyes scanned whoever was behind me before he glanced at me, a new twinkle of something in them.

"What are we celebrating?" His voice was low, though held humor. And I recognized it immediately.

Davis.

I didn't look behind me, too unsure how to react. How exactly did a guy react after he'd kissed a stranger and then run out without even a backward glance, let alone a goodbye? I paused at that, thinking how I'd react if it had been a woman I'd run out on. Truth be told, I wouldn't have given much of a shit, as the kiss would have been forced and gone against every natural instinct inside me. I wished I didn't know that from experience.

Aware of not only the silence but of the bartender looking at the figure behind me, then back at me with a smirk, I held back the grimace that tried to break free.

"What'll it be?" Ted asked.

Davis moved to my side, and I swallowed hard before gathering the nerve to look his way. His eyes were firmly on me, his mouth fixed in a careful smile. How I even knew it was careful was beyond me, but I was able to deduce enough to recognize caution when I saw it.

"Hey, Scott." His voice was smooth, calm, and a little quieter than his previous words.

I nodded. "Hey." But I couldn't muster a smile. I glanced away, no clue how to react or respond. If there was ever a time that I wanted to punch myself —and admittedly there'd been several such occasions over the past few weeks—now was the perfect moment. I felt pathetic and so out of my comfort zone, a hit of pain was a possible solution to getting me back on track. My whole life I'd played the part of arrogant and privileged. The truth was, though, there'd been no playing. I had been those things. My only chance of redemption was knowing wealth had been a noose and arrogance had been a ruse. But still, I'd lost who I was, and that was one heck of a hard pill to swallow.

I gripped my drink and took a big gulp, not even wincing at the burn.

Davis's arm brushed mine when he angled himself closer to the bar, leaning over slightly with his outstretched hand. I willed myself to remain relaxed and ignore the contact, blindly and unsuccessfully refusing to pay attention to the heat traveling across my skin or the buzz of electricity the contact created. I had no idea how successful I was at concealing my reaction. I was just relieved I hadn't broken into a cold sweat.

"Hey, the name's Davis. New owner, right?"

Ted smiled and shook Davis's hand. "There are no secrets in this place, huh?" I didn't miss that Ted's gaze landed on me briefly. "Ted. Nice to meet you." He tilted his head to the side. "Another outta towner, right?"

I could imagine the grin on Davis's face. I didn't dare look at him; my fear stilled me.

"That's right. We've been here about a year now. I

own the Split Bean in town. The coffee shop." I stilled at the news, wondering how I didn't know that. The Split Bean made the best coffee in town. Admittedly, there wasn't much competition, but it was still good. They also made amazing cakes. When I'd worked at the clinic, it was usually one of the receptionists or a nurse who grabbed orders for everyone at lunch, though, so I'd rarely been in there. "Not sure I'll ever be classed as a local though, until maybe I've been here for thirty years or so," Davis continued with a chuckle.

Smiling, Ted said, "I can imagine." He wiped the bar top. "Beer?"

Davis nodded. "Yep, what's on tap will be good."

"Sure thing." Ted took a glass and started pouring Davis's drink. "You said we?" he pressed, his eyes flicking up to Davis at my side.

This time I risked a glance at Davis. He was smiling, apparently his natural state. The guy seemed so damn happy. My gaze roamed the side of his face, landing on the small creases around his eyes, and my gut clenched. Shit. Reality hit me. I was sitting silently at the bar like a spare part. I had no idea if I should get up and leave to find a table or stay. My inability to handle the situation made me jolt, or at least made my knee jerk. What the hell was with overanalyzing? I could play this game, right? Act like a goddamn human being at least. I told myself that playing was what I was meant to stop doing. In my world, playing tended to equal lying to myself and those around me. This was meant to be the new, brave, no-bullshit Scott.

Shrugging off my tension, I paid attention to the conversation taking place around me and jolted for real this time when one of Davis's words registered. "You have a daughter?" I spun in my seat to look at him full on.

With a glance my way, he nodded, though his brows dipped in amusement, confusion—I had no idea what. Though he did seem to be working out what my outburst was about. His lips quirked into a smile. "I sure do."

"But you're gay." The words fell out of my mouth before I could stop them. My filter shattered. I would swear blind to anyone who asked that I wasn't usually this way... this dim-witted or dense, but hell.... Daughter? Rattled wasn't a strong enough word to describe what the hell my brain was playing at. It was trying and failing to make sense of every-thing. Not only was I still in a spin with my own revelations, but I was ridiculously affected by Davis. Apparently, so much so, common sense and all pretense of subtlety flew out the window. In its place, stupidity had taken root and made my brain its home.

Davis pursed his lips. I couldn't help but be distracted by them, remembering all too clearly how they'd felt against mine. "Shit," I managed. "Sorry?" Yes, it came out as a damn question. My eyes widened in horror, gaze firmly on Davis. I didn't even glance when I heard Ted snort and place Davis's drink down before his footsteps moved away.

With a raised brow, Davis asked, "Are you?"

Was I what? Sorry about asking? Sorry for saying something so inappropriate? Absolutely. But admittedly, I was as curious as hell.

CHAPTER SEVEN

DAVIS

A WIDE-EYED SCOTT STARED AT ME. A MIXTURE OF horror and embarrassment swirled across his features, but I didn't miss the interest either. He could've so easily turned away from me, just as he could've easily pleaded ignorance. Hell, he could have simply downed his drink and run. Instead, the confusion written on his face was intriguing and somewhat adorable.

For the briefest of moments, I contemplated playing a game, winding him up. But considering all I knew about Scott, I didn't think that wise. "Libby, my baby girl, she's almost one now."

His attention was rapt, focused, and he was seemingly listening to every word. I paused a moment, waiting to see if he would respond. When he didn't, I continued. "So…." I didn't know where I was going at all with this half a conversation. It was on the tip of my tongue to ask him about the other night, about his running off, and of course about the whole my tongue in his mouth incident. I was convinced he'd dive through an unopened window to prevent that conversation, though. I needed to think fast, as this was all levels of awkward. Hell, why had I even approached him? I ignored the obvious answer to that question and instead said, "You come here often?" I froze at how absurd I sounded. I seriously should have just backed away slowly, but then something happened that I didn't expect, and damn if it didn't make my gut tighten.

The handsome bastard smiled. It reached his eyes, and his mouth spread enough to show perfectly white teeth. "Do you need a moment to take it back, or are you just going to go with it?"

I laughed, possibly a little too loudly, but Scott was a conundrum. He appeared to teeter in fight-or-flight mode, while apparently throwing in an extra *F* of flirt for good measure. While the latter was definitely something I could get on board with, I didn't trust how long this flirtatious Scott would last. A voice inside told me to be sensible and grab my drink and run, but I remained rooted to the spot, unwilling to pull away. "Not quite sure yet the best way to handle it, but perhaps it puts us on an equal footing of awkward moments and questions."

Scott's brows lifted a little, his mouth still curved upwards. "Touché."

"Perhaps we can rewind just a little?" I reached out to pick up my beer and took a large mouthful. Cool and crisp, the liquid gave me a moment to collect myself. After swallowing, I angled a little more toward Scott, aware his gaze remained fixed on me. "So, you come here often?" My smile changed to a laugh in response to his deep snort and ringing laughter. "For real though, I mean with the new owners and such. You've been here a couple of months, right?"

With a bob of his head, Scott sobered a little, but there was still humor in his eyes. I hadn't lost him completely. "Yeah, just a bit longer than that, but no, never this place. I wanted to check it out though, as I'd heard decent things about it." His brown eyes remained connected to mine, and he smoothed his hair off his brow. "The owner, Ted, seems like a good guy." He glanced around, possibly searching for Ted. I saw him standing off at the far side, pouring a drink and in conversation with a woman.

"Yeah," I agreed. "I've only been here for about an

hour, and Ted seems really friendly." I cleared my throat, hoping inspiration would hit for how to continue to hold a conversation. I was struggling, majorly. Was I so out of practice that I could no longer hold a decent conversation with a guy, who I admittedly found attractive, but whose presence confused me? I spoke to people all the time. Yeah, I liked to hide away in the kitchen whenever possible at work, but I could hold my own and carry conversations all day with customers. So why was I failing so spectacularly? I had no doubt at any moment he'd find a reason to leave, or hell, maybe he'd just tell me to fuck off.

I threw Scott an awkward smile, hoping it came off more relaxed and natural than it really was. The creases around his eyes dropped a little. I was losing him. "You been busy today?"

He gave a noncommittal shrug. "Not especially."

"What, no wo—" Slamming my mouth shut, but not quick enough, I changed route. "Yeah, days like that are good. I'm trying to take on a new hire so I can take a few more hours off, and hopefully the weekends off too." While I hadn't lost Scott completely, he was definitely more closed off. There was a tightness in his shoulders that hadn't been there a few moments before. "It makes juggling work and parenthood tricky at times, you know?" Holy crap, how the hell would this guy know anything about kids and balancing work?

To my surprise, he leaned an elbow on the bar and turned a little toward me. While he was still guarded, something else flashed in his eyes. Curiosity? Understanding? Interest? I had no idea, but I hoped to find out.

"Yeah, my sister works full-time and has two young children. My nephews are only five and three."

I tilted my head in surprise at what he was sharing. And a sister? From the secondhand info I had of Scott, I'd deduced several things, none of them especially pleasant, if I chose to ignore the hot-as-hell kiss we shared and the kind things Carter said. As well as arrogant and a dick, I'd also assumed he would be a spoiled only child. My powers of deduction were worth shit, it seemed. That actually boded well for Scott, and I relaxed a bit more, liking that he'd shared something personal about himself.

"Is she a single mom too?"

"Too?" he asked, his brows dipping.

My lip quirked. Confusion looked good on him. A flash of the extreme confusion that had plastered his face at Tanner's party invaded my thoughts. That confusion wasn't quite as hot, admittedly. "Well, yeah, but exchange that with single dad."

His eyes sprung open even wider. "You're a single dad?"

I nodded, my gaze roaming his face. I'd figured he'd known, but then remembered, unsurprisingly, that there was no reason for Carter and Scott to talk about me. Carter was the only loose connection I had with the guy. Come to think about it, he had been surprised as shit to discover I was a dad in the first place. "Yeah."

"Wow." My chest puffed out when I saw something akin to admiration in his gaze. "That's something."

I shrugged. I wasn't looking for an ego boost for simply taking care of my daughter. She was my world. I didn't need any approval or praise from anyone. "It just is. I'm her dad. It's my role, you know?"

"So…" He chewed on his bottom lip a moment. "Libby's mom?" The question was tentative.

I understood why he would be confused. Between the two of us making out and the rarity of single custodial dads in the world, let alone bisexual ones, it could paint a confusing picture. Carter had called me a rare magical unicorn once. Tanner had sensibly taken that moment to usher him out of my home before I'd jumped all over that bullshit. While I didn't generally tell anyone my business—though I rarely had to tell it due to the gossip in town, especially after Libby's mom left—I was happy to share some of myself with Scott.

While his dick status hadn't completely been swept clear after how he'd treated Carter, Carter had insisted on a second chance and a clean slate. Plus the dude looked like he was in serious need of something: a friend, maybe, normalcy—hell, talking about someone else's shit rather than his own? All of the above were genuine possibilities.

"She gave up legal custody when Libby was born."

His mouth gaped. It took him a moment to ask, "So you and her…?"

And there it was. The question that regularly left me rolling my eyes. Scott's tone, though, teamed with his hesitant eyes, stopped me from sighing or sneering, and instead I overshared the fuck out of my history.

"We just had a one-night thing. Nothing more. That night resulted in Libby. I moved here as this was where Mags wound up for one reason or another. From the beginning, she made it clear she didn't want to be a mom. She agreed to have Libby and signed all parental rights to me the day Libby was born."

"And you haven't seen her since?"

One good thing about chatting this way was that Scott appeared relaxed. No longer was he peering around or stumbling or pausing over his words. Instead, he seemed to be intently listening to all I had to say. It gave me a moment to pause and consider him.

He was good-looking, there was no doubt about that. He seemed as if he came from money, but I couldn't quite put my finger on the reason behind that. It wasn't his clothes or even the way he spoke. Maybe it was more to do with the way he carried himself, his mannerisms. But who the hell knew? I wasn't from money. I hadn't been poverty-stricken as a kid or anything, but with the loss of my parents when I was at college, I'd had to fend for myself and work my ass off. There were many days I worried about keeping on top of payments and wondering if I'd done the right thing venturing into a new business with a baby, but I'd decided the moment I knew I was going to be a dad, I'd do everything in my power to ensure I gave my child everything they needed. That didn't involve just the material shit, or the important stuff like love, but also things like a work ethic.

On too many occasions over the years, I'd witnessed silver-spooned assholes not appreciating all they had, yet still taking advantage of everything they were given or thought they deserved. And I hoped to God Scott wasn't one of those pricks. He didn't seem like it. Maybe he had been once, but with all of the changes in his life, I hoped decency and common sense overruled the rest.

I completely lost track of Scott's question while I debated who he was and where he came from. Though I supposed the latter didn't matter. It was the now that was important. The now I was becoming increasingly interested in.

"Nope," I finally answered. "She has no legal rights to Libby. We didn't mean anything to each other." I didn't intend for my words to sound harsh, as I had zero animosity about my situation. I also knew a lot of people didn't understand how a mother could leave her child, but Mags had her reasons, and neither she nor I ever needed to explain them to anyone, other than to Libby one day.

He tilted his head as if studying me. "And you're okay with that?"

I nodded without hesitation. "Of course. I have my girl. There's nothing else I need."

Scott straightened up a little at that, and I considered how my words could be perceived. Hell, I didn't really know the guy, so sharing with him my plans for the future on top of my place in the world seemed like I'd be pushing it a little too much.

"Right," he eventually said. "That makes sense." He nodded and picked up his beer and took a drink.

And we were back to awkward again. Maybe I was best off taking the moment as my out and heading back to Lauren. She was a cool chick, uncomplicated. I enjoyed her company, so had no question we'd have fun tonight, yet my ass decided to make a decision for me and planted itself on a barstool next to Scott.

He looked surprised when I sat next to him, his eyes widening a little.

"So what about you? I know the basics of your story." He stiffened, his forearm becoming taut as he gripped his glass. "Not from gossip. Well, sort of"—I hastened to add—"from Carter."

Scott snorted, the sound surprising me. "Not sure that's any better."

"No?" I asked, my brows lifting as I angled to look at him. "I would have thought he was the best guy to hear anything from, since he's Team Scott and all."

This time abrupt laughter spilled from his mouth. He shook his head, a smile on his lips. Fascinated, I watched the movement and his mouth closely, liking the smile I'd somehow put there. I happily took credit.

"Team Scott, huh? Is that what the locals are calling it?" His gaze moved to mine. While the smile still sat on his lips, there was a shift in his eyes that looked a lot like desperation, and damn if that wasn't a kick in the nuts.

"It's just what I call it." He raised his brows, apparently knowing I was full of shit. "Okay," I admitted, "I started it to rub it in Tanner's face. Carter caught on to it and ran with it, and we both gang up on Tanner whenever we have the opportunity. I'll take any ammo I can to wind the bastard up." I smirked after I told him the absolute truth.

"So what's the opposing team?"

I clamped my mouth shut, then twisted my lips together in thought. "So, maybe I never thought it through. There's just you."

Scott's lips twitched and his shoulders noticeably relaxed. "Does Tanner still want to kick my ass?"

I shrugged. "Not so much these days. I think

Carter's worn him down, or gone down on him so many times he's managed to pretty much take control of Tanner's thoughts and feelings when he wants to, or at least his actions." I snickered, knowing Tanner would attempt to kick my ass for talking about how dick-whipped he was.

Scott turned in his seat to face me more fully, his expression full of curiosity. He raised his right eyebrow, something I was envious about, as I couldn't do that to save my life. "Are you always like this?" His question was a little quieter than the rest of his conversation; it was also dipped in something akin to wonder.

"What?" I had no idea what he was talking about and wasn't quite sure if I wanted to know. My mouth got me into trouble a fair bit, so I could never really tell how people would react.

He lifted his hand and waved it in my general direction. "Like this?"

"Gorgeous?" I hedged. "Fuckable?" I laughed hard at the look on his face and allowed my mind to consider how perfectly my dick would fit into his mouth when he opened it like that.

Scott coughed loudly, laughter breaking free as he did so. "No," he said with a shake of his head, but I was sure he silently agreed with me. "I meant honest, talking like this." He paused. "You were telling the truth, right?" Hesitation flashed over his features.

"Always." I nodded. "Well, pretty much. Sometimes I have to rein myself in or be more selective about what I say, but I find it helps cut through a hell of a lot of bullshit if we speak the truth, right?"

"Right."

I wasn't even sure how we'd reached this point, but somehow we'd got here.

"So, who are you here with?" He eyed a few people in his periphery. "Libby, that's your daughter's name?"

I nodded, a rush of something I was unable to grasp sweeping over me that he remembered Libby's name. "Yeah."

"She'd be with who, Tanner and Carter?"

I nodded again. "I'm here with Lauren and some of her friends. Guys from y—" The moment his face blanched, I stopped talking, immediately understanding his reaction and the discomfort no doubt racing through him. That had to be awkward as hell.

He sat frozen a moment, then took a swig of his beer and placed it down, offering me a smile that was more like a grimace. He stood and pulled his wallet from his back pocket, threw some cash on the bar, and I watched as he looked over at Ted, who angled his head a little, seeming to take in what was happening. Rather than coming over, he offered Scott a head lift, his lips pulling at the corners just barely.

I was sure my expression was similar. I hadn't even considered how Scott would react being in the same place as the people he used to work with. As far as I was aware, only Lauren knew the truth about what had happened. But communities like this, as great as they were, could also be cesspits of gossip.

My gut ached a little as I observed Scott's abrupt movements. It was obvious he was trying not to freak, and I could tell that after just sharing two conversations with the guy. Unable to hold back, I stood too, putting some cash beside his. I knocked on the wooden bar and saluted Ted my thanks and goodbye. "Come on, let's get out of here."

Scott's head whipped around, his startled eyes roaming my face. Not sure what he was looking for, all I could do was offer him honesty. "It's too early to go home, and I can imagine the last thing you want is a shitty, uncomfortable conversation with that lot." I flicked my head in their direction. Scott's gaze didn't leave mine, however. "Let's get out of here." I turned, not waiting to see if he followed. On the way out, I caught Lauren's attention and signaled I was leaving. She raised her brow and threw me a wink. I knew the moment her eyes landed on Scott. A frown crossed her lips, and her gaze jerked back to mine, a question pasted all over her face. I returned her wink and tugged open the door, holding it open for Scott, and was pleasantly surprised when his hand reached out to hold the door barely a second later.

Now what the hell were we going to do?

CHAPTER EIGHT

SCOTT

THE COOL EVENING AIR WRAPPED AROUND US, AND immediately I was able to breathe again. It didn't take a genius to figure out why I was struggling or why my brain felt as if it would explode at any God-given moment. On top of that, my nerves were close to tatters. And I hated it. While I knew I had to stop comparing then to now, how I was to *who* I was… doing so was so much easier said than done.

I wasn't emotionally crippled, despite my upbringing and even though I was sure it had been my father's mission, but that didn't mean I was completely comfortable with emotional stuff either. I didn't want to harp on about what could've, should've, would've been. It wasn't cathartic. In fact, it felt debilitating.

I inhaled again and looked up to the night sky. While I was all too aware of Davis beside me, most probably wondering if I'd lost my mind, I didn't quite have it in me to care. Okay, I sort of did. I liked the guy. Maybe. Possibly.

It was time to let go of the hurt of my past and focus on the present. Only then would I be able to focus on the future, and that started with looking at myself in the mirror fully and liking what I saw. Not literally at the moment, since I was outside and I truly hadn't lost my shit—I didn't think—but I knew the way forward.

And fuck, that was freeing as hell.

But only I could do this—work my shit out. There'd be no leaning on anyone to do so.

"Ah, you okay there?" Davis's voice snapped me into focus, and I dragged my eyes from the starry night sky to him. Amusement and I was pretty sure concern flitted across his face.

I nodded. "Yeah, I think I will be."

"Shit."

"What?" I tilted my head in question.

"Were you having an epiphany moment or something?"

He was so wide-eyed, genuinely appearing serious, that all I could do was laugh. It was belly deep, loud and gruff, and traveled quickly to my chest and spilled over. "And shit, yeah," I admitted between my laughter.

He scratched the back of his neck. "Did I totally spoil your moment and piss on your mojo or something?" He looked a little shifty, but his lips quirked in amusement.

"I think I'll survive." My laughter calmed and I looked at the man beside me. With his dark hair and stubbled chin, he seemed all too real, too present. I took that as a good thing despite the feeling being alien to me. "So," I pushed myself to be bold, "where to?"

He'd rescued me. Legitimately allowed me to save face by getting me out of the bar when I couldn't cope. I hadn't been ready to face Lauren or anyone else from the clinic. Davis was so far from being a typical knight in shining armor… well, I didn't think so, but he'd read my panic, read the situation, and selflessly helped me. I'd lived a fairly sorry existence to date, too used to the philosophy of nobody doing anything for nothing. Having to keep the real me so close to my chest had made it all but impossible to let down my guard.

Just maybe things were on the up and I could change all of that.

"Well." His gaze remained on my face a few moments before he glanced around, as if deciding his options. "Come on." Reaching out, he tugged the sleeve of my shirt lightly. "Come with me. I've the perfect place."

I followed without hesitation, and we walked in companionable silence. Side by side, we headed in the direction of the main street. We were far enough apart not to brush shoulders, but that didn't mean I didn't feel the heat radiating off him. I was all too aware of his proximity.

Once on the main street of town, he came to a stop. I glanced at him and then beyond him to the storefront. He'd brought me to his coffee shop. Warmth tentatively traveled across my chest. While I didn't know if he came here out of hours regularly, or even brought people here when the place was closed, I didn't spare another moment considering it. Instead, I focused on the gesture. Not only was he bringing me to his domain, I liked to think he was sharing a little something with me.

I expected I was making a big deal over nothing, but it didn't make him bringing me here any less of a big deal—for me.

With a smile curving his lips, Davis pulled keys

out of his pocket and opened up, motioning me in. I followed immediately.

"Hold on. Let me just throw the light on out back before you trip over your ass." Davis's voice was light and easy, the tone calming.

I did as he asked and waited in the dark shop. The only light came from the streetlights dotted down the sidewalk. My eyes had just started to focus when the lights out back, in what I assumed was the kitchen, flickered on. Davis then filled the open doorway and beckoned me over.

"This way." His grin was easy and natural, pretty much fitting for the man I was getting to know.

I walked around the tables and the counter. Just before I reached Davis, he stepped out of the door-way, leaving it free for me to head right through. Stainless steel filled the space, everything pristine and clearly in its proper place. Out of my periphery, I watched Davis step in front of a huge refrigerator. He pulled out a few items and came to the large island in the middle of the kitchen.

"Grab those for me, will you?" He indicated with a nod toward the back wall. I followed his gaze and spotted the stools. With a bob of my head, I made my way over, grabbed two stools, and took them toward him. "Right," he said as he continued to unpack his loot, "before we start, have you ever actually been to my place before?" Davis paused and looked at me expectantly.

"No," I admitted. "I've had takeout coffee and a couple of pastries before, but it was via order and brought to the practice by one of the staff." My gaze drifted to about six different pastries and cakes. I legit had a sweet tooth. For all of my healthy-ish living, put a sweet in front of me, hell, put five in front of me and I'd try my hardest to clear the plates. Sweets were my one weakness. With everything else in my life I'd learned to hold back, control, or use moderation. But cake…. I'd been known to throw a fit something major a time or three at college when a housemate ate one of my stashed cakes.

With a raised brow, Davis perused me. I had no idea what he was looking for, but before I could overthink or become uncomfortable, he smiled and pulled open a drawer, his focus switching to collecting utensils.

"Okay, I've decided I can forgive you for not coming here before, since you've tasted my savories." I gulped, having no idea if he'd intended to assist in dragging my mind into the gutter. His expression was far from the picture of innocence. It was already clear that with Davis, there was too much mischief, too much laughter and fun to ever make it appear he wasn't up to no good. I had no idea if he was flirting or just being friendly. I latched on to the latter. It was the safer option, and hell, I could openly admit I was in desperate need of friends.

"Right," I said cautiously, not sure where he was going with this whole visit, beyond hoping the sweets before us would be offered up. It would certainly help to smooth out my anxiety from earlier.

"But," he continued, "I do expect you to stop by every now and then. I'm always trying new stuff out and could do with a taste tester." I grinned at that, more than happy to comply. "For now, take a seat, grab a fork, but no sampling just yet. Give me a sec."

I did as he asked, my chest feeling light. Waiting as Davis stepped through another door just to the side, I picked up the fork and spun it around between my fingers. A moment later, I glanced up. Davis was back with a bottle of red wine and two glasses.

"Not perhaps what I would have selected to go with the sweets before us, but it's wet and it's red." He shrugged and indicated the bottle. "Also, I've no wineglasses here."

"A glass is a glass, right?" I grinned.

He nodded, his eyes connecting with mine and a generous smile flitting across his lips. "Good answer."

Placing the glasses down, he then opened the bottle and poured.

"Thanks." I picked up my full tumbler.

"No problem." He chinked his glass against mine. I brought the glass to my lips and took a sip. "Good?" Davis asked.

"Red, wet, booze, and tasty." I laughed and threw him a wink.

He snorted and shook his head. "I had you pegged for a connoisseur and half expected you to be talking bold and oaky." He took another sip and lifted his brow in my direction.

I offered a small shrug. "In a previous life, maybe."

"And not anymore?"

With a slight shake of my head, I answered truthfully. "Screw that."

Davis guffawed. "Screw that indeed."

With my eyes locked to his, I struggled to pull away. Not only did I remember the press of his lips against mine and the sensation of his tongue in my mouth, but having gotten to know Davis and having shared more than a few syllables with him, attraction tightened my gut and awareness sprang to life. I realized, and without the reaction I expected, that I would happily kiss him again.

But not yet. Maybe when I was ready, and maybe if I thought he'd reciprocate, and hell, maybe if I could get my head around the whole "Davis has a kid" announcement, then perhaps I'd consider it.

For now, cake and wine were in my immediate future. And while it would mean the continuation of many countless nights of sexual frustration by not testing the waters with kissing a guy again, it was cake. One of the best consolation prizes ever.

"So," he began, sitting beside me, his fork raised and pointing at a pastry that had me already salivating, "this one is only my second test batch. Wanna taste?" He angled himself toward me, and I was already nodding before he finished. Davis's laugh filled the small space between us. "You like pastries?"

I scoffed. "Like doesn't even come close to how I feel about sweets." My grin stretched my face as I drifted between ogling the deliciousness before me and the deliciousness that was Davis. He was fun, gorgeous, and I was sure—based on what I'd eaten via takeout—he was one heck of a baker or pastry chef. I had no idea of the correct term, but if the spread before me tasted as good as it looked, I imagined I'd be calling him god before long.

When I noticed he hadn't responded, and just how quiet it had become in the room, my gaze flicked to Davis. He stared at me, his eyes roaming my face. Holding my breath, not quite sure what he was reacting to, I remained focused on him. Immediately, I became lost, my breath rushing out of me when his eyes connected with mine. Not quite sure how to describe the look or emotion in his eyes, I deduced enough to know whatever he was thinking wasn't bad. It was enough to get me breathing once again.

"You okay?" After only just finding such freedom and normality with Davis, the last thing I wanted was to lose it. At the bar, he'd made it clear he was open, almost to the point of being so direct it made people uncomfortable, or at least unsure how to react or respond. I liked the concept, regardless of others' reactions.

With a barely perceptible nod, his eyes searched mine before he said, "Smiling and laughing looks good on you. You should do it all the time."

Despite my heart that had taken flight and was fluttering around like it was trying to escape, I raised both of my brows. "How do you know I don't?"

His lips curled. "Call it a hunch."

Mulling over how to respond, I didn't waste time in pretense. "Thank you." I gave a sharp nod. "I'll try."

Seeming pleased with my response, he looked away and placed the pastry down before me. "Pear tarte tatin. Admittedly, it's much better when warm, but I'm sure it'll taste just as sweet tonight. Dig in."

I didn't need a second invite. Cutting a piece off with the edge of my fork, I placed it in my mouth and appreciated the flavor before I started chewing and unapologetically groaning. "Holy shit." I reached for another forkful and happily inhaled my second piece. The sweetness, the caramelized pears, teamed with the light pastry was pretty spectacular. Hearing Davis's amusement, I cast him a glance. He wore a shit-eating grin.

"Don't fill yourself up with just that one. There's more."

"I don't think that would ever be possible."

"What?" he asked, his voice light and amused.

"Eating so much cake or the good stuff"—I indicated the pastry—"that it would stop me from having room for more."

His eyes roamed my chest and traveled lower. I ignored the heat spreading across my chest under his scrutiny. "You must have amazing self-control, or you work out all the time."

I snorted, relieved there was no salacious undercurrent to his tone. He was simply making an observation. Admittedly, I liked to think he'd eyed me with some appreciation. "The latter. Sort of. Cake is kryptonite."

He chuckled. "Death by cake would be an interesting way to go, I suppose."

"It sure would. Okay, what's next?" I took a couple of sips of my wine, ignoring the sharpness after the sweetness of the pear.

Humor creased Davis's brow as he gathered the next treat.

We spent the next thirty minutes sampling Davis's creations, drinking wine, and chatting about nothing that required thought, and specifically nothing personal. While I was all too aware of the safe topics, I appreciated every one and eased into each conversation happily.

"Shit. I think I've broken you," Davis said with a laugh as he eyed me up and down.

I was angling back on the stool, and if it hadn't had a backrest, I would have fallen on my ass. My stomach was chockful of sugar and wine. "Apparently," I said, exhaling, "you have. You're not going to tell me you're my nemesis, are you? It's quite nice being on the same team." I clamped my mouth shut, and heat hit my cheeks. I chose to ignore the look of amusement on Davis's face and moved on quickly. "Thanks for tonight, and for this." I paused, meeting his deep brown eyes. "It was… unexpected, so thank you."

Davis grinned. "My pleasure."

"Listen, I'd better—"

"What are you—"

We both started speaking at the same time. "Sorry." I smiled widely. "You first."

Davis angled back a little, appearing casual and comfortable. I envied his ease. "What are you doing the rest of this week?"

My eyes widened in surprise. Was he asking because he was interested in seeing me, or was he being polite? The idea of the first sent tingles to my skin. It had been a long time since I'd felt anything like it. "Ah…" I cleared my throat. "To be honest, not much."

He bit his top lip and sucked it in just a little, his brows dipping. "The job thing, right? You've still not made up your mind?"

I shook my head. Unlike every other time I thought about my work situation, whether I should return, quit, or even leave the town for good, I didn't feel the usual pit of dread in my gut. I had nothing and nobody to stay for, but since my life had blown up, there was nowhere else I'd rather be. "Not yet, no. I will, I need to… make up my mind, that is. I just have some shit to figure out first."

"That makes sense." A flash of seriousness crossed his face, his tone losing the lightness when he said, "I don't think you're ready to talk about what happened between us"—my face caught fire, shouting my answer loud and clear—"and that's okay. It's a lot. My own sexuality was a mindfuck, and trying to explain to others I'm bi and shooting down all the stupid-as-shit stereotypes that come with it is exhausting."

He was bi. While I'd figured that out or had assumed as much, it felt different hearing it for his truth. Relief swept through me. Knowing he had a child had admittedly left my mind reeling when I considered the heat of our kiss at Carter's house-warming. Having Davis confirm he was into men and what we'd shared wasn't a mistake—I damn well hoped not, anyway—tore away a heavy weight that had set on my chest. I could breathe a little easier and actually found a real smile curving my lips as he continued.

"What I'm saying is I really do get it, and I do think we need to talk about what happened, but more than that, I'd like to see you again. You look like you could do with a friend."

I was all in with his plan. I'd have time to over-think and freak out later. He held up his hand, though, as if he thought I'd challenge him in some way. I wondered what exactly he was thinking. "And this isn't some sympathy shit." I held back my grin as he continued. "It's not like I'm drowning in buddies since moving here, and with Tanner… well, you know he and Carter are inseparable, so yeah, next week, stop by here and I'll take a break and we'll have coffee."

I widened my eyes and waited to see if he had more to say. I liked that he'd spoken so much, liked how while he didn't appear at all nervous, he'd spoken more than necessary. When he laughed and shook his head and gestured for me to continue, I said, "Sounds good." I stood. "Let me help you with the dishes, and I'll get out of here."

"I've got it."

"You sure?" I stacked a few of the plates before he put his warm hand on my wrist, stopping me. Heat zipped up my arm from his touch. My eyes connected with his, and while nerves bubbled in my chest, anxiety wasn't fighting its way to the surface.

"Honestly, please let me." I released the plates and nodded, his palm moving away. "I'll finish up in the morning."

"Okay." I backed up a step.

The room remained quiet a few moments, the only sound coming from the hum of the huge refrigerator. While I wasn't uncomfortable, I had no idea of etiquette, overthinking every move, every gesture. All too aware of how ridiculous I was being didn't exactly help the situation. It wasn't even as though I could rationalize by comparing how I'd behaved over the years when I'd found myself in similar situations with women. There had never been a situation like this.

I'd had sex with a couple of women over the years—each time I'd been drunk. It had been sloppy, awkward, and had been the exact opposite of what I'd truly wanted to be doing. Living a lie took its toll, just like it had forced me into situations I hadn't wanted to be in, and that included behaving like an arrogant prick, and worse, lashing out at Carter, the only openly gay man I'd ever worked with.

It was only right that my life had cracked right open after hurting him so badly.

"I've lost you again." The soft, smooth voice of Davis filtered through me, and I focused on him.

"Yeah." I flushed. "I keep doing that recently."

With a purse of his lips, Davis reached for his keys, his eyes still remaining on me. "Something we can chat about in the future." He stepped past me and made his way to the doorway. The smile on his face as he looked over his shoulder was sweet and reassuring. "When you're ready." He winked, and I all but swooned at the gesture.

Quickly pulling myself together and telling my hardening dick to chill the hell out, I followed Davis out. Once he'd locked up, we headed down the street together, aware we were going in the direction of my place, but with no idea where he lived.

Davis's snort drew my attention to him. I glanced over, and he was looking at his watch. Barely anyone seemed to wear a watch these days. The thought popped into my head, completely insignificant, but I liked that he did. "It's not even ten." A laugh fell from his lips and he angled to look at me.

My mouth curved into a smile. "I imagine you're tired though, right, and barely get time to yourself." It didn't take a genius to work that out. As well as owning his own business and working full-time, he was also a single dad. I couldn't imagine that would leave much room for anything else. The thought gave me pause. So why did he want to invest time in me?

"True that." As if on cue, Davis yawned and covered his mouth. "Shit, sorry," he said, just as a second yawn broke free.

Inevitably, I yawned after him and laughed. "They're contagious."

A snort was his answer.

"Do you live in this direction?" Living just a few doors away from Carter and Tanner, I figured he knew where I lived.

"No. The other side of town. It's not far."

My heart stumbled as a shot of adrenaline raced through me. He was walking me home. That's what it meant, right? No one had ever walked me home, but then why would they have? On the bullshit dates I'd had over the years to ensure I portrayed the dutiful son expected of me, I'd dropped the women home as soon as I could get away with it. Even my college friends and some work colleagues I saw socially never made the effort, apart from perhaps me being dropped off first when sharing a cab.

Yet again, another simple and seemingly insignificant thing made it impossible not to like Davis even more. Not that there was anything wrong with that,

I didn't think. He had a child, but we could be friends—at least to start. Things didn't have to be complicated, and for the first time ever, I saw the possibility of a future, one that didn't involve hiding and getting blown in the restroom of seedy gay bars, which admittedly happened once.

"I really should take advantage of having no responsibilities tonight and not having to deal with a 5:00 a.m. wake-up call from Libby, but the house feels crazy empty." Davis looked at me as we crossed the street and continued on. "Is it all levels of pathetic if I crash at Tanner's?"

Amused, I shook my head. "Not pathetic. A bit crazy for not taking the opportunity to sleep in maybe, but I get it."

"You do?" He paused the briefest of moments before saying, "Ah, your sister, right? Did you say she was a single mom?"

I hadn't. I'd been too distracted by learning more about Davis's situation. "No." I shook my head then looked both ways as we crossed another street. While the night sky was pitch-black, a splattering of stars lit the way, and the moon was high and bright. It was one of the things I liked about living in this small town. It had none of the light pollution of cities. "She may as well be though."

"Oh?" Davis's arm brushed mine. The touch was brief, but I felt the moment's warmth.

"Yeah, I'm sure she would've divorced Stan if it wasn't for my dad. Her husband is a waste of space and does jack shit to help her or the kids. Plus he's away all the time." Guilt slammed into me. I'd been a crappy brother. I loved my sister, and especially my nephews, but I hadn't been present in their lives. Not only was that due to the distance of the past few months, but when I had lived just a short thirty-minute journey away, I'd been so involved with my own issues, not only my sexuality but keeping as far away from my dad as I could manage without being called out for it, that I hadn't supported her either.

"That sucks. Are you close?"

I blanched. At one point we had been fairly close, but things had changed when we were teenagers. It hadn't stopped me from loving her though. I really had to call Jenna. "Once," I admitted. "I'd like to be again."

When my eyes landed on Davis's, I saw no reproach, no judgment, nothing but simple curiosity, as if he were trying to figure me out. I understood that. If I told him I actually enjoyed a simple life, I was sure he wouldn't believe me. My past made that tricky to swallow. But to me, nothing about my life seemed simple these past thirty-two years.

"That's good," he finally said as we turned the corner to my street. "Reconnecting with someone you clearly love has to be the right thing to do."

While he was right, I couldn't hold back my grin. "You also a trained therapist as well as a business owner and chef?"

Davis chortled. "Nah, this is just my inability to keep my mouth shut and my opinions to myself. You know"—we slowed down as we drew closer to my gate—"I wouldn't be offended if you told me to fuck off."

My brows lifted.

"Okay," he chuckled, "I may be a bit offended and tell you no, but it's okay to shut me down and tell me you don't want to talk about it. Honesty, right?"

I thought back to our earlier conversation in the bar. I could be honest, and wanted to be, especially with myself. "No telling you to eff off tonight, so you're in no danger." Stopping outside my gate, I turned to face Davis. He wasn't so close that I could feel his warmth, but if I reached out, my hand would touch skin.

"Good to know." I could barely make out his eyes in the darkness and had forgotten to leave on the porch light. But between the stars and the moon and the streetlights, his smile was bright and genuine. When he continued to speak, I exhaled a relieved breath. I didn't want awkward or weird. "Right, thanks for the company."

"Thanks for the cakes," I quickly added.

"No problem. So I'll see you for coffee this week." It wasn't a question. "Now I'm going to be a sad, overprotective father and go and sleep in Tanner's spare bed." With a grin, he held out his hand, and I happily gripped it and shook.

Friends. I could totally do friends.

CHAPTER NINE

DAVIS

In the past few days since my impromptu evening with Scott, I'd spent time shooting the shit with Tanner and Carter, while the former of the two mocked me for sleeping in the spare room on my night off. I'd also survived work with no drama and a steady parade of customers. Not only that, I'd finally pulled my finger out and advertised for some help. I wasn't sure how I'd work the roster yet. It would all depend on who I selected—assuming I had applicants—and what their strengths were and in what area. It was something I hoped to work out, ideally ASAP.

While I'd been fully aware balancing being a parent and working would be tricky, I worked more hours than I liked and felt guilty as shit for it. The truth was, I wanted to spend time with Libby. I didn't want to keep missing out on so much. There was also the fact I was exhausted from the hours I kept.

I glanced at the time on my kitchen wall. "Shit." I was running late.

"Sip, sip, Dada."

I cast an anxious glance at Libby, who was elbow deep in toast and jelly; she gurgled at me and giggled. I clamped my mouth shut and forced myself not to react. Libby had been gurgling and muttering words for the past month or so. It was fucking awesome, especially when she said Dada for the first time and wasn't pointing at Rex but instead had her arms open to me. But I really had to curb my language, or at least get creative. The last thing I wanted was her daycare calling me up complaining that Libby'd been teaching all the other toddlers creative curses.

"What's that, baby, you want a sip from your cup?" I picked up her sippy cup from next to the sink and placed it on her tray table.

She eyed me speculatively then shook her head. "No. Ship, ship."

Fuck me dead. She was getting too damn close. "Alrighty. Daddy said ship, *ship*. We can play with the ship, your boat in the bath later, okay?" With my fingers pressed against her soft tummy, I tickled and was treated to her cooing laughter. After dropping a kiss to her head, I swiped a cloth, dampened it, and proceeded to wipe her down so she was sort of presentable. I was certain the remnants of butter and jelly in her hair would be sticky for later, but it would have to wait for tonight. "Come on then, kiddo." Unbuckled and in my arms, I collected Libby's bag and grabbed what I needed for the day and headed to the car.

It didn't take long to reach her daycare, Daisy Chains. It was a nice place, and they'd looked after Libby from when she was just a few months old. I took pride in knowing they adored her. It made leaving her every day that little bit easier. "Hey, Jenny," I greeted when I stepped into the sunshine-bright room.

With a push of her glasses up the bridge of her nose, Jenny gave me a small wave. "How are two of my favorite people?" She stepped around the entrance counter toward us.

"Great, thanks, if not a bit late."

She nodded. "I can take her from here. Just sign her in and you're good to go."

Before I released my girl, I pressed kisses to her

cheeks and forehead. She smiled and grabbed my nose and blew a raspberry, remembering a game we'd been playing together. I laughed. "Hey there, stinker." I blew a small raspberry on her cheek. "Love you, baby. I'll see you a little later. Uncle Tanner's picking you up."

With wide eyes, she looked at me. "Ump."

"Yep, Uncle Tanner." Ump was the best we'd managed so far. We all understood, so it worked for us. It just became hilarious when Carter was Carp. I handed Libby and her bag over to Jenny before stepping over and signing her in, adding the note that Tanner would be collecting Libby today for me. "Thanks, Jenny." I waved at my girl and blew her a kiss.

"No problem. Have a good day."

The morning air was fresh, with just a small amount of chill to it. I liked mornings, probably as a result of so many early starts baking and preparing food in the early hours. It didn't make getting up with Libby any easier though. She'd been through a stage of waking up every hour or so for three months straight at one point. This parenting shit was hard, and doing it by myself while working full-time... hell, I didn't know how I managed it. Wasn't quite sure how any parent, single or a couple, survived. Coffee, I expected. It was one of the pros of owning my own coffee place.

There were times I wondered just how easy life would have been or could be if I had someone else to share my life with. I wasn't actively seeking, but that didn't mean I wasn't lonely, or horny. Scott's sweet face, complete with haunted eyes, flashed in my mind. Admittedly, I didn't want to like the guy, but I did. I definitely didn't want to think about fucking the guy, but again, I did. It had complicated and messy written all over it. While I couldn't be certain of that, navigating through a relationship with someone who was still coming to terms with themselves, their sexuality, was a hell of a thing. I didn't know if I had the energy, truth be told. It didn't matter if he could be totally worth it. If I didn't have the energy to spend one night away from Libby staying up past ten, then I didn't see how I could even consider Scott as anything more than a possible friend.

It didn't mean he couldn't star in a few of my fantasies, though.

Just a few minutes later I parked and stepped into the welcoming scent of fresh coffee and the pleasant chatter of customers. I smiled, welcoming the locals, which seemed to be everyone currently here. It was rare we had unknowns pass through.

I stepped behind the counter. "Morning," I greeted Katie. "Everything okay?"

Along with her usual bright smile, Katie nodded and answered happily, "All good, boss. Libby okay?"

I bobbed my head in reply. "She sure is. Thanks." I took a quick glance at Phil, who was serving a regular, before allowing my gaze to roam over the tables and my customers. Everything appeared to be running smoothly. There was a decent crowd in, some whizzing in and out getting to-go coffee and pastries, while others took the time to sit and relax, seemingly in no hurry.

Pride bubbled in my chest. I'd previously managed a coffee shop, one that specialized in crepes. The owner had let me run things completely, which had really allowed me to get a full understanding of starting and running a place of my own from the ground up. The pay hadn't been that great, but it had been worth it. This was the reward. I'd gained the knowledge and the experience, made the mistakes, all without risk to myself. It had made the decision to move to Kirkby about eighteen months or so ago completely worth it. Without it, I'd never have had the balls to start up.

And I was so glad that I did. All I needed now was to continue to step back a little and hand over the reins. My aim was to focus on baking while employing the staff I needed to do all of the front counter work. I was so close to achieving that.

Balance, I reminded myself.

"You good here," I said to Katie, "if I head on to the kitchen?"

"Sure thing."

With a knock on the countertop, I retreated to the kitchen. Before I could start on the few items I wanted to work on, I had to step into my small office out back. It didn't take long to fire up my PC. Once online, I headed to my account on the job site where I'd advertised the position I was hoping to fill. While I had access on my smartphone, I'd made a deliberate decision not to check work when at home with Libby. It was a slippery slope to mix work with family time or my rare downtime. Hell, I even paid Katie to manage the social media pages we had.

There were seven applications. Surprise flittered through me. Town was relatively small, with just a few thousand residents, so there wasn't exactly a huge pool looking for a job in a coffee shop. I wanted someone with some experience. While I'd trained up Phil and Craig myself, I didn't want to start from scratch again. Not if I could help it.

I skimmed over all of the applications and scrunched my nose. I thought I knew three of the applicants, possibly. I rarely knew last names, but knew enough of the first names of our regulars—as well as gossip—to work out who three of them might be. None of them would work out. Heck, Larry dropped at least one cup of coffee a week—we now only served him in takeout cups—Joanie had that god-awful spit thing going on around her mouth that would cause us to lose customers so damn fast we'd probably get whiplash seeing them charge out the door, and Calvin swore like a sailor, regardless of where he was.

The other four didn't exactly fill me with hope either. One could possibly result in an interview, but I wouldn't hold my breath.

Frustrated, I pushed out of my seat and headed to the kitchen. There was nothing I could do about the position at the moment, so it made more sense for me to focus on something I had control over. Chocolate eclairs. Perfect for the afternoon rush.

It was midmorning when Katie called out, "Hey, there's someone out front asking for you." I nodded and quickly glanced around the kitchen to make sure the stove was off before I stepped to the front. Lightness filled my chest when my gaze landed on Scott. He stood near the counter, his side to me, his hands deep in his jeans pockets. I hadn't had time to study or enjoy the angles of his face before, too involved with conversation or that one hot time we made out. I swallowed hard at the thought. With his high cheekbones and perfectly cut jaw, he was handsome, but not to the point where he looked airbrushed or unattainable. Instead, despite his prominent features, there was a softness that drew me to him.

He did admittedly look well-bred. I would have smacked myself around the head if I didn't care about causing a scene. *Well-bred?* But it was sort of true. While not preppy, the way he carried himself, the straightness of his back, his trim body that he clearly took care of, it screamed of a high-class upbringing. I imagined he was usually clean-cut, perhaps prior to his coming out and figuring out who he wanted to be, but his beard growth was definitely more pronounced than a simple shadow. The bristles were evident with the sun as his backlight, a slight blond in his otherwise dark hair. It looked soft, and I spared just a moment wondering how good it would feel under my fingers.

Caught up in ogling Scott from the open door-way, I hadn't realized I'd stopped short to get my fill. Phil's "Holy crap!" dragged me out of my daze as he managed to prevent himself from plowing into me. "Geez, I didn't see you there. You okay?"

Scott's gaze snapped to mine in that instant. Sure I was wide-eyed, I whipped my head to look at Phil. "Shit. Sorry. Yes, I'll get out of your way."

Phil's brows dipped low as he took a moment to consider me, but he stepped around me. Pulling myself together, I flicked my eyes back to Scott. This time my smile was instant, as was his.

"Hey," I greeted as I stepped around the counter and made my way over to him. I reached out for his hand. Warmth met mine as he clasped it, and we shook while I forced myself to not think about his firm grip, the strength evident in his long fingers, or the sensation creeping up my arm from the contact. His nearness bled into me, affected me, and I wasn't quite sure the best way to handle that.

"Hey," Scott finally said a moment before he released my hand. I wondered if he was as reluctant as I was to sever the contact.

"Good to see you. Have you ordered a drink?"

Scott bobbed his head. "Yeah." He cleared his throat. It was quiet but noticeable since I was all too aware of how close we stood. "Is it okay that I'm here?" His eyes searched mine, hesitancy apparent.

The look, his uncertainty, sat heavily on my chest. "Of course it is, man. It's good to see you. Let me fast-track your order, and I'll take thirty."

His eyes brightened while his shoulders lost some of their tension. "Sounds good."

"Perfect. Just grab a seat." I jerked my chin at the empty table in the corner of the room. With a smile, he turned and headed in that direction. And when I dragged my wandering eyes from his ass, I sighed and went to make our orders.

At the machine, I told Katie I was taking a break and that the eclairs were ready to be brought out the front. With a nod, she told me she'd collect them while not so subtly casting curious glances in Scott's direction.

"Isn't that the vet?"

I didn't lift my gaze as I heated the milk. "It is."

"He's kinda hot."

"Kinda?"

She snorted. "Well, you know, for an old dude."

"Hey." I angled toward Katie and raised my brows incredulously. "He's younger than me."

Her grin was wide. "Seems perfect for you then. Young and hot, but not so young you'd be a cougar."

I rolled my eyes. "I don't think men can be called cougars, even gay or bi men."

Katie shrugged and released a snorting laugh. "Whatever. You know what I mean. But still, nice work."

With a shake of my head, I didn't bother setting her straight. She was nineteen, and I swore to God nineteen-year-olds were getting younger every year. Had I ever been that young? I sighed and finished the drink. After giving Katie a friendly wink, I took our drinks over to Scott, who surprisingly sat looking around, possibly people watching rather than having his nose stuck in a phone. It was strangely appealing.

"Thanks," he said when I placed his coffee before him.

"My pleasure." Setting mine down, I offered Scott a small grin as I pulled out the chair and sat opposite him. "It's good to see you." His mouth curved upward and the slightest hint of pink touched his cheeks. I tucked the image away. "What have you been up to the last few days?" I continued.

With the barest of shrugs, Scott picked up his drink and blew before taking a sip. He sighed contently, and I straightened. "God, that's good."

I laughed. "Why, thank you."

"For real, it's good coffee. I was so relieved and surprised as hell to discover decent coffee out of the city."

"That was my hope when I moved and set up. Decent coffee, hell, good coffee is a necessity in life. It certainly is for my survival anyway."

"I can relate." Scott pulled his lower lip between his teeth and nibbled at the center before continuing. "And not much these past few days. I've been running in the morning."

"You jog?"

"Run," he said with a grin. "Go hard or go home." His eyes almost bugged out of his head as soon as he'd finished, and I couldn't hold back a snort.

"One of my favorite sayings." I chuckled.

Even though his cheeks heated and turned a little brighter, he took it in stride and gave a toothy grin. He shook his head. "Anyway." His mouth was still wide with a smile when he spoke. "So yes, run. It's been a while, so I thought while I had this time, I should start getting fit again."

"Good plan." The urge was there, bold and determined, but I fought hard not to allow my gaze to roam his body to truly appreciate how fit he was. *Friends*, I reminded myself. At least until we could be something more… maybe… hopefully. "And how are you going with working things out and the whole 'future' stuff?"

His lips flattened out a little. "To be honest, I don't know."

"And you're okay just to be not working, you know, not earning money?" I was genuinely interested—as well as a nosey bastard apparently.

"I'm lucky and am living rent-free still. It meant I was able to save a good percentage of my earnings. I don't think Denver's planning on returning for a while."

"That's your uncle?"

"Godfather, but he's as good as my uncle. He went to college with my dad. He's a really nice guy. Hell, I'd be lost without him, to be honest."

"Oh?"

He took another drink and brushed a drop of foam off his top lip. "Yeah, we're close. He's been a good ally at times"—my brows dipped in confusion—"when I need support with dad and stuff."

I was still none the wiser. "Why do you need an ally against your dad?"

Scott shifted uncomfortably in his seat. While I talked a fair bit and tended to ask questions that most wouldn't, I could also read discomfort well.

"A conversation for another time maybe?" I

offered. When relief flitted through his brown eyes, an honest to God pang jolted in my chest.

"Yeah. Maybe."

I smiled at that. There was no way I'd push him for more. Not today, anyway.

"How about you?" He nodded in my direction. "A busy few days?"

I leaned back in my seat a little and stretched my legs out, ankles crossing. "Always," I admitted. "Between baking, running this place, and Libby, it doesn't give much time for anything else. Not that I'm complaining," I quickly added.

Scott's gaze met mine, and he gave a slight shake of his head. "I didn't think you were."

Fuck me, he was sexy when his voice softened like that. I swallowed, shaking off the desire to stare at his mouth and ask for a replay of the other night. It was a miracle I'd held out for so long. I kept surprising the hell outta myself that the words hadn't sprung out of my mouth already.

"Do you run?"

His question startled me. After I cleared my throat, I shrugged. "Not really. I went through a stage a few years back, but it was never really my thing."

Wide-eyed, I froze when Scott's eyes openly

roamed my chest. My breathing shallowed, reacting to his scrutiny. I liked it. Liked being his focus. Liked he felt confident enough to check me out. Regulating my breathing, I raised a brow. Yeah, I could have let it slide, but to hell with that. I was more than happy to let it be known I saw him.

When Scott's eyes returned to my face and our gazes connected, surprise flittered through me. While there was a hint of pink, he didn't look embarrassed at being caught. Apparently, he didn't give a shit. I grinned widely at the thought.

"So what's your thing?"

Laughter burst free at the loaded question, the tension dissipating. Scott joined me, then continued, "I mean, clearly you keep fit. You bake, so I'm sure you do lots of sampling and don't make a habit of inviting guys 'round to sample your creations." I saw the doubt immediately, just as I heard his voice lower and fade a little, and was quick to address it.

"No." I shook my head. "No regular taste testers. You're the first unsuspecting taste tester I dragged back here." I offered a reassuring smile. "And I do try to exercise." I rubbed my hand over my not-so-hard stomach. "But this guy here," I indicated my stomach, "isn't so much fit, more like thankfully compact-ish." While I wasn't in bad shape, I was also a guy in his thirties with little time to indulge in exercise. It really did seem indulgent to take time for myself. Hell, I barely had the energy to do anything beyond tidying my toy store-cum-home.

"You're doing a good job at keeping *compact* then." His eyes lit up with humor.

I snorted a laugh. "Thanks." I brushed a hand through my hair before returning it to my thigh, pleasantly surprised when Scott's gaze followed my movements. "I have some basic gym equipment in my garage, and a jump rope to at least give my heart a workout, but just enough to get me by."

"So that's your thing? A skipping rope?" he teased.

"It's a training rope," I challenged, my lips quirking.

"Right." He dragged the word out. "Do you have songs, like melodies or rhymes and stuff you use—"

I picked up a packet of sugar and hurled it at his head with a laugh. "Maybe, smartass." My shit-eating grin was a dead giveaway to just how much I was enjoying spending time with this guy. He was not the man I thought he was at all. Hell, Tanner'd never believe me if I told him about Scott teasing the crap outta me.

"It'll help when your Libby gets older though, right?"

Fuck me dead. Not only was the dude making me laugh, but he had to go there and give me a hard-on. He wasn't shying away from Libby. Wasn't ignoring her existence. I had very few flirt-worthy, potential hookup moments these days, and usually I couldn't go through with them. Mainly because they'd recoiled once they'd discovered I had a child. Funnily though, guys tended to hightail it in the opposite direction, while women seemed to swoon at the sweetness, only to choke at the thought of taking on someone else's kid.

It was hardly a surprise my dry spell had lasted so long with so many idiots in the world.

Then there was Scott.

He was unexpected.

A closeted jerk-cum-outed sweetheart.

Sweetheart? Hell. I didn't see him coming at all, but now he was well in my sights, I really had to figure out how to handle that—and him.

"Yeah." I finally found my voice. "I'll even learn all the rhymes she needs to kick ass when she has rope offs in the playground."

Scott tilted his head, both brows raised. "Rope offs? Is that even a thing?"

I shrugged. "Hell if I know," I answered with a wicked grin. "But she'll still kick ass and take names."

A smirk played on his lips. "I have no doubt about that."

We continued chatting about everything and nothing, only stopping for breath when one of us drank or laughed too hard to form words. It wasn't until I felt a presence over my shoulder that I reluctantly dragged my focus away from Scott.

"Sorry." Katie flicked her gaze to Scott and offered him an apologetic smile. "I didn't want to interrupt, but we could really use some help."

With a quick nod, I told her I'd be there in a minute, my gaze registering that the café had filled up a lot while we'd been talking. Movement from Scott immediately caught my attention.

"Sorry for dragging you away. I knew you were busy."

Shaking my head, I offered him a smile. "I'm pleased you stopped by." I really was. The past thirty minutes or so had flown by, offering me a welcome break from the norm. "I do have to head back, though," I begrudgingly admitted. "Life will get a bit easier when I've finally hired someone."

The man before me quirked his lips and stood. "Easy would be good, right?"

"Right," I said with a small laugh.

"So…."

Scott looked as awkward as hell, and once again I took notice. He may have class, a shitload of education, and a history of being a prize asshole, but his discomfort and uncertainty were disarming and endearing. While I knew what I wanted to do about that, *to* him because of that, I knew better. I offered him an out. "We'll catch up soon, yeah?" I reached out, and his strong palm connected with mine. The touch was just like the previous time, one that sent awareness through me.

"Yeah. That would be good." He released my palm and tucked his hand in his pocket. I made sure not to let my gaze linger, but his hand was temptingly close to his zipper.

Before I could respond, he stepped fully away, gave me a head lift, and made his way out of my place. I remained rooted as I watched him leave, only getting my ass into gear when Katie's less-than-subtle clearing of her throat cut into my lingering gaze and heated thoughts. I cut the latter off immediately. *One day, maybe,* I said to myself, knowing full well I was full of shit.

Shaking my head, I faced the counter and shifted my eyes away from a grinning Katie. Just as I was about to take a step, my name had me turning and my eyes widening. "Hey." I tilted my head. While happy Scott once more stood in front of me, confusion made my brain swirl. Not only because of his return, but because he looked nervous as hell. "What's up?" I cast my gaze to where we'd sat, wondering if maybe he'd left something behind. Coming up with nothing, I returned my focus to him.

"I was just wondering—" He lifted his hand to his head and rubbed his palm over the top. My eyes were immediately drawn to his corded bicep as he made the movement. The gesture appeared unnatural, too nervous for a guy like Scott.

"Yeah?" I asked. I took a step toward him and gestured to the side of the shop so we'd be out of the doorway and away from prying customers.

He swiftly stepped with me, positioning himself directly in front of me. It was nice being evenly matched in height. Nice being able to look someone in the eye without being towered over or getting a crick in my neck by staring down.

"I was—" He cleared his throat, his eyes shifting around the shop before returning to make contact with mine. "I was wondering if you'd consider letting me work for you."

My eyes sprung open so widely I had no doubt I'd give a cartoon character a run for its money.

"Just until you find someone permanently. You know, as an interim job," Scott rushed out.

Aware I, or rather my dumbfounded expression, was no doubt the cause of the heat creeping across his cheeks, I quickly smiled at him.

"I know you're looking and are struggling. I have this free time on my hands and could do with a bit of extra cash to tide me over, but more, I need to busy myself, you know? Until I work out what I'm going to do. I just thought maybe it would be doing us both a favor." He shrugged.

I tilted my head at the poor guy who was looking more and more perplexed with every word he spoke. Fuck, he was all levels of hot when he was nervous. A lick of flame sparked to life in my gut. Did I really want to be putting myself in such close proximity to this guy?

Ignoring the flashing warning signs building at the back of such a thought, I nodded, probably a little too quickly to be casual or suave. "Yeah, sure. Great. Yeah. That would be great." I slammed my mouth shut. *What the heck?* It was that bastard flame. Apparently, it had grown a head and a mouth, or grown fucking something, enough to put stupid-ass words in my mouth and get me behaving like a stumbling idiot.

I needed to douse that shit out real quick.

"Yes," I said around an amused smile. I mentally high-fived myself for keeping my voice controlled and normal. "That could actually work out really well." Katie prevented me from continuing, calling out my name once more. "Shit. I have to go and deal with whatever Katie needs me for. I'm off in a couple of hours, how about—" I cut myself short. I had Libby to collect and wanted to head to the park after.

Scott's brows lifted, no doubt wondering why I'd stopped.

"Sorry, I was going to suggest we hash out the details, but I'm going to the park with Libby as soon as I've picked her up."

He nodded. "Perhaps I can just call you tonight when she's in bed or something?"

My lips kicked up. "Yeah, that would be great." I was far too tempted to invite him along, but was sure that would be all levels of weird, so I held back, which was so unlike me. Scott was tying me up in knots, and I wasn't yet sure how to handle that.

"Davis!" Katie's voice carried over.

"Listen, how about I grab your number from

Carter, and I'll call you once she's settled. Will that work?" I edged away from him, backing up toward the counter and Katie.

With a grin, he nodded. "Sounds good. Thanks."

"Talk to you later." I waved him off and spun to a harassed-looking Katie. "Sorry."

She narrowed her gaze at me, but the twitch of her lips told me she wasn't that pissed off.

I rushed past her and almost stumbled over my feet when she called after me, "With an ass like that, I can totally get why you wanna take a bite."

I snorted my way into the kitchen.

CHAPTER TEN

SCOTT

CHRIST ALMIGHTY, WHAT WAS I THINKING? I SWEPT MY hand over my face as I stepped out of the shower and reached for a towel. I patted myself dry while considering if I needed my head checked out. Nothing I was doing, nothing about the way I was behaving was the norm.

Wrapping the towel around my waist, I cast a wary glance at the steamy mirror, relieved I couldn't see myself fully. I couldn't recognize myself anymore. And that wasn't because of the messy scruff I'd taken to wearing over the last few weeks.

For the first time in my sorry-ass life, not only was I reaching out and genuinely trying to do someone a kindness, but I was also lusting over a guy. The significance of the latter was not that it was the first time, but rather, for the first time ever, I was actually in a position to do something about my attraction. Openly. With no darkened cubicle in a dodgy club in sight. No looking over my shoulder in fear of discovery. And the most significant, it was with a man who was kind and cocky and intelligent and as hot as sin.

Shit, being with the guy at work…. Ha! I scoffed and shook my head at my reflection. I didn't know the first thing about working in a café, serving people, or making coffee. I used pods, for Christ's sake, but still, I wanted to do this for him. And admittedly, a little for me too. But still, I was fully aware I was playing with fire when it came to Davis.

He was not a guy to fuck with.

To fuck… maybe.

Goddamn flutters ran riot in my stomach, and my cock twitched at the thought.

But still, he had a kid.

I looked at myself hard. "He. Has. A. Kid." And I couldn't wait to meet her. Pursing my lips, I tensed and gripped the sink, waiting for it. The panic, the need to smack some sense into myself. Nothing. It didn't happen. I was left white-knuckled, hard, and still wondering why, for such an intelligent guy, I could be such a fool. Burn. That was what was going to happen. It was inevitable when I played with fire, especially with a damn flame so out of my league.

Shit, it was no good.

Just like the past few weeks, I switched into a version of autopilot. When I thought too hard about being gay, it scared the shit out of me. Dressed and with keys in hand, I pulled my front door closed and locked it. A few steps later, I was knocking on a bright red door that still looked freshly painted. Footsteps made me shake out my hands to loosen up, while a deep bark reverberated around the space. I was too tense. Too everything these days.

Tanner. The guy still struggled with me, I knew, and I was pretty sure he hated sharing his space with me, but desperate times and all that. Carter had become something more than just a former colleague over the past few weeks. Shit, I was sure he was the first true friend I'd had ever. He knew one of the most real versions of me, one no one else really knew, one I'd held back all these years. As such, Carter made no qualms with the fact that he'd taken me under his wing. Tanner had begrudgingly accepted that.

Didn't mean he'd forgiven me or stopped being a dick though.

"Come in," Tanner said with a sigh. He turned

and was heading toward the kitchen before I could even respond.

I stepped inside and closed the door behind me.

"Dr. Dickwad's here." I heard the voice coming from the kitchen. "What?" Tanner continued. A moment later, I heard a loud *oomph*. "What was—"

"Stop being an asshole, or you can cook your own food tonight…." The voice quieted a little so I couldn't quite hear, especially as Rex took that moment to barrel through the open doorway, almost taking my legs out.

"Jesus, Rex." I reached down and stroked behind his ears. "I bet Tanner's trained you to do that, huh?"

Carter's snort drew my attention up and to him. "I wouldn't put it past him." He rolled his eyes. "How're things?" He reached out for my hand. I extended my arm and shook his hand, offering a genuine smile.

I was right to have stopped by. There was no way I'd survive the night or get any sleep if I was left with my own thoughts and didn't have the chance to talk this stuff through.

"I'm not interrupting dinner, am I?"

"Not quite, and even so, you're more than welcome. I'll set you a plate."

There was no point in feigning politeness and

arguing. Early on in our friendship, Carter had made it clear that BS of any kind in his home wasn't allowed. Just like refusing a meal was a cardinal sin, apparently. I didn't mind the latter, as Carter was an excellent cook.

"Thanks." I followed Carter into the kitchen and relaxed in the warmth of the room. Food was on the stove, soft music was playing, and something smelled so good my stomach rumbled.

"Come on. You can prep the salad." Carter headed to the refrigerator and pulled out the ingredients for me while I went to the sink to wash my hands. "Drink?" he asked.

"No. I'm good for now, thanks." While I could definitely do with a drink, I'd found myself all but wading in booze over the past few weeks and had made a conscious decision to cut back. Drinking my woes away wasn't a habit I wanted to fall into, and with me starting at the café tomorrow, the last thing I wanted was to be cloudy. I imagined I'd be tired as hell, based on how wound up I was, and alcohol wouldn't help that any.

"I'm just heading out to the shed for a few." Tanner approached Carter and pressed a kiss to his temple before his eyes momentarily passed over me.

Carter grinned at him, and I didn't miss the wink

he sent Tanner's way. As soon as it was just the two of us and I was washing the lettuce, Carter moved around the center island and perched on one of the high stools facing me. "So?" He dragged the word out and his brows lifted when I looked at him. "Care to share?"

I rolled my eyes. "By that, I'm assuming you already know everything, so what's the point?"

His lips twitched. "Well, I don't know your version or reasons…."

With a sigh, I focused on slicing the tomatoes. "Two birds and all that." I cast a quick glance at Carter, who didn't look impressed. Instead, both brows were still raised, and his lips were pressed together. "He needed some help and was struggling. He's a good guy. I need something to do, even if for a few days or weeks while I get my shit straight."

Silence greeted me and the same pressed lips, but this time his brows had dipped and his eyes seemed almost sad. I did not want anyone's sympathy for this clusterfuck of a mess I'd got myself in, especially not his. I didn't deserve it.

"What?" I placed the knife on the chopping board, pressing both palms on the countertop, preparing myself.

Carter released a deep breath and slowly blinked. "Okay."

I waited for a beat and then five, but he remained silent.

"Okay?"

"Yep, okay."

"Really, that's it? No smartass remark, no pulling my reasons apart and dissecting them for deeper meaning? No clapping your hands in glee—"

"I don't ever clap my hands in glee."

This time I raised my brows at him, a smirk quickly finding a place on my lips.

Carter huffed. "That was one time, and I was teasing."

"Uh-huh" was my noncommittal response. When he squinted at me and gave his version of a scowl, I laughed.

"And no, to all of the above," he said, ignoring my laughter. "Simply okay."

I chewed on the inside of my cheek, trying to figure out his game plan. Carter rarely held back. I should have been relieved, should have felt my shoulders relax, but I'd come here to… hell, to offload maybe, be reassured I was doing the right thing, or maybe even have some sense talked into me. An "okay" was not what I expected.

Fuck it. "So you think I'm doing the right thing?"

He leaned back on his stool and picked up his wineglass. "Do you think you're doing the right thing?" He had the audacity to quirk a brow and take a sip from his glass and looked far too damn happy with himself doing so.

The asshole thought he was funny. I clamped my mouth shut, worried I'd overshare Davis's effect on me. He had me in knots, had me believing in the possibility of a world and a future that wasn't quite so shitty. Not only that, but he made me so hot and needy I struggled to know how to behave. My jaw twitched in discomfort, and I quickly eased the tension before I strained myself.

"I think you've massacred the tomato. Let me take over."

I glanced down, and he was right. If I carried on, the salad wouldn't survive.

"How about you set the table?"

It was probably a safer option. "Will do." I headed to grab the utensils. As I set the table, Carter's voice stopped me short.

"You need to set for four, and an extra space with the plastic utensils, please."

My eyes widened and I flicked my head up so damn fast to look at Carter I was sure I got whiplash. He snort-laughed. I made to speak but was cut short.

"Holy Stitzel, are you cooking Moroccan?" Davis.

His voiced washed over me. Goose bumps scattered over my skin, lifting the hairs there. I fought hard not to close my eyes. There was no chance in hell I'd be caught mooning over a guy. I never mooned, ever. I didn't even know what the hell it really meant, other than my mom had used it a time or two when describing her friend's daughter and how she apparently "mooned" over me.

"We're in here."

My gaze snapped to Carter, who'd just spoken and whose eyes were already on me. The bastard was amused, focusing solely on my reaction. Standing a little straighter, I shot him the finger before gripping the fork in my hand more tightly. I would not react other than the usual greeting to someone I knew… to my boss. My stomach dipped.

I was so screwed.

"It smells so damn good in here I could—"

It was inevitable that my eyes flew to the doorway when Davis entered. My gaze traveled to his mouth, which was slightly open before it lifted into a smile. Then it moved lower to the child on his hip. Soft wisps of hair framed her pretty face, her eyes wide and alert, taking everything in. When they landed on Carter, she grinned and wriggled.

Davis bent, his eyes still on me. "Hey," he said in my direction, his smile still wide.

I grinned back, my heart hitting my rib cage hard. "Hey." I followed his movements and watched as he placed his daughter on the floor. Once her knees were on the tile, she whizzed off in the fastest crawl I'd ever seen. My grin stretched impossibly wide, amusement bubbling in my chest. She was cute as hell as she raced to Carter. When she reached his legs, she clambered up to her feet, using him as a crutch, babbling away.

"You staying for dinner?" Davis's deep voice caused that damn extra beat in my chest again. I flicked my gaze at him. He was still crouched low and peering up at me, his stare intense and that ever-present smirk on his face.

"Ye—" I cleared my throat and fought hard to keep color from rising in my cheeks. "Yeah." I glanced around, seeing Carter was fully occupied with Libby, and Tanner was still absent. "Is that okay?" There was no exact reason behind the question that spilled out. I was just all too aware that he and Tanner were family and my being here meant I was encroaching on family time.

Davis frowned as he stood and stepped toward me, pausing when he was directly opposite, the table separating us. "Of course it is." He paused. "Is there a reason why it shouldn't be?"

I allowed myself to shrug, a gesture that had been banned when I'd been growing up. I'd been slowly training myself to rebel against old teachings and challenge my fears and habits. I stumbled at the thought and considered rebelling and going ahead, but some fears were hard to challenge, and now didn't exactly seem like the best time. Instead, I said, "I just didn't want to intrude on family time, is all." My answer was as truthful as I could make it, fully aware of what Davis had previously shared with me about being open and honest. I was trying my utmost to do just that.

Davis's mouth slipped once more into a grin. "You're not. And from what I've heard, Carter has pretty much adopted you or some sh— erm…" He cut a glance at his daughter. "…something, so that makes you practically family. Right?" He winked, and this time heat lit my cheeks, but amusement played on my lips.

Acceptance was a strange and definitely surreal concept. But somewhere along the way, it had happened. I'd been gifted with it by Carter, and in turn by those who cared for him. I just had to continue to work at pulling it into myself and embracing it. I'd get there, though. I knew it.

I was a stubborn asshole when I wanted to be. I hoped that would be in my favor in my current battle.

Refocusing and trying to ease into this new sense of normality, I glanced around the table. "Does Libby have a high chair or something here?"

"Yeah." He indicated toward the pantry. "It lives in there."

"Okay, thanks." I placed the fork that had remained in my hand down and made my way to get Libby's chair. Casual. Normal. I could totally do this. And if I lied to myself about it enough, eventually it would become the truth. Right?

With focused movements, I set up Libby's chair, all too aware of her garbled baby talk. Davis had told me she was almost one, which made sense since she was crawling and trying to stand. Seeing her chattering away and not making a lick of sense reminded me I really had to pull my head out of my ass and call Jenna.

"I'm impressed."

I looked up at Tanner, who openly observed me.

For once he didn't have a pissed-off stare fixed on me. "About anything in particular?"

He quirked a brow. "You know how to handle a high chair, and you're not running from the house screaming."

It was my turn to look confused. "Is there a reason you expect me to run away screaming?"

He appeared to contemplate my words for a moment before saying, "Well, I know you've been spending time with Davis, and I know this is the first time you've met Libby."

"I actually haven't met her yet," I interrupted, then slammed my mouth shut. Was it weird I'd said that? I wanted to get to know her. Yeah, she was a baby, or an almost toddler, or whatever, but still, she was Davis's, and I was curious. They'd been here for only about fifteen minutes, and Carter had whisked her away. Davis had disappeared too, so that left me focusing on anything else so I wouldn't track Davis down, or do the same to Libby so I could get a decent glimpse of her.

My eyes sprang open, honest-to-God surprise smashing into me. Tanner smiled at me. It wasn't a half-assed attempt at a smile either, one that appeared more like a grimace. Instead, it seemed genuine, and I had no idea how to react to that. I was spooked the hell out.

Tanner then tilted his head, and my skin prickled. He was fully taking me in. I had no doubt he didn't even spare the barest of moments checking out the shell of me. Nope. He measured me up, and I could only assume it was all because of Davis and because I was apparently "spending time" with him.

I didn't know if that was technically true. While I wanted to, as I did want to get to know him better and build on the tentative friendship we'd started, I didn't think for one moment that Davis would go out of his way to form anything beyond friendly-ish acquaintance. The last thing I was after was pity or an ego stroke. I was simply all too aware I was an asshole.

"Right." Tanner nodded, spun, and left me alone in the dining area. Had I passed his inspection? Hell if I knew. I supposed only time would tell.

I headed toward the kitchen, uneasy. Davis's presence had changed the dynamics of me being here. Still finding my feet in Carter's house, I was becoming better at navigating through tasks without instruction and trying to feel comfortable in his home. I needed to latch on to that so I wouldn't feel on show.

I ignored the ball of disquiet in my gut. Uncertainty was not me; well, not in my previous life—the one where I'd hidden my sexuality. I was all too aware of how messed up that sounded, since I'd been hiding in the closet all my life. Bringing that part of me to the surface for the world to see was unsettling, but bringing it forward in a home with four individuals…. I could do this. I had to.

"So," I said when I entered the kitchen, "what's next?" I eyed the scene before me. Tanner was standing close to Carter, who had Libby in his arms. Tanner looked to be in the process of taking her from Carter. Davis was at the side watching on, a bemused expression on his face. They carried on, despite my entrance. No awkward pauses, no stopping the action…. My ache eased.

"Libby," Tanner pressed a kiss to the side of her head when he took her from Carter, "meet Dr—Scott." Tanner took the few steps toward me. They were controlled, deliberate, and the whole time his eyes were on me. "Scott," he said when he was directly in front of me, "meet Libby. She's a hell-raiser. You've been warned." He thrust her into my arms, his focus intently on me and no doubt my reaction.

"For sh—ugar's sake, Tanner. Give the guy a break. Are you for real?"

I didn't look at Davis when he spoke. Rather, I immediately placed Libby on my hip, forearm under her backside and hand splayed on her back while my other arm remained free. My attention was solely on her. "Hey, Libby."

Big brown eyes stared back at me; they were identical to her daddy's. She pursed her pink lips and pulled a face, her nose scrunching up. I could not let her cry. Hell no. Not with everyone looking on and Tanner pushing me into performing for him.

I mimicked her movement and crossed my eyes, then stuck out my tongue. "I can do those silly faces too." I lightly tickled her tummy. "Can you stick out your tongue too?" I did it again and mentally pumped my fist when the first signs of a smile formed on her mouth. "I bet you do them all the time to Uncle Tanner when he's not looking, huh?"

I heard a snort but wasn't sure who it came from. The sound gave me the courage to carry on. "All right, I imagine you're hungry. Shall we get you strapped in your chair and look for the messiest food possible to paint Uncle Tanner's walls with?" I didn't attempt to hold back my grin. I tickled her stomach again and was rewarded by her laughter.

The urge to look at Davis was strong, as was the urge to flip Tanner the bird. I restrained both desires and instead looked at Carter.

I could have easily stumbled over my words with how he was looking at me. Pride. While it was an emotion I rarely felt, and even more rarely had sent my way, I recognized the look immediately. I quickly swallowed and kept my grin fixed, allowing Carter's pride to sweep over me and settle on my shoulders. It felt light and uplifting. "Is Libby's food ready?"

Carter nodded, and I was sure he was close to being teary-eyed. Hell, I couldn't handle that. All I'd done was sweet-talk a kid and not freaked out when she'd been unceremoniously placed in my arms.

"Do you have wipes or something for her hands?"

"Yeah." A smooth caress... every damn time he spoke. I turned in Davis's direction, not quite sure what to expect. My eyes widened a little at the so damn hot and smoldering look that was being fired my way. "There's some in her room. I'll take you."

He stepped toward me and indicated for me to follow. I did so immediately, my heart in my throat the whole time.

"What about your ba— *Oomph.*"

I glanced over my shoulder to see Tanner rubbing his stomach and Carter staring daggers at him. Alrighty then. Curiouser and curiouser. As I followed Davis out, I asked, "Libby has her own room here?"

"Yeah." He spared me a quick glance, his eyes holding mine for the barest of moments before he headed up the staircase.

I held on to the oak rail, using it to steady me as I carried Libby, my gaze drifting to Davis's ass. It looked firm and the right size to grip and bite. I glanced away quickly. I had to stop with my wicked thoughts when holding his baby girl in my arms. It was so damn wrong, but still… yes, it did look definitely bitable.

"Carter insisted she had her own space." He shook his head. "I only live a few minutes away." I could imagine him rolling his eyes. "It's hardly an epic distance to get her home to bed."

"I imagine they're trying to give you some downtime."

He snorted. "Yeah, downtime to twiddle my damn thumbs and polish my dick."

My eyes widened so much I was convinced they'd pop out of my sockets. I managed to keep myself from swallowing my tongue, though. Slamming my gaping mouth shut, I carried on in silence, with no idea how to respond to that.

"But yeah, they're great, family, you know?" I didn't really. I cringed when I thought once more of my sister. "They do so much for the two of us," he continued, "and it's good that she'll have a place to escape to when she's a teenager and PMSing." He laughed. "Stroke of genius, really."

My lips quirked. I could imagine these three men dashing around looking after a teenaged Libby. Fighting off asswipes trying to date her and throwing chocolate in her room once a month to keep her at bay. On the rare occasion as a teenager when I didn't have a stick up my backside, I'd done the same for my sister. I shuddered. Not only did the thought of vaginas make me tremble in horror, but the whole menstrual thing absolutely terrified me.

"I'll give her a quick change while we're here too." Davis stopped and opened a door. He waited in the doorway, his gaze flicking between Libby and me. "I usually change her on the bed." He tilted his head and indicated the single bed in the room. At the end sat a cot, and on the other side of the room a wooden box. I brushed past him, my shoulder touching his chest, so very aware of the contact. Gaze fixed ahead, it didn't stop me from feeling his on me the whole time.

Placing Libby on her feet on the floor beside the

bed, I sat beside her. She held on to the mattress while I remained at her side, one hand on her back—lightly so she wouldn't squirm away. She bounced on her feet, her knees bending up and down. She then garbled something and latched on to the comforter with her mouth, giving it a good munch. I grinned. "Taste good?" I asked. "Is she teething?" Angling my head, I looked at Davis. He remained in the doorway, an expression I couldn't read on his face. My stomach tightened. Not being able to know what he was thinking was perplexing. Just as he was brutally honest, his reactions and expressions were usually an open book to his thoughts. Admittedly we didn't know each other well, but still, right now I was getting nothing other than an intense stare that I had no idea what to do with.

Finding my voice, I asked, "You okay?" I couldn't just leave it there. There was an uncomfortable need to rush on, figure out what was going on in his head. "Have I overstepped?" Had I? I racked my brain trying to think of what specifically I could have done wrong. "Is something the matter? Do you need me to leav—"

"No." The smallest of head shakes joined his response. "Just give me a second."

My brows dipped. "Okay." I dragged out the

word, my hand smoothing over Libby's back as she continued to move her knees like she was in training for some sort of sport. And I waited. Alternating my gaze between a perturbed—which was now the look present—Davis and an oblivious Libby, I remained quiet.

The moments ticked by, each fraction of a second uncomfortable. I should really just run, do exactly what Tanner expected of me. This sitting here in awkward silence thing was too much; plus my ass was going numb from sitting on the wooden floor.

"I really want to kiss you."

My heart stopped. A quiet ringing started in my ears. I needed to breathe.

"But I can't."

Thud. There it was. My heartbeat punched against my chest, brutally hard.

"But I will."

Fuck. Me. Dead. That was going to be my mantra around Davis. I could just tell. "Erm, what?" I hoped my voice was strong. There was no way of telling with the blasted ringing still going on.

"You're not ready yet." His face was solemn, certainty coloring each word. And then he smiled. "And I don't think we're ready for you yet."

"We" as in him and Libby? Me and him? Hell, I

was so damn confused, and hot, and that ringing was still going on.

"No?" While the word wouldn't clear anything up, monosyllabic was all I could manage.

"No." He shook his head. "But we will be." Davis nodded. It was short, decisive, and seemed final.

I opened my mouth to speak but was pulled away when Libby turned and grabbed hold of my T-shirt.

"Pu, pu." Wide-eyed, she stared in me in expectation. I had no freaking clue what she wanted.

"She wants to get up."

I cast a quick glance at Davis and nodded. I swept Libby up and placed her on the bed, but rather than letting go, she held on and used me as her balance so she could really go for it. She seemed to jump as hard as her light weight and small legs could manage, barely making a dent on the mattress, but by her smile, you'd think she was touching the stars.

I dislodged her grip and held her hands, allowing her to bounce a little more freely. Her giggle was sweet and loud and contagious. I joined in with her laughter. "Higher," I encouraged. "Up as high as the sky."

"Pu, pu," she gurgled before throwing herself as far backward as she could. She was a heart attack waiting to happen. My stomach lurched, my heart stuttered. It didn't matter that rationally I knew she couldn't go anywhere—my grip was secure and held true—but Christ, for a moment there….

Davis snorted beside me. "Come on, stinker. Let's get you changed and ready for dinner. You're going to give Scott here nightmares."

A sound of agreement slipped out of my mouth. "She do that a lot?"

"Yep." Davis laughed as he took Libby from me and pushed her lightly to the bed, guiding her down, but from her reaction, it was clear she not only thought she was falling but that the whole thing was hysterical. "And usually she manages to break free. She can be a slippery creature."

I grinned. Flat on her back and still giggling, she wriggled around, even as Davis tugged her toward him. He swiftly changed her diaper and had her standing back before me, asking me to hold her up while he wiped her hands.

"You're a bit of a pro at this." I flicked a quick glance at Davis as I spoke. "I'm impressed." And I was. My brother-in-law, Stan, admittedly the only guy I'd ever really seen and knew with children of his own, did the bare minimum when it came to parenting—and being a husband. I knew not every parent was as great as my sister or Davis.

"Thanks." He stepped closer so that I sensed his heat at my side, and the pitch of his voice lowered. "Before we go down"—I turned to look at him while he spoke, fighting hard to not gulp at the close proximity or the intensity in his eyes. Libby remained securely bouncing around—"I shouldn't have to say I meant what I said, as I hope by now you believe I really don't bullshit. But just to be clear, it's going to happen." His dark gaze roamed my face, no doubt looking for my reaction. Despite the heat that I knew colored my cheeks, I gave nothing away. Mainly because I couldn't pinpoint one specific emotion or reaction amongst the many racing around. "When we're both ready."

This time I had no doubt he was talking about him and me.

I want to be ready. The thought came to me loud and clear, strong and assured. Any conflict brewing faded away. It was absolutely, a hundred percent, positively a truth I could get behind. I wanted to be ready. More than anything. It would be my prize, what I would aim for. A moment with Davis, even if the outcome didn't amount to much, was a target I could get behind.

The journey was my own for sure, but focusing on someone else, reaching for something I was keen to savor, it helped. The pressure eased a little; the burden, while far from gone, weighed a bit less. "I can get behind that."

If Davis was surprised by my words, he didn't show it. Instead, he winked and stepped back, not touching me once. Disappointment at the lack of contact warred with common sense. I had to find *me*, and stumbling into something with a man, with Davis, headfirst would be my cock doing the thinking. While tempting, the baby in my arms was enough of a reason to make sure we did this right.

CHAPTER ELEVEN

DAVIS

THERE WAS DEFINITELY ZERO ARROGANCE IN SCOTT, not anymore, and not after his frozen face of horror connected with my semi-amused one when he dropped and broke his fifteenth cup. Katie, Phil, Craig, and even Ted, one of the new bar owners I'd met a few weeks back, had wagers going about Scott's epic fails.

"I'm so sorry." Mortification colored his words. He quickly looked around and I saw his shoulders visibly relax when he realized there were only a couple of customers present. We were the only two staff here closing up. "I'll pay for it." He squatted and picked up the pieces while I reached for a pan and brush and stepped over to him.

Crouched beside him, I nudged him a little. "You know I have to mark it down, right?"

He groaned, knowing I was not talking about payment, but rather about the bets. "Seriously? Can we not hide this one?" He glanced over his shoulder, then returned his focus to me, saying, "Bill's here. He could have easily knocked this one off the table picking up his trombone."

"I heard that." Old Bill's voice echoing around the quiet café had Scott widening his gorgeous gray eyes and me laughing my ass off. "I'm in on that bet too. Just two more and I win two hundred," Bill said, finishing with a gruff laugh.

He really did carry his trombone with him everywhere. There were a few residents like that around the place: quirky, openly outspoken, and often hilarious. It was one of the things I was really fond of about this town.

I swept up the debris and stood at the same time as Scott. "You sure you did surgery and shit, are still licensed, actually cut animals and stitched them up?" I jested.

Scott gave me the evil eye, his middle finger snaking up to his nose and subtly rubbing. I snorted. Definitely no arrogance, but there was so much more to Scott than I could have ever realized. The past two weeks of him working for me had presented a very different Scott to the one I knew, the town knew, and I thought on some level, Scott knew. He was quick and witty, he was surprisingly observant of the needs of those around him, and of course, he was as clumsy as all hell. It was all a revelation, but the latter confused me the most.

From what I knew about him, mainly from the tidbits Carter had passed my way, Scott was an excellent vet, and despite the obvious, had an exceptional reputation in his field. Clumsiness, I assumed, was not a prerequisite for successfully practicing veterinarian medicine.

"Are you in on it?" He stood as he spoke, gaze still on me.

I smirked. "Maybe."

"Any chance of you winning?"

"Well, that depends."

He walked behind the counter and threw away the broken cup. "On?" he asked over his shoulder.

I followed close behind him. "The pool closes tomorrow. Your second week of shifts. Only dishes counts, and they have to break." He shook his head at me as I spoke. There was no embarrassment in his face; instead, there was a mildly amused acceptance. "So no chips, no spillages, no dropped cutlery."

"And I'm on fifteen?"

I bobbed my head. "Yeah."

"What was your number?" he asked while he started shutting down the coffee machine.

Leaning against the counter, I studied him. There were fewer lines around his eyes, suggesting he was sleeping better at night. The darker flecks in his eyes also seemed a little brighter than they once had. I didn't think "content" was the right word—he broke too much for me to believe that—but he did seem more relaxed and together. "I'm not sure I should tell you."

"Oh?" He raised both brows in my direction, and I grinned and lifted one of mine back at him, knowing it got to him that he couldn't lift just one eyebrow. I'd spent one morning getting him to try and had laughed so damn hard tears had spilled down my cheeks. He'd somehow ended up looking like a constipated rodent. And for a good-looking guy, I still had no idea how he managed to pull that off.

I laughed when he squinted at me. "You might try to sabotage me. You know, drop one too many or one too few."

With a roll of his eyes, he shot a blast of steam

out of the machine, cleaning it down and cooling it off. "It's not like I intend to do it."

"Hmm… that may be the case, but still, I'll take my chances and keep quiet." I turned in the direction of the scrape of chairs and called out to both Bill and Margaret as they left. Scott did the same. "I'll get the door." Scott nodded, and I went to flick the sign to Closed and lock up. I only did two shutdowns a week since Scott joined. And while he was a bit of a disaster, he was capable of making coffee and helping out in the kitchen. I'd been able to rejig all of our schedules so I was doing far fewer hours a week, which meant I was not only spending more time with Libby, but I also ensured I had about three hours to myself a week while Libby was in day care so I could do chores or shop.

When I headed back toward the counter, Scott was in the process of refilling the condiments, having already cleaned out the display cabinets. We were almost done for the night. "What are your plans tonight?"

With a flick of his gaze, his eyes connected with mine and he grinned. "I have a date."

My breath caught in my lungs and my tongue stuck to the roof of my mouth. I needed to breathe, but it was so hard when my gut tightened, painfully so, and my heart had spurted out a hit of painful adrenaline at his words.

Something akin to panic washed over Scott's features. His eyes widened, his face ashen. "Shit, I mean with my nephews. My sister. I actually got my head out of my ass last week and called her. We're FaceTiming tonight."

Air hit my throat, filling my lungs as I took in a whoosh of breath. My reaction scared the shit out of me.

He appeared to hesitate a moment, and then resolve filled his eyes. "You okay?"

"Yeah." I needed to say more, but the strength of my response to the possibility of him dating…. I shook my head, trying to clear it.

"It's just a phrase I use with Jenna. Date. I have no idea when or why it started. It's kind of weird, I suppose." His explanation made it clear he'd witnessed the effect his words had on me. And he wasn't gloating, wasn't behaving indifferently; instead, he was trying to soothe and reassure me. The ice that had taken hold of my body just moments before thawed immediately.

"I don't want you to go on dates," I admitted. "That's probably a shitty thing to say, but I can't…." Since the words I'd spoken to him a couple of weeks earlier about kissing him, I'd thought about doing so every day, regardless of whether we saw each other or not. When I wasn't focused on Libby or work, Scott occupied my mind. It was no accident that his work schedule was almost identical to my own. Katie was more than confident to train him up with the basics, and it wasn't like I had the spare time, but I wanted the opportunity to be with Scott and get to know him better.

He didn't smirk. There was no visible swallowing or other sign of nerves, and there was no whitening of his face. What there was instead was a steady gaze on me. "I'm gay."

It wasn't the time for a smartass comment about shit and Sherlock. Rather, I nodded. This was huge for him. I wasn't a hundred percent sure, but it was probably one of a handful of times he'd ever said those words aloud before, let alone to anyone else.

"I'm gay and I'm terrified, and I'm excited as hell. I also want to vomit."

I got it. I really did. How could I not? It didn't matter what label I stuck on myself, or others for that matter, the task of coming to terms with your sexuality was momentous. Personal acceptance was just one thing in a long list of hurdles many people had to tackle. Pride swelled inside me and spread in my chest, desperate to break free and let Scott know.

"And I want to kiss you, but I'm not ready yet. You were right. Don't get me wrong, I'm so ready. Hell, I'm *really* ready, but I'm not, you know?" He continued talking while I nodded my understanding. "And I don't want a unicorn tattoo, and I like rainbows, but I don't want to wave one"—my lips twitched—"and the last thing I want to do is listen to Cher, and I don't think I'll be able to handle anyone asking me if I'm the man or the woman in a relationship, because seriously…?" He shook his head, a bewildered, slightly frenzied look on his face.

"It's just… I'm me. I'm just a guy. I've always felt this way, always known. Nothing's changed, but I feel like everything has."

At that, I stepped around the counter to his side. He watched me coming. My heart ached for him, for his uncertainty, his confusion. He'd needed to offload and expel all of the crazy things rushing through his head. I would have liked for him to look more relaxed for it, but he was wound up tightly, every muscle visibly taut.

I reached for him and wrapped him up in my arms, not quite sure how he'd react to my gesture. Scott wasn't a tactile guy. He rarely reached out and touched anyone, beyond a firm handshake. The most I'd ever seen was when he was with Libby. But this moment warranted contact.

With his head pressed against my shoulder, we remained silent. I lightly squeezed the back of his neck, encouraging him to relax and release the tension threatening to consume him. "You know," I said after a beat, "somehow, someway, it'll all work out."

He pulled back, and I dropped my arms to my sides. He didn't look convinced at all.

"Yeah, it sounds like a bullshit phrase meant to placate, but it's true."

"How d'you figure?" he asked.

With a small shrug, I said, "Because it has to. What other choice is there apart from living the life you were given and dealing with everything that comes with it?"

His chest moved as he snorted. "So hard-headedness will solve my problems?"

"Yeah. And that's all on you, you know?" And it had to be that way. No one could sort out our shit for us. I was a firm believer in facing life head-on, just as I believed we made our own luck with sheer determination and hard work.

He nodded.

"So...," I drawled, "you're almost ready for a repeat." I wiggled my brows, wanting to pull the conversation around.

"Ha!" He shook his head and continued to clean up.

"Ha? Really, that's your response?" His saucy grin didn't look the least bit apologetic. Bastard.

It didn't take much longer before I was kicking Scott out and sending him home. It was great he was making that call and reconnecting with his sister. He'd mentioned her a few times now, and I hoped her being more fully in his life would be really good for him. Meanwhile, I had an almost one-year-old to collect from Tanner's, and at some point I had to get my shit together and organize a birthday party for her.

She would be one, and I'd been seriously tempted to throw a party hat on her head, bake a cake, take some photos of her face-planting in it, and be done with it. She wouldn't remember it when she was older but would have photos as evidence of us celebrating. Carter had told me I was an asshole, while Tanner had simply laughed and shaken his head. A party for a one-year-old addled my brain. Who the hell was I meant to invite, and what was a one-year-old meant to do? Beyond bouncing on her feet, trying to walk, and doing little else in terms of entertainment, I thought the whole concept was ridiculous. A party for a kid her age must be for the adults. Right? I considered that as I locked up and jumped into my car to pick her up.

A few minutes later, I entered Tanner's and called out in greeting.

Carter stepped into the doorway from the kitchen. "Hey."

I frowned. "Is there a reason why you're whispering?" I glanced at the time. I wasn't late. Libby still had a good hour before her bedtime.

He flicked his head toward the kitchen, and I followed him. When I stepped inside, my eyes immediately settled on Tanner, who was slowly rocking on his feet, Libby in his arms fast asleep. I angled around to have a look at her face pressing against his shoulder. It was blotchy.

I stepped away from her so I could speak to Carter. "She not well?"

Shaking his head, he said, "No. It's taken about two hours to finally settle her. We've given her some medicine to take the edge off and help with her fever."

My chest tightened. I hated Libby being ill. It hurt my heart every time.

"She's fine. It was only slightly elevated. I had a feel and think she's cutting a couple of teeth. I think she also has a stomachache. She's been vomiting, but was able to keep her last bit of water down."

I nodded, taking it in, and fully aware I was so lucky to have both Tanner and Carter looking out for the two of us. "I can't imagine she'll be well by tomorrow. I'll make arrangements at work."

"Sorry, if I didn't have appointments at the clinic all day, I'd offer, and you know Tanner's on that crazy deadline with the florist in town."

"No." I shook my head. "I don't expect you to change things around, nor apologize. Hell, you do so much already." I glanced at Tanner, who pressed a kiss to my daughter's head. "Thanks, guys. I'll just get her home and prepare for a rough night." I hoped it wasn't; not for my sake, but Libby's.

"I'll get her in her seat," Tanner said quietly.

"Thanks." He headed out to my car. I glanced around, picked up the backpack she used for child-care, and followed, Carter on my heels. "Thanks again." I nodded at Carter, and he squeezed my shoulder.

"Just call us if you need anything, okay?"

"Will do."

In the car, Libby was still sound asleep and in her

seat, strapped up safely. Tanner closed the back door and stood at my side before I got in.

"You good?" he asked.

"Absolutely. It's not the first fever she's had or tooth she's cut. It's just shitty for her."

"True, but still, we're here if you need anything." He pulled me close and patted me on the back. "It doesn't matter if it's the middle of the night. Got it?"

I stepped away and opened the car door. "Got it." I smiled at him. "Go and relax with Carter. I'll yell if I need anything."

With a nod, he backed away, giving me a small wave.

Before long, I was at home and running Libby a bath, hoping it would help her relax a little more and hopefully exhaust her so she'd have a better chance of sleeping. While the water was running and Libby, who'd woken with a lower temperature and a happier mood, was crawling around my bedroom floor, I took the time to shoot out a couple of texts to organize cover for tomorrow. Thankfully, tomorrow's specials were already prepared, and would only need twenty minutes in the oven to get ready for the morning rush.

I had faith Katie would manage just fine filling in for me.

I contemplated letting Scott know I wouldn't be around, even though it was one of the rare shifts he wasn't working with me. My fingers hovered over my cell before I shook my head and placed it in my back pocket. He'd said himself he wasn't ready for more, and while a text wasn't a big deal in the scheme of things, I didn't want to push him any harder. But that didn't make me not want to reach out to him.

I turned off the tap when the water had reached the right level, and double-checked the temperature. Rounding up Libby was next. She was standing on her bare feet, sans clothes, sporting just her diaper while gripping the side of my bed.

"Hey, cheeky girl. What are you up to?"

She angled her head in my direction, her mouth forming a smile. "Da Da."

That never got old. Every time she said my name, my heart became fit to burst. I'd never known it was possible to love another human being to the extent that I did Libby, and every day, it managed, some-how, to grow that little bit more. I had no idea how that was even possible.

"Come on then. Bath time."

Bath time was never a hardship. She loved them. Yeah, the bathroom always ended up looking like a mini tsunami had occurred, but her happiness while splashing around was worth the cleanup.

"Ba, ba." With her knees bobbing up and down, she squealed.

"Yep, bath time. Come on then, baby girl. Bath, then bed."

By this point, she'd angled herself to grip the bed with just one hand and was fully facing me. And then, holy shit, she did it. She released her death grip and took a step forward, then a second, and a damn third and fourth, squealing in delight the whole way before she toppled over on her ass.

Wide-eyed and heart pounding, I'd stood there transfixed, too overwhelmed to cheer her on or react beyond the grin I shot her way. I raced toward her, dropped to my knees, and pulled her into my arms, raining kisses on her face and blowing a raspberry on her neck.

"Da Da." She tapped my face and wriggled in my arms. I held on tighter for the barest of moments, wanting her to feel every ounce of my love and pride. And then, reluctantly, I set her down. She gripped my hands and then released, and I was sure if she could speak, she'd be telling me to get the hell out of her way so she could carry on. Independent to the core, my Libby had known her own mind from day one. And I wouldn't have it any other way.

I edged out of her way and got to my feet, creeping backward to give her room to walk. If she fell, or likely, when she fell, there was nothing around to injure her. After five stops, stumbles, and restarts, she was finally in the bathroom, butt naked and happily splashing around.

Kneeling on the floor beside the bath, I played with her, some of her toys, and the water until I was soaking wet and her eyes had become glassy. "Come on then, buttercup. Out we come." When she was tired was the only time she held out her arms to get out of the bath. "Ready for some milk?"

"Boc boc."

I wrapped her in a large towel and carried Libby to her room. While she seemed less grumbly than I imagined she had been for Carter and Tanner, I still expected she'd have a difficult night, so once she was in her sleep clothes, I rubbed some teething gel on her gums and gave her some more pain relief. I then sat down with her in my arms, and she drank from her bottle. As she did so, I stroked her whisper-soft hair from her forehead and smiled as her eyes drooped and her suckling slowed.

I was lucky to have Libby. Nothing about

parenting had come easily or exactly naturally, but she made every single moment, the wonderful and the terrifying, worth it.

Finally asleep, I lowered her into her crib, turned on the baby monitor, and headed to the kitchen. I stared around the quiet room, feeling strangely at a loss. With Libby already in bed and not being well, unease thrummed through me. I rolled my eyes at myself as I pulled out some ingredients to make a simple pasta dish, frustrated that a break in routine shook me. It wasn't like life was monotonous, per se, but having a quiet house earlier than usual and being on tenterhooks that Libby would be unsettled through the night made my home feel kinda off.

I chopped a few veggies and fried them up, putting the pasta on to boil. My phone weighed heavily in my back pocket, the urge to reach out to Scott niggling at me. With a bemused sigh, I pulled it out and opened my messaging app. After hesitating for the barest of moments, I typed out a quick message.

Me: Hey, did you manage to catch up with your sister?

I watched small bubbles appear and stared at them expectantly, casting a quick look at my cooking food.

Scott: Yeah, thanks. Saw the kids too. I think I convinced her to come over for a few days to visit. Yeah, not quite sure if that's a good thing or not.

Me: Why not? The whole coming out thing?

I didn't even falter as I typed out the words. I assumed that was his reasoning, so I figured it best just to come right out and ask him.

The bubbles were back.

Scott: Lol. Yeah, the whole "coming out" thing. *insert eye roll* It's fine though. She's the one person who I know loves me despite... yeah, despite it all.

I breathed heavily through my nose as I took that in and switched off the stove. It was no good, I had to call him. I hated texting at the best of times, and a conversation like this needed a little more care. There was too much that would be left unsaid.

As I drained the pasta, I hit Call. It rang three times before he answered. "Contemplate not picking up?" I asked without preamble, sure he could hear the amusement in my voice.

A chuckle reached me. "Maybe. Then I figured there was no getting out of the call, so I thought, screw it."

I grinned widely, placing my pasta in a bowl. "Good call. So, what's the despite bullshit?"

He was quiet a beat. "You caught that, huh?"

I spooned the sauce on my pasta, took it to the bench, and sat on one of my high stools. "Sure did." I left it at that, leaving him room to speak.

After a small sigh, he said, "I was going to say despite me being gay, and I may have considered tagging 'and an asshole' on the end of that."

I grinned widely at the latter. "I can imagine it takes someone special to forgive your asshole ways for sure." My gut tightened at my words, knowing full well him being an asshole was no longer on my radar. I knew him well enough already to be sure he was a decent guy who was trying to make a life for himself. "I have to ask though, man, why is being gay tagged to despite?"

In truth, I knew why. That didn't mean I liked him thinking it, and I sure as hell didn't like him believing it.

I heard movement before he spoke. "I know it makes no sense, and I know it shouldn't matter, and hell, I'm trying my hardest above all else to make sure it doesn't matter to me, but there are too many people in the world who are bigoted dipshits." He snorted. "What's worse, I think I could vomit because of the way I treated Carter because he's gay."

I pressed my lips together, wanting to interrupt,

but I sometimes even shocked myself and had moments when I knew to keep my trap shut. This was one of them. He needed the floor.

"At the time I was saying and doing those things, I knew. Not even deep down. The knowledge was fresh and clear, and I was freakin' terrified that he'd know somehow that I was gay too." His laugh was disjointed, and I wasn't sure if it was forced or simply one of disbelief. "How stupid is that? I'm an intelligent guy. Shit, I'm a vet for Christ's sake, but still, honest to God fear whiplashed through me as soon as I found out he was gay." There was a pause before he said, "I was one of those bigoted shits. Who does that?"

His heavy breaths traveled through the line, his emotions riding him if the shake in his voice was anything to go by. Sure he was finished, I started in the way I always did. "You were a dickhead." A burst of laughter from Scott made me smile. "The truth... you're not, nor were you, bigoted. You were terri-fied, naïve, and yeah, a little moronic with your thinking and how you handled the situation, but it's time to fuck that all off and move on."

"As easy as that?" His voice dipped lower, as if he truly wanted the answer, the solution.

"Yeah, as easy as the hardest thing you'll ever do

in your life." I grinned as I spoke. "Did you mean anything that you said to Carter or about him, or hell, any other person you've come across who wasn't straight?"

Scott cleared his throat. "Well, Carter did look ridiculous that one time when I saw him doing this random booty shake with Lauren in the staffroom." His voice sounded lighter as he continued. "But no," he said with a sigh, "everything was for show, to create an idea, to save face, and to, I don't know, distract him from noticing me."

"And are you different now because you've admitted to yourself, to me, to Carter that you're gay?"

"I'm a bit disappointed, actually." I was sure he was smirking.

"Oh yeah?"

"I was expecting to all of a sudden know how to dress sharper, to wake up and have good hair, hell, to… I don't know—"

"You have great hair," I admitted easily, having spent too much time wondering what it would feel like under my hand when I gripped his head to kiss the crap outta him. "And you know I'm fresh out of BS stereotypes, so I'm not filling in the blanks."

He laughed. "You like my hair?"

"Concentrate. We're talking about you. Answer the goddamn question." I attempted to throw some sternness into my voice, but I wasn't sure how convincing I was.

"Fine." He seemed to sober a little. "Other than being terrified, but in a different way, I feel lighter… happier…?"

"Did you cringe when you said that?"

With a snort-laugh, he said, "Seriously, are you watching me right now? Do you have a camera trained on my bedroom window or something?"

My eyes narrowed and my voice dropped. "You're in bed."

"Concentrate." Laughter followed as he threw my words back at me. "Yes, there was cringing. I sound like a dick for saying it aloud, but there you have it. I'm shitting bricks but smiling when I'm doing it, apparently. But other than that, I'm fundamentally the same. My beliefs are the same. I suppose with the exception being I'll never lash out at someone again in a warped attempt to save myself."

I closed my eyes at that and breathed lighter and a little easier. He'd get there. He was so damn close. I opened my eyes and stared down at my untouched food. "So your sister, when is—" Libby's cries filled the room through the monitor. "Shit. It's Libby."

"She okay?"

My heart did a weird palpitation thing when I heard the concern in his voice. "Sort of. She'll be fine. She has a fever and has been sick. She's teething." I stood as I spoke and headed toward her room.

"Is there anything I can do?"

"Nah. I was just about to eat, but that's already gone cold and will taste like crap." I sighed. "We'll be fine. I'll settle her down and just head to bed or something, try and get some sleep when I can."

"You need to eat."

That erratic beat spasmed once more in my chest. Concern. Someone looking out for me who wasn't obliged to. "Honestly, I'll be fine. I won't be at work tomorrow, so I can recoup and look after my girl should she have a bad night." With my hand on the door handle to her room, I said, "Thanks, man, but I've gotta go. I'll catch up with you later, yeah?"

"Sure. I hope Libby feels better."

After we said goodbye, I tucked my phone away and stepped into Libby's bedroom. She lay in her crib sounding utterly miserable.

"Come on, pretty girl." I scooped her up, and she immediately placed her head on my shoulder, obviously exhausted, sobbing a little quieter. I hushed her, reached for the high cabinet in her room, and pulled out the teething gel. It was still too soon for more medicine. I sat with her in the soft chair in her room and took in her teary face. She looked back at me, her bottom lip sticking out, and sniffled. Her tears were settling, but the stray one still broke my heart. God, I hated it when she was so upset.

I maneuvered her so I could open the gel, then rubbed some into her gums. She was definitely cutting two teeth. "Better than going through this another time by doing them double-whammy, right." She continued to sniff as I spoke, allowing me to rub her gums without a struggle. Once done, I placed her against my chest, her favorite position for settling and drifting off, and she snuggled against me.

I started singing her a lullaby, completely off-key and making up the words halfway through as I was useless at remembering lyrics. No doubt she'd give me shit for it when she got older, but at eleven months, I could get away with it for a little longer.

After about twenty minutes, and too many weird songs later, her breathing settled, her sobs completely gone. I eased out of the chair and placed her gently in the crib. After tucking her in and placing her blankie next to her, I double-checked her monitor was still set and headed out. As soon as I closed the door, my text alert pinged, and I froze. I listened to see if Libby stirred, knowing I was so lucky it had gone off now rather than when I was settling her.

Opening the text, I grinned, seeing it was from Scott.

Scott: I didn't want to knock, but there's something on your porch. Be sure to eat it while it's hot. I hope Libby feels better.

What the hell?

I headed to the door, careful not to bound down the staircase and make a heap of noise. As I tugged open the door, I saw Scott's car pull away and watched his lights disappear as he turned the corner of my street. When I glanced around my porch, my gaze quickly landed on the brown paper bag. I grinned, my curiosity piqued and my stomach somersaulting.

I didn't open the bag until I was in the kitchen. Noodle soup. Scott had brought me soup so I wouldn't go to bed on an empty stomach. It was crazy sweet. What the hell was I meant to do with that gesture apart from swoon and fall for the idiot even more? Screw a quick kiss. Scott was going to be mine.

CHAPTER TWELVE

SCOTT

BRIGHT MORNING SUN FILTERED THROUGH MY uncovered window and for once made me smile. Rather than duck under the covers, I grinned like a loon and stretched. I glanced toward my phone and couldn't resist grabbing it and taking a look. A new message from Davis waited for me, and my cock twitched.

Last night, nerves had thrummed through me, my heartbeat fast and urging me on to pick up some noodle soup and drop it at Davis's porch. I hadn't wanted to be caught, soup—and balls—in hand and left stuttering at the ground, looking and sounding like a fool. I was not one for grand gestures. There'd never been a cause or a need. But hearing Davis, the exhaustion in his voice, knowing he was going to have a nightmare of a night, I'd simply reacted and found myself ordering food and racing away from his place as soon as I'd sent him a text.

His text back had made my chest expand and my cock take notice. I'd then spent an hour watching porn, the whole time making mental notes of what I would seriously like to try with Davis, while being turned on to the point I'd exploded. Twice. On the flipside, my ass had seen zero action from a real penis. My cheeks heated when I thought of the dildo I'd ordered a few weeks back and had been experimenting with.

I opened the message.

Davis: Coffee's on. Get your lazy ass over here.

I threw my bedcovers off after shooting him a quick reply letting him know I was on my way. It didn't take long to get myself together, and then I was in my car and pulling up outside his place. Taking a deep breath before I exited, I swallowed the nerves attempting to force their way to the surface. I felt giddy and ridiculous, sure this was how I'd have felt going to collect a guy for a date should I have had the opportunity. I hadn't. I liked Davis, a lot, more than I'd ever liked anyone, and admitting that to myself was one heck of a rush.

Before I knew it, I was in front of Davis's door and knocking.

"Come on in," his voice called, and I smiled as I opened the door and entered. "We're in the kitchen." I continued through and stopped short when I took in the scene before me. Davis was shirtless. His jeans sat on his hips, leaving very little to my imagination. Hell, I'd already spent countless hours imagining the happy trail that lay beneath his beltline. He was half turned toward me, a smile on his face and a shirt in his hands. "Hey."

I removed my tongue from the roof of my mouth and remembered how to speak and breathe. "Hey, all good in here?" I couldn't resist another slow examination of his bare skin.

His small laugh had my gaze meeting his. His eyes were wide, amusement dancing in their depths. "We are indeed."

Right, Libby. My gaze jerked in her direction. Covered in what looked to be oatmeal, she looked thoroughly happy. "Da Da." She whacked her plastic spoon on her high chair tray and giggled.

A wide smile stretched my lips. She was freakin' adorable. "You want to retract that statement of being all okay?" I lifted both brows high, a lightness sitting happily in my chest at the domestic chaos I'd walked in to.

"This?" He glanced around, his lips tilting up. "This is nothing. You should stop by when there are multiple food groups on offer."

I nodded in Libby's direction and took a step toward her, being careful not to step on any oats. "And you seem better." I picked up the second spoon on her tray and looked at Davis. "Can I try?" My mouth went dry when I took in the expression on his face. There was no longer amusement in his eyes; instead, a softness I hadn't seen before hit me with a force so hard it took my breath away.

He nodded without speaking, his soft expression on me for a moment longer before it drifted to Libby, then back to me. This time, I took note of the breath that left his lungs—it was heavy, almost a sigh. His Adam's apple worked before he cleared his throat and turned away.

Not giving myself time to get my thoughts under control, since Libby thumping her tray drew my attention back to her, I managed to force a smile. It only took a moment for the smile to settle and become real and at ease. It was impossible not to when Libby had her fist in her mouth, oatmeal oozing out the sides. My heart remained pounding though, Davis's look still burning brightly in my memory.

With a deep breath, I scooped up some oatmeal. "Does your hand taste good?"

"Ba ba baba…," Libby chanted happily.

"Alrighty then. How about we try this spoon instead?" I made a show of moving the spoon in her direction before saying, "Nope?" I sighed dramatically and puffed out my cheeks, my lips vibrating loudly. She giggled. "For me then?" Once again, the spoon was moved slowly, this time toward my face.

Libby yanked her fist out of her mouth and reached for my hand. "May may may may."

"Yours, huh?"

She nodded so fast I was worried her head was going to bobble off. "May may may."

"You sure?" I took the spoon to her, and inwardly fist pumped when she opened her mouth wide and smacked her lips around the spoon. I pulled out the empty spoon to her *mmmm* sounds.

"You know that's just beginner's luck, right?"

I peered up at Davis, who was at my side, his heat brushing over me a welcome warmth. I winked. "I have the element of a fresh face, something of a new shiny toy that she can con and no doubt decorate with oatmeal when I least expect it."

He snorted and set my coffee on the table out of Libby's reach. "For you."

"Thanks." I nodded and spooned in more porridge when Libby opened her mouth wide for me.

"I swear, she's going to have all guys wrapped around her damn finger." Davis pulled a chair next to mine. "She generally feeds herself, she's so independent, but every now and again she'll allow us mere mortals to fawn over her."

"There's nothing wrong with that. Isn't that right, Libby?" From the gummy smile she threw my way, she knew exactly what we were talking about. "So she's better?"

"Yeah, thanks. One tooth has finally cut, another is almost there, but her fever's down and she hasn't thrown up for about five hours, so I'll take it as a win."

I nodded. "That's great."

"And thank you." Davis reached out and placed his hand on my arm when he spoke. I watched, mesmerized, as he squeezed lightly. "For yesterday."

I nodded, my eyes traveling across to him. I didn't need or want him to say any more. Yeah, I was a little embarrassed by my actions of yesterday. I felt like a dick for rushing out to do something nice for him, which was ridiculous, I knew. When had doing something nice for someone meant you were a dick? But still, his reaction was worth it. Rather than rambling and giving reasons and excuses, I bit my tongue and composed myself. "You're welcome."

The moment passed as he handed me my coffee. I smiled when I took a sip; it was made just how I liked it. That he knew something as mundane as how I took my coffee felt good. Outside of work, I'd never had that before, had never allowed myself to be in a situation where someone could get close to me.

I attempted to shrug off my thoughts of wasted years and focused instead on the present, the guy at my side who had me in knots, and his baby girl who was crazily adorable. No sooner had I finished the thought than the half-full bowl upended on my lap, splattering on my tee and somehow managing to land on my face, my arms, my jeans, and my shoes.

"Holy crap," Davis said with a laugh, jumping out of his seat and racing into the kitchen proper. His laughter trailed behind him as I looked at a wide-eyed Libby, who was leaning over and looking at her upturned bowl that sat on my groin. She seemed to contemplate the situation a moment, taking it all in, my reaction, the mess, her dad's laughter. Understandably, she found the whole damn thing hilarious.

I was standing by the time Davis returned with a cloth. With the damp material in hand, he pressed his lips together and scanned my body. "I don't think this is going to cut it. I'm so sorry." Amusement laced every word.

"Uh-huh, you seem truly mortified over there with your clean, naked chest." I paused. "Why is it you're partially dressed again?"

His smile turned wicked. "That may have been Libby's second bowl you were feeding her."

I snorted. "Of course it was." I was legit covered in oatmeal.

"Come on. Both of you need hosing off." He unfastened Libby, who was happily chattering about her perfect aim and expressing how grateful she was that she had us for entertainment. At least, that was how I interpreted her delighted baby chatter. Once she was in his arms, he indicated I should follow. I did so, walking like some sort of deranged oatmeal monster, trying not to leave a trail of oats behind me. He led me to what I quickly figured was his bedroom.

It smelled of his aftershave. I took in the room,

surprised by how light and airy it felt, as he led me to an en suite bathroom. "Here. You can grab a shower in my room while I give Libby a superfast bath in the main bathroom. There are clean towels in the cupboard." Before I had time to respond, he'd waltzed out the room with a grubby Libby in his arms and left me standing there all too aware I was going to be stripping off and taking a shower where he did.

Swallowing hard, I pushed the door closed, pulled out a towel, and then turned on the shower. I stripped down, wondering what to do with my soiled clothes. I really hadn't thought this through. Too late to turn back, so I folded them up and placed them on the floor. Steam filled the room as I stepped under the spray. Just a quick wash would suffice to get the congealed oatmeal off the pieces of skin it had managed to attach itself to. Glancing around, I spotted shower gel and reached out for it. I sniffed it like a creeper, a rush of lust spiraling up my spine when the scent was familiar. After the light after-shave he sometimes wore, this was my second-favorite scent on Davis. Shit, I seriously was a creeper. That didn't stop me from washing myself down and taking a few seconds longer than neces-sary to wash my balls. I should not have ventured there. This situation was not the right time to be getting turned on by Davis.

Pulling my hand away, I switched off the hot and gasped when the cold spray hit me, effectively shriveling my cock and sucking my balls into my stomach. I gritted my teeth and waited till all thoughts of a wet Davis in this shower were frozen from my mind before I turned off the tap and stepped out.

After patting myself dry, I edged toward the door. Nerves worked their way through my system. This shouldn't be a big deal. With that thought, I stepped out into Davis's bedroom just as he came through the door. He was still shirtless and looked hotter than sin. I held on to the knot in the towel around my waist, making sure it was secure. I didn't need to humiliate myself by flashing the guy. "So, clothes?"

He nodded, his eyes no longer on my face but instead roaming my chest. I was confident it mirrored how I'd checked him out when I'd first arrived. His tongue darted out, giving the barest of licks to his bottom lip as his gaze traveled higher. It took a great deal of willpower not to allow my body to react as he perused seemingly every inch of exposed skin. "Yeah." He nodded again.

When our eyes finally met, it was impossible to

miss the flare directed my way. I just had no idea if now was the time to do anything about it. I cleared my throat and tilted my head. "Libby?"

"Bouncing around in her cot with some toys."

I bobbed my head, unsure of my next move.

I needn't have worried.

In three long strides, he was before me. His hand around the back of my head, he angled himself and pressed his lips to mine. I'd prepared for urgent, a clash of tongues, a bruising push of lips. Instead, the kiss was so much more.

Davis stroked his lips over mine, the touch so soft, so light that only the feel of his hand and the brush of his stubble kept me grounded. My eyes closed. He repeated the move with the gentlest press against my lips, until finally, his tongue darted out and connected with mine for the briefest of moments. Lights danced before my closed eyelids at the rush of sensation. The fumbling kiss as a teenager, the uncomfortably forced kisses with women, the disappointing kiss that one time with an unknown man... they were all meaningless, memories I was happy to let dissolve in this blast of heat.

Kissing Davis was everything I had always hoped it could and would be since finally knowing him. The barest of caresses of tongues, the tender pressing of our mouths together. Not rough and hard, not now, not for this first time. I hoped to God there'd be time for that.

An unbidden groan left my mouth when my arm wrapped around his back, and I pressed closer to him. His heated skin touched mine, the hardness of his muscle combined with the scratch of the small amount of chest hair I'd previously admired feeling so right against me. As if sensing my growing need and urgency, Davis gently pulled back, dotting two more sweet kisses to my mouth.

With the small distance, my ears tuned in to his daughter chattering in her room. This was most definitely not the time and place.

Pulling back a little more, I focused on Davis's face. A slow smile quickly found its way to his mouth, and his eyes connected with mine. Slowly, his hand released the back of my head, and he trailed his fingers to my cheek, then my lips. He stroked my bottom lip, and I was tempted to take one of his fingers into my mouth but resisted. Libby's garbling voice was growing louder.

"Okay?" His question had me flicking my eyes once more to his mouth, and I nodded silently.

He groaned, and my eyes widened before lifting to his. "Fuck." After one quick, hard press of his lips to mine, he pulled away completely and backed toward the door. Lazily, he trailed his gaze down my body, and I became all too aware I was standing with a towel wrapped around my naked body with a raging hard-on. I didn't even have to look to know I'd created a tent. He shook his head and groaned once more before spinning on his heel and leaving the room.

Alone, I exhaled loudly, then gasped for fresh air, welcoming the rush to my lungs. *Holy shit. That just happened.* I would have fallen onto his bed, needing a moment to regroup, but the fear of breaking my erection was real. I didn't think there'd been a time I was this hard in my life. Instead, I looked down at myself, perplexed. I still hadn't figured out what to wear.

When I heard Davis already heading downstairs, no doubt with Libby, I took the risk and tugged open his drawers. Bingo. Sweatpants. I took hold of a pair and pulled them on, then reached in the drawer below, hoping to find a tee. Smiling at my success, I removed a green T-shirt and put it on too. The time to dress gave me the moments I needed to cool off. Not wanting to overthink it, I headed downstairs and walked into the kitchen, slamming to a halt when I realized we were no longer alone.

Both Tanner and Carter spun in my direction, their eyes widening when they took me in, both pairs of eyes landing on my bare feet.

"I didn't know you went to culinary school too, Scott. You really are a man of many talents." Carter's eyes lit with amusement, and I glanced down at the tee I'd selected.

My eyes immediately sought out Davis's, who was on his knees cleaning up Libby's breakfast mess. He winked at me and shook his head. With a roll of his eyes, he said, "Cut it out, wiseass. Scott had to change because Libby took advantage of his good deed."

My shoulders relaxed a little, but I still noticed Tanner staring at me, hard.

"Hey." I found my voice and headed further into the room, debating my next move. I side-stepped them both and reached for my cold coffee. Knowing I couldn't stomach it, I took it to the sink. "I should get g—"

"No chance." I whipped my head in the direction of Davis's voice. "Ignore these jerkoffs." He stood and clipped Tanner around the head. "Stop shooting fu—dging daggers at the guy, for Satan's sake."

"The hell?" Tanner jolted and rubbed his head. "I wasn—"

"You were, babe," Carter agreed, reaching for Libby, who'd been tentatively wobbling over to him and had made a grab for his legs. He took her hands before she fell, a proud smile on his face at Libby's walking.

Tanner shrugged and huffed out a sigh. "Aren't you supposed to have my back, *babe*?"

Carter shook his head and tickled Libby under her chin, bobbing his tongue out at her. "Not when you're being an a-hole for no reason."

"It's not for no reason." He slammed his hands in his pockets, looking genuinely perplexed that he was being called out.

Carter snorted at the same time as Davis. "And what is the reason exactly?" Davis asked, coming to my side after throwing the dishcloth in the sink. His shoulder touched mine. He leaned back against the countertop, his hand landing behind me, his finger reaching out and brushing against my lower back. I tensed, surprised as hell I didn't jump at the unfamiliar contact. His finger continued stroking until it dropped into the waistband of the sweatpants and tugged. I half stumbled, half stepped back so my ass was pressed against the counter.

There was nothing subtle about the action, nor anything subtle about Davis's hand taking hold of my waist, squeezing lightly and then settling there. One finger managed to bunch the T-shirt's fabric and found skin.

Both Tanner's and Carter's reactions were pretty priceless, if opposites. I was concerned Carter was going to hurt his face with how big his smile was, while Tanner's frown deepened as he took us in. Me? I didn't know what to do. It felt good to be at Davis's side, for him to make such a physical statement in front of his friends, who I knew were as good as family. But we had only just kissed. There had been no declarations, no discussions, leaving me unsure of how anything that was transpiring really worked.

"And that right there is my reason." Tanner's voice was surprisingly level. There was no anger in his voice, but concern thrummed from his body. I got it. Truth be told, I was just as concerned. "Do you really think this"—he gestured the two of us—"is a good idea?"

"Tanner—"

"No, Carter, I know you have a weird sort of friendship with this guy"—*this guy?* I supposed it was a step up from dickwad—"but, Davis, come on, really?"

Davis's hand paused and he stood a little straighter. "Tanner, you need to back off. Nothing about what you're saying or how you're behaving is okay. I'm a grown-ass man, a dad—"

"Exactly—"

"—and because of that do you not think I'd have the good sense to make decisions without simply thinking with my dick? Do you not think Scott being here means I've already worked out, *know* he's a good guy, good enough to be around my daughter, my fucking heart?" There was no censoring of his words this time.

Holy crap. I was going to vomit or swoon, one of the two. I'd never heard anything so hot or as equally terrifying before. I willed myself to stay strong. There was no way I could flake out on Davis after this showdown with Tanner. I clamped my mouth shut and concentrated on breathing evenly.

I didn't know where to look. Carter looked stricken, kind of like how I thought I looked. He was biting his bottom lip, visibly upset, but I wasn't quite sure if he was moved by Davis's statement or wanting to kick his boyfriend. Tanner's neutral expression softened a little, but I had no idea how his friend's words were affecting him. I finally peered at Davis, who, probably feeling me move, turned to look at me. I'd never seen him look so serious, so fierce. That one look was all it took to strengthen my resolve. I moved the hand between us behind him and hooked a finger in the waist of his jeans. His eyes searched mine for the barest of moments before a softness entered his gaze. His taut body relaxed, and he squeezed my waist again. Turning his attention back to Tanner, his words came out calmer, quieter. "We don't know what this is yet, but you need to trust me to navigate through this and know what's best for Libby and me. You're concerned. I get it. But you need to support me with this, and if you can't, you need to keep your mouth shut when it comes to Scott. I love you, man, so what's it going to be?"

Tension filled the room, and I held my breath, hating the guilt rushing through me at coming between them. After a few more beats, Tanner sighed. "Fine, I get it. I'm sorry." He paused. "Scott, I'm sorry. I'll back off, but I will kick your ass if you hurt either of them. Got it?"

"Tann—"

I cut Carter off. "No, it's okay. I've got it." My promises weren't for him, though. Anything else that needed to be said was for Davis alone.

"Okay," Carter said, dragging the word out. "If anyone else cuts me off, I won't cook for at least a month, and I may just put laxatives in someone's drink."

Davis snorted, and I all but melted at his side as tension drained from me.

"We're over to check on Libby."

I frowned at that. "Aren't you meant to be at the clinic?"

"I booked a couple of days off as there was a delay with a delivery Tanner was waiting for."

"So you decided to spend precious boinking time being pains in my ass instead?"

"Boinking. Really?" I laughed as I angled to look at Davis.

"What?" Davis shrugged, not looking at all fazed. "Yes, boinking. I'm trying to curb my language a bit, when I remember."

Tanner shook his head. "You're such a dick. Since Libby's redecorating your kitchen and whizzing about the place, she's better, right?"

"Yeah, thanks." I heard the warmth in Davis's voice when he responded. While Davis had nothing like a traditional family, he was lucky to have Tanner in his corner. I couldn't imagine how it was being a single parent, especially with a newborn, and knew Tanner had been something of a lifeline to Davis.

Because of that, I'd take his threats, knowing every sharp gaze was because he loved Davis and his niece.

"In that case, come on." Tanner indicated Carter with an outstretched hand.

"Are we not staying for co—"

"Nope." Tanner took Libby and pressed a kiss to her cheek before placing her on the floor next to some of her toys. He then took Carter's hand in his and led him toward the door. "We've got boinking to do apparently."

Carter's laughter drifted after them, and I smirked.

When the front door opened and then closed, Davis moved and stood in front of me, the barest of gaps between us. "Do we need to talk about Tanner or upstairs?"

I took a moment to consider, all too aware of Davis's desire to be upfront. "Not about Tanner," I started. "I understand his need to protect you. I'm pleased he's got your back."

Davis nodded. "It's why he's in my life so deeply. He's one of the good ones, family."

I bobbed my head in understanding.

"And upstairs. The kiss?"

With a loud swallow, I zeroed in on his mouth. "The kiss."

His lips quirked, and my gaze lifted to his eyes. Amusement danced in their depths. "You okay with what happened, what I said to Tanner?"

"I—" I clammed my mouth shut before restarting. "I want to do it again. A lot." He beamed at me as I continued. "The whole defending me was hot." I shrugged, aware my face was hot, and I felt awkward as hell. This telling the truth shit was hard freakin' work. I didn't know how he did it so effortlessly.

"That's good. Go on."

I held back from rolling my eyes and attempted to form words I knew I was more than capable of, despite behaving like an awkward teenager around him. And I would never admit it to anyone, but all of those broken cups and plates were all directly linked to Davis distracting me in some way. This was what he did to me, and more often than not without him even realizing it. "I didn't know how to handle everything you were saying at first. Yeah, it was seriously sexy, but then I couldn't help thinking of Libby and about the bigger reality of us doing… this. When you said you were unsure about us too, what we were, I was able to breathe again. It's a lot."

"Too much?"

I shook my head. "No, not that, just a lot. I don't want to mess this up. Having Libby in the mix changes everything, and do I sound like a complete idiot if I say I don't want to let her down?" I certainly felt like it for saying those words aloud. She wasn't even one, so none the wiser, but still, getting close to her and then somehow screwing this up… the possibility didn't sit well with me at all.

Davis glanced over at his daughter, who'd crawled over to the small play area set up in the corner of the dining area. She seemed content picking up and playing with, sometimes throwing, her toys. When he returned his focus to me, he said, "I need you to not worry about messing up. Sometimes relationships work out; sometimes they don't. As long as we keep telling each other what's going on, we'll figure it out." He took hold of the bottom of his tee I wore and stepped right into my space. He lowered his voice. "And I'm relieved as fuck that you want more." He shook his head as though contemplating something. "I'm so aware being openly gay is new and scary as shit, and part of me knows jumping into something with you when you're not sure—"

"I am sure." I was. What I felt was real, right. It didn't mean I had everything worked out just yet, but I refused to ignore my attraction to Davis.

"Okay." His hand gripped my waist. "But I need

to be really clear. If we're going to see where this goes, I don't share. I don't mess around."

I nodded emphatically. "I wouldn't—"

With a press of his lips against mine, he cut me off, and I breathed him in. Happily allowed him to take control of the kiss, aware Libby was a few feet away. I reached up and touched the stubble on his chin, and goose bumps dotted across my skin. After a few small kisses, he pulled away.

"So no screwing around, no overthinking, not quite casual, but no labels just yet?"

My heart stuttered as hope pushed its way to the surface, desperate to break free and take a big, gulping breath. While a dull knot swirled in my gut that we weren't ready for more, for labels and every-thing that entailed, acceptance bloomed. "Sounds doable." I sealed our agreement with a brush of my lips against his.

When he stepped away, I lost his heat but gained something far better.

Contentment.

I really was going to figure my life out. This was the next major step.

CHAPTER THIRTEEN

DAVIS

A WEEK LATER, I WAS IN THE KITCHEN PREPARING tomorrow's baked goods while Katie was up front serving and Scott was running the register. It had been a week of stolen kisses between working, parenting, and life, and a whole week of Scott not destroying a single thing. I took it as a win.

"Hey, boss." I lazily looked up at Scott, not so secretly loving when he called me that. I would take any moment of time I could get luxuriating in the extra time with the guy, even if it was in these small moments at work. The reality was he wouldn't be here for much longer. We'd already briefly chatted about him returning to the clinic, and while he tended to change the conversation, I saw a longing in him that he didn't seem ready to admit to.

I picked up a towel and wiped my hands. "Hey."

"It's kinda quiet out there, so I was wondering if you needed a hand."

I didn't even bother to glance to check. Instead, I called him over with a nudge of my head. "Get your hands washed, then get your ass next to me." He grinned and did as asked before moving to my side. His arm brushed against mine, and I threw him a wink. "Grab those apples for me and get chopping."

"Yes, sir." He mock saluted, looking far too pleased with himself. It looked good on him, this lighthearted side that I'd seen more of recently.

With a raised brow, I gave him a once-over, deliberately taking my time. When a hint of pink made an appearance on his neck and traveled higher, I grinned. I couldn't deny I made it my mission whenever I had the chance to get him hot under the collar. "You know," I leaned into him, "I could get used to you saying yes to me when I ask for something."

His breath hitched before his jaw tightened, and I watched, amused, as he pulled himself together. "You know," he leaned into me this time, and I didn't fight my grin, "perhaps you need to start asking questions where my *yes* will be mutually beneficial."

A burst of laughter sprung free, and I shook my

head, willing my semi to calm down. "Touché," I responded and nudged him. "Now chop."

As he chopped, I continued preparing the pastry. "So what did you do last night after I spoke to you?" We'd fallen into a routine of speaking to each other every night after I'd put Libby to bed.

He shrugged. "Not much. I did speak to Jenna, though. She's finally given me a date when she's going to come and stay with my nephews." His voice took on a different tone when he spoke about his sister and the boys. For that alone, I liked Jenna already.

"That's great. When are they coming?"

"By the end of the week."

"Oh wow."

"Yeah, she kind of sprung it on me, but that's cool. I don't need any time off or anything."

He sounded so worried that I laughed. "It's fine if you do, Scott. Geez, how long's it been since you saw them?"

"Too long," he admitted. "But honestly, she's already said she's not sure how long she's going to stay, plus she's going to drive rather than fly, which is crazy with Toby and Hunter. She said something about a road trip or something."

It would be good to discover a different side of

him, and what I already knew I liked. "Are you okay for room and things?" I'd only been around his place a couple of times and wasn't quite sure of the situation.

"Yeah." He nodded. "Thanks. Denver has made a really great home. There's a bedroom for everyone, but the boys can bunk together if they want. All the rooms are doubles."

I nodded and started gathering the chopped apples to put them over the heat. "Will you grab the cinnamon and brown sugar for me please?" A moment later he handed them to me, and I measured out and placed them in the pan over the heat with the apples. "Have you spoken to Denver recently?"

"Yeah, actually." He rubbed the back of his neck, and I zeroed in on the sliver of his stomach exposed by his raised shirt.

"And?" I asked, distracted.

A grin lit up his face. "The old guy's actually met someone on his travels and is relocating. He wants to sell."

"Holy shit." I wondered immediately what this meant for Scott, who was staying in his godfather's place, and for Carter as well who worked at the clinic.

"Yeah, that was pretty much my response too."

I stirred the contents of my pan and lowered the heat. "Grab the pastry for me, please."

"Sure."

"So," I started, giving him a smile when he placed the trays on the counter to my side, "what are you going to do?" He could leave. The possibility of that, which to be honest was very real considering this news, sat heavily in my gut.

Scott leaned against the counter, facing me. "I'm not sure." He blew out a weighty breath, and I glanced his way. He worried his bottom lip between his teeth.

"Well, what are your options?" I was impressed with my ability to be a grown-up when I needed to be. It seemed fatherhood did that to a guy.

He shifted and his brows dipped. I couldn't figure out if he was nervous, uncomfortable, or possibly even embarrassed. Maybe it was a combination of all three.

"What?"

"Denver actually asked me if I wanted to buy him out." He gave a shallow laugh.

"On the house?" My heart leaped at the possibility of Scott being more permanent, but I tamped my excitement down. What he was talking about now was pretty significant to his future, and while I was definitely interested in being a part of it, our newness meant that I couldn't hope or expect for him to be thinking about me, or Libby for that matter.

"Yeah," he finally answered after a beat. "Not just that, but the clinic too."

I turned the stove off and turned in his direction, eyes wide. "No shit."

"No shit." He nodded, looking like a deer caught in headlights. "I just can't process it, you know? Why'd he offer it to me? He knows what a jerk I was, how unprofessional I was." He shook his head, disgust with himself written across his face.

"Hey." I reached for him and turned so his back was to the counter and I was before him, my legs wide and straddling him in a standing position. "Cut that shit out." I gripped his hips and squeezed lightly. "You made a mistake, and I'd say there was a significant extenuating circumstance to factor in. Right?"

He shrugged, a frown creasing his brow.

"Do you miss it?" When his eyes connected with mine, I knew his answer without even speaking. "So what the hell are you doing here working with me?"

"You don't want m—"

I slammed my mouth to his and kissed him for a few long seconds before I pulled away, taking pleasure in his heavy breathing. "Shut the fuck up and don't be ridiculous. You know that's not what I mean. You didn't go to school for what, five—"

"Seven."

"—seven years to be working a register when you have these crazy magic hands to save animals and this bulging brain that's going to waste." When a small smile curved across his mouth, warmth filled my chest. He was finally getting it. "So I'll ask again, despite being here for a piece of my fine-looking ass, what the hell are you doing here, Scott?"

He reached out and dipped his hands in my back pockets. "It is a fine ass."

"I know. I already said that. Quit stalling."

"I really want to consider it. I trained so damn hard, went to the best school and was in the best program in the country." He shook his head. "I worked my ass off for this."

"And?"

"Part of me wanted to rebel and to give my dad a big eff you. How screwed up is that? I'm a grown-ass man in his thirties and wasted time rebelling. I'm kind of pissed off with myself."

It was the first time he'd shared so much about his dad. I was curious for more, so kept quiet.

"I hated the idea of going into a branch of the family business. It was either veterinary school or pharmaceuticals. I wanted to hate it so much, but instead, I love it. I had no choice, beyond those two options, in any of it. It was made really clear I had to go into medicine, to keep up with the good name. Whatever the hell that even means." His tongue darted out and he traced his dry lips before continuing. "My family is pretty much a household name for pet owners, did you know that?"

I shook my head.

"Yeah. My grandfather got into bed with a huge pharmaceutical company, was the lead consultant on staff, became a joint partner. It was left to my dad, is meant to be left to me."

"Wow. Okay, so not what I was expecting. So is that what you want?"

"Hell no. I just want to practice, get my hands dirty and heal, you know? Plus there's no chance it'll be left to me anyway, not now." His face fell. "My dad's not quite so accepting of having a gay son."

Shock shot through me. "He knows?"

"I was fifteen and caught making out with my friend Tommy. I never saw him after that. He and his family up and disappeared, while I had to have a week off school with broken ribs."

Nausea churned in my gut. I wouldn't ask him to repeat himself, despite the incredulous *what the fuck?* forming in my head. I knew it happened, knew people who stepped out of the hetero "norm" were at risk and vulnerable every day, but that didn't make the knowledge of him being hurt by someone who should have protected him any easier to swallow. "Did that happen a lot?" My voice was gravelly with controlled emotion.

"Only when he suspected something was going on with me and another guy." He gave a humorless snort. "Nothing ever did though, go on, even when I was at school and at Davis…" He paused a moment, and I wondered if it was because of the link to my name. "…for my veterinarian studies, I was too chickenshit."

"Understandable." My eyes were wide, my tone edged with a need for him to believe that one word.

"Maybe." He looked defeated for a moment before his gaze refocused on me. "You know, when Denver offered me the job to come out here, I was already in a great position, waiting to become partner."

"So why did you?"

"Denver convinced me. He never talked about things openly to me, but he knew I was terrified of my father, and the more I think about it, the more I suspect he had an inkling I was gay." His lips kicked up. "It was the best decision I ever made."

My heart stumbled, a rush of feeling pulsing through it and making my chest ache. A lick of flame traveled across my skin as I searched his eyes for the barest of seconds before our lips touched in a bruising kiss. His chest was plastered against mine as our tongues collided. I breathed him in, tried to memorize every moment. Everything he'd shared, everything he'd been through, all of it. I couldn't take it away and wouldn't even if I had the magic to do so. The very fabric of the man before me was made up by not only his fierce determination, but the battles he'd survived. And he shared it all with me in my goddamn café kitchen with Katie out the front, customers clanking cups, and us in a position where I couldn't show him how his story had affected me.

Reluctantly, I pulled away, both of us breathing heavily, and not a moment too soon as my name was called to head out to the front.

"Come and have dinner at my place tonight."

He bobbed his head, his cheeks flushed and need sparking in his eyes. "I can do that."

With a brisk nod, I disentangled myself, needing the distance so I didn't go all Neanderthal on the guy and drag him home now in the middle of the afternoon.

CHAPTER FOURTEEN

SCOTT

THERE'D BEEN A SHIFT IN ALMOST EVERY ASPECT OF my life since that unexpected moment in the kitchen. Not only had I spent several hours video conferencing Denver about returning to the clinic, but I'd also met up with Terry, who was managing the clinic in my godfather's absence. I'd made it clear that if I was to purchase the practice, I didn't want to be the manager. While I'd obviously be involved in key decisions and budgets and such, the day-to-day running would be far better in Terry's capable hands.

Not only would this keep the existing staff settled, but Terry was doing an excellent job. I'd witnessed how good he was myself when I'd been working there. With the basics hashed out, I then had met with the business manager at the bank to look at funding.

It wasn't complicated. It was just figures and therefore exhausting. While I excelled at math, I had no desire to be buried in it. But still, together we worked out options to look at financing not only the house but also the clinic. Denver had tried asking for a ridiculously low sum, knowing full well I wasn't going to be asking my father for funding. He knew me better than I'd originally given him credit for.

The opportunity was beyond anything I'd envisioned for myself, outside of the financial support of the Anderson inheritance. And while I was grateful for the low offer, I pushed him for a more realistic agreement—but nor was I a fool. I needed all the support I could get.

With reams of paperwork to go over, contracts to be properly drawn up and signed, licensing to be acquired, it would take a few weeks to get everything settled. It would mean financially I was going to be tied to a loan that made me feel slightly queasy, but I knew I'd make it work. I wanted this.

It also helped that with this purchase, I was making a commitment to stay. There was new ease between Davis and me, and I was sure it was because I was finally settling. With no chance of me up and leaving, the very real chance of a future was a little more attainable.

An edge of fear still remained, but largely to do with the unknown. I was just relieved that excitement kept me high and pushed me forward. It was always close to the surface whenever Davis was around or in my thoughts.

I looked out of the front window when I heard a car pull up outside. With a grin, I headed to the door and stepped out to greet Jenna and the boys. While my smile didn't falter when I saw them, my brows dipped when I saw just how full her car was. Boxes sat on the passenger seat, and the station wagon's rear window would have been impossible to see out of, it was stacked so high with bags and boxes.

I opened the door and felt my eyes light up when I took in my two favorite boys in the world. Toby and Hunter's bright eyes widened, and they sprang into action unbuckling their harnesses; it was at that moment I was grateful for video calls so that despite not seeing them regularly, they knew exactly who I was.

"Hey, monsters." I leaned in and helped Hunter with his straps, relief trickling through me that they seemed as happy to see me as I was them. It had been so long since I'd seen them, a real pit of dread had sat in my gut at how they'd react at our reunion. I shouldn't have worried.

Both boys launched themselves out at me. A loud laugh burst free as I gingerly managed to maneuver us out to the side of the car without banging their heads along the way.

"Uncle Scottie," they called in chorus.

I rained kisses on their cheeks and blew raspberries for good measure.

"How are my two favorite boys?" I repositioned them so I had one on each hip, trying to get my head around how much they had grown. "You ready to cause chaos and stretch your legs after your long journey?"

They both nodded, and Hunter shouted, "Yes!"

"Hey, you."

My sister's voice had me looking in her direction. She looked dog-tired, but the smile on her face was real. "Hey." I grinned and indicated with a nod for her to follow me in.

The sound of the car door closing and the doors locking followed me into the house. Once inside, I set the boys down, crouched, and ruffled their hair. "Do you want to go and explore and see if you can work out where you're sleeping?"

Hunter bobbed his head excitedly up and down while Toby said, "Yes, please."

"Go on then. There may even be a couple of surprises for you both." I'd headed to the toy shop in town and had bought them both a couple of small gifts each. They grinned and raced in the direction of the staircase. Standing, I turned and faced Jenna, not quite prepared as she hurled herself at me and broke into a flood of tears.

Hands gripped the back of my shirt as she sobbed. Wide-eyed and confused, I held her close. "Hey." I hushed her and placed a kiss on the top of her head. Guilt threatened to claw at my chest. Something was so very, very wrong, and I'd had no idea. "Shh, it's okay, you're here now. It's okay."

Her sobs calmed a little, her breaths broken. Jenna nodded against my chest. I heard her expel heavy breaths as her shoulders lifted up and down in time with the forced inhale and exhale.

"Let's head to the kitchen." The boys were distracted, but I wasn't sure for how much longer. I heard little feet still thudding above us. She pulled back, but she didn't lift her head to meet my eyes. Instead, she tucked herself under my arm and allowed me to lead the way into the kitchen.

"Sit." I directed her to a chair at the kitchen table. "Tea, or something harder?"

This time she glanced up at me and offered a watery smile. "Coffee, please."

"Coffee?" Jenna never drank coffee.

She snorted a little and nodded. "Yeah. I've been hitting the hard stuff recently."

I cast my eyes over her, my worry for her bubbling to the surface. "You start speaking, and I'll make coffee." I paused and listened to the boys. I heard them both squeal and then laugh; a louder thud followed. They'd found their gifts, so should be occupied a while longer.

I started preparing coffee but glanced over my shoulder when Jenna remained quiet. She was almost bug-eyed, a mix of surprise and confusion in her eyes. Her lips tipped up though. "What?" I asked.

"You." She tilted her head as her gaze roamed my face.

"Me what?" We were meant to be talking about her, so I had no clue what she was thinking or talking about.

"Something's happened. Changed." She brushed her thumb across her closed lips. "On our calls, I could tell something was different, but I didn't know what."

I froze, not quite sure how to proceed. I really didn't want to be focused on me right now, especially as something major was going down with her. Why else would she have turned up with a car filled with what looked like all her possessions?

With her narrowed eyes focusing so intently, I fought the urge to squirm. "I meant you were to talk about you and what the hell's going on."

She nodded, but her gaze didn't waver. "You look good. Happy." Tears sprung once again in her eyes. I was not cut out with dealing with emotional stuff. I wasn't good at it.

"Jenna." Her name came out as a sigh as I frowned in concern.

"No." She waved me off. "It's so good to see you like this. I can't remember the last time I saw you this relaxed, this happy. I don't know who or what's made you this way, but it's wonderful. Truly wonderful." She sniffed and wiped her eyes, her mouth splitting into a grin. "Gah." She sniffed again. "I suppose I'm just sad that it's so obvious. That I honestly can't remember seeing you so… I don't know, at ease and carefree." I stepped over to her, placed my hand on her shoulder, and squeezed. She leaned her head against my hand. "Is it crazy that seeing you like this gives me hope?"

Fuck, I'd seriously let her down if she was reacting this way at seeing me happy. What the hell had she been through to be so broken? I pulled out the chair next to her and held her hands on top of the kitchen table. "Fuck, Jenna, you've got to give me something. I'm freaking the hell out here. What happened? What's going on?"

Jenna swallowed, the sound loud. "I've left him. I just couldn't do it anymore." She shook her head. "I had to get out of there before I was pushed over the edge."

Loud ringing burst in my ears. "Did—" I slammed my mouth shut, trying to take control of the shake in my voice. "Did he hurt you?"

Her shoulders sagged, her eyes still connected to mine. "Yes and no." She removed one of her hands to wipe at her free-falling tears. I frowned, not knowing what that meant. "He's been having an affair, or affairs." Her lip curled into a sneer. "He was drinking more and losing his temper. He pushed me over in front of the boys. I hit my head pretty badly and needed a couple of stitches. He didn't hit me with a fist, but—"

"You thought that he might do that next? And shit, Jenna, stitches?"

She bobbed her head and touched her brow. "It

was coming. He raised his hand a couple of times, but both times he didn't go through with it because he was interrupted." Jenna's lips thinned. "Things haven't been going well at work. I think Dad found out he was having an affair with one of the admin staff. She was fired a few weeks ago, but that made things worse at home."

"What have Mom and Dad said?"

She gave a humorless snort. "I tried talking to Mom, but she shrugged it off, saying 'men would be men,' and offered to make me a martini. Dad told me to keep my mouth shut. You know he won't allow anything to ruin the family name."

Didn't I just. I would have liked to say I was surprised at my parents' lack of support, but considering my own history, I was fully aware that reputation was paramount for the Andersons, appearance everything. We were a family of bulging rugs and stuffed closets. My father would have likely paid off the woman and threatened Stan to show more discretion. Sickness churned in my gut that Jenna, the nicest and sweetest woman I knew, had felt no other choice but to live this way.

"When it became clear you were more settled and you actually started calling me again, I knew it was my chance. I couldn't look myself in the mirror anymore, bringing the boys up with such a bastard of a father." Fire lit her eyes, and I smiled despite the heaviness in my chest.

"I'm pleased you came. Wish I had—"

"Nope." She shook her head vehemently. "This is not your fault, and wishes are pointless. I'm here, the boys are here, you were actually not tense a few minutes ago." She laughed. "Now I'm here, so it'll be okay."

While she didn't ask a question, her eyes did. I stood and tugged her up and hugged her hard. "It will be okay. Shit, it'll be fucking perfect."

She snorted a laugh and hugged me back. "Thank you."

I stepped back and grinned. "Why don't you finish making the drinks and take a few minutes, and I'll see what those kids of yours are up to. It's suspiciously quiet at the moment."

She heaved a breath and blinked while nodding. I could virtually see the first layers of tension drifting off her, and my heart eased a little. I would do everything in my power to make sure she and the boys found their place in the world, and I was more than happy if that place was here in Kirkby.

ONCE AGAIN LIFE KNEW HOW TO KEEP ME ON EDGE. That wasn't to say things weren't falling into place; in fact, almost every aspect of my life seemed to be charging full speed ahead. It was as exhilarating as it was making me shit scared. In truth, it was the reality that everything seemed to be falling into place that kept me wary. I wondered when the other damn shoe would drop.

Pessimism was hard to shake. After too many years of hiding, of resisting, it was proving difficult to step out of its clinging shadows and break free completely.

"What time are you heading to the clinic?" My sister swept past me, a dirty sock in one hand and Christ knew what in the other. The house, my *almost* house had become a manic place to be for the past week. And while squeals and the thudding footsteps from the boys had moments that made me wince, I loved spending the time not only with them, but Jenna too.

"In fifteen." I glanced at the time on my phone. It was my second trip to the clinic this week, but so far I'd kept my head low, not ready to cause a stir. I was aware from Carter that rumors were already rampant about Denver selling, but no official announcement had been made. I still had paperwork and funding to organize, but the whole process was going scarily fast, with Denver seeming to be in a hurry and happy to fast-track as much as possible while nudging his lawyers to be as proactive as possible.

It wasn't just that though that had my gut threatening to push me off balance.

"And then you're seeing Davis, and he's coming here for dinner, right?"

That was the second reason.

On Jenna's third night here, we'd sat down with liquor once the boys were in bed, and I'd built up to telling her the truth.

She'd cried, devastated I'd been unable to come out and share with her before, while becoming incensed over Dad's involvement. I'd wondered how much she'd known or seen about Dad's treatment of me, but she admitted between sobs and shots that she'd been so caught up in our parents all but trapping her in the house and fixing her up with Stan, who she was determined would be her *ex*-husband, that she'd wallowed in her own angst and hadn't even considered what I'd been hiding.

It made sense. I just wished life had been different for us. All too well I knew many wouldn't understand that. Shit, we'd been brought up with goddamn silver spoons in our mouths, but wealth and education were not the making of a man. It was only since moving to Kirkby that I'd allowed myself to embrace that belief fully.

I cleared my throat. "Yeah."

She grinned widely, while my nerves were as obvious as the heat touching my cheeks. When she waggled her brows ridiculously, I couldn't help but mirror her amusement. She was excited, and that knowledge slammed into me so hard, I caught my breath.

Davis was incredible. And sharing him with Jenna and the boys was something I'd never expected to be able to do. Life had a funny way of panning out sometimes, and it was that I had to grasp on to rather than allowing the shadows to seep back in.

"What about you?" I asked.

She washed her hands, having discarded the offending items while I'd been blushing. "I have an appointment at the day care in thirty minutes."

It was that permanent, this move. The morning after our talk, she'd approached me wearing sunglasses and let me know that she planned to stay in Kirkby. Resolve had held her voice steady when she'd told me this place was exactly where she and the boys were meant to be. I hadn't hesitated when I'd tugged her close and hugged her so hard that she threatened to vomit on me.

Her plan was to settle the boys into the same day care as Libby. Davis had recommended them when I'd discussed everything with him a couple of nights ago over dinner at his house. Toby would be able to start school at the beginning of the next school year, but rather than wait till then, Jenna hoped the boys being together would help settle them in easier, plus she was resolved to find a job.

She hadn't worked since the boys were born and was determined to make sure she could care for them financially. There was still the fallout of leaving her husband to deal with, but she wasn't quite ready to handle that just yet.

"Okay, well, I'll be home at maybe four so I can start on dinner." I rolled my eyes when her waggling brows started up again.

"I can—"

"Nope. My... Davis." She grinned when I hesitated. "So I'll get food prepared."

"Even the kids'?"

I nodded, sure I could wrangle together a meal for us all. "I've got it."

Amusement lit her features. She knew I wasn't

the best of cooks, but I was determined to try. I pressed a kiss to her cheek, did the same to the boys who were glued to the TV in the sitting room, then headed out to the clinic, trying to shake the nerves away as I traveled closer.

When I pulled up out front, I took a deep breath, grabbed my files, then headed inside. Emily, one of the receptionists, was at the desk. Her eyes widened a little before she smiled. I was aware how lucky I was that all the shit I'd caused with Carter, which seemed like a lifetime ago but in reality was only a few months, had been kept on the down low. Only Lauren and Terry were aware of the events.

"Hey, Emily." I bobbed my head in greeting.

"Well, I'll be. If it isn't the elusive Dr. Anderson. I heard talk that we may be seeing more of your handsome face around here again."

Genuine laughter escaped, relieving some of the tension I carried in my shoulders. "Is that right?" Emily nodded, her gray-white hair staying miraculously in place. "Is Terry in his office?"

"He sure is."

"Perfect. Are you okay for me to head back—"

"Do you really need to ask…, boss?" she hedged.

I snorted and shook my head. "Thanks." I made my way around the familiar hallway, rightness settling in me. While I hadn't been at the clinic long before I'd messed up, there was nothing like the stinging scent of disinfectant and the underlying smell of animals to make me feel like I was at home. For all my moments of arrogance and idiocy, medicine was in my blood. Healing animals made my blood sing and heart soar. Hell, I'd missed this place.

As I approached Terry's office, Lauren stepped around the corner. Her eyes zeroed in on me, her smile slipping as she continued my way. I paused, knowing it was time I addressed her. "Lauren."

"Dr. Anderson." There was an edge to her voice.

"May I speak to you privately?"

Her gaze was assessing as she nodded. "The staffroom is empty." She turned back, and I followed her on through, closing the door behind me so we had privacy.

Once we were alone, I didn't give her the opportunity to speak. Instead, I launched straight into my apology. "I need to thank you."

Her eyes widened; no doubt it was not what she was expecting me to say. "Go on."

I didn't dare allow my lips to twitch at her focused tenacity. "You did the right thing reporting me. I'm grateful that Carter has you to support him, and the clinic is lucky to have you." I waited for a beat as her head tilted slightly, her eye contact unwavering. "Thank you for stepping up and reporting my behavior. If it wasn't for you, and if it wasn't for Carter, I would never have had the courage to admit I was gay"—her brows shot high at my admission—"and I wouldn't have been lucky enough to earn Carter's forgiveness and friendship."

I took a deep breath, proud of myself for keeping the shake from my voice. I'd had no intention of sharing so much with her. My personal affairs were my own, but it had felt right in the moment; plus the words felt freeing.

"I'm sure you've heard the rumors—"

"So they're true? You're buying the place."

I straightened up a little. "Yes." When she didn't respond, I continued. "One day I'll step into the role of managing the clinic too, but I don't plan for that to be until a few years have passed. I love practicing, so am not ready to give that up for an admin role. Not just yet. Plus, Terry is doing an excellent job."

She nodded. "He is."

"And I apologize for putting you in a position where you had to step in to prevent a situation that should never have happened." While I wanted to rush through the words, I owed them the time and respect they deserved, just like I owed the same to her.

When Lauren smiled, breath rushed out of my lungs. She stepped toward me and held out her hand. "Congratulations, and thank you. I look forward to working with you and for you." I took her hand and gave a firm shake, surprise making my head fuzzy. After she released my hand, she looked up at me. "You need to know I do speak plainly, and sometimes I say more than I should." I knew this about her for sure. "I'll always show you the appropriate amount of respect as my boss, but respect has to be earned. You didn't have to apologize, so I know it took some pretty impressive balls to do so." She smirked, and I mimicked the gesture.

"We all do stupid shit sometimes and fuck up along the way. Carter's sung your praises so much recently that I'd already started coming around, but still, I appreciate it." She glanced at her watch. "I have to go."

"Okay. Thanks for being so understanding."

She bobbed her head. "Doesn't mean I won't call you out on shit in the future though." She smirked. "With respect, of course."

I laughed lightly. "Of course."

"Also," she threw over her shoulder as she tugged

open the door, "there's nothing quite like a new coffee machine for your soon-to-be dedicated staff to help make us loyal as hell."

I shook my head as she left and ran my hand over my face. My return to the clinic couldn't start fast enough. A smile drifted across my lips as I left and made my way to my meeting.

CHAPTER FIFTEEN

DAVIS

I STOOD AT THE DOOR AND STRETCHED MY NECK FROM side to side. Libby, oblivious to the rare nerves taking flight in my gut, wriggled in my arms, desperate to be put down. She was so eager to explore and walk. She was growing too damn fast.

"In a few, wriggle ass." I tickled her tummy, and she squealed in delight. The door opened midsqueal, and I glanced over at a smiling Scott. "Hey."

"Hey, back." He stepped outside rather than waiting for me to step forward. His lips landed on mine, but for nowhere near long enough. "Here, let me take this little lady."

Warmth spread in my chest. I loved his confidence with Libby, his eagerness to not only help but to get to know her. I lifted Libby so he could take her and shook my head, my lips curving upwards when I heard the raspberry he blew.

"Come on in."

I did so and was immediately aware the house no longer looked or sounded like it did the last time I visited. Instead, the sound of Scott's nephews playing filled the house, with what sounded like a kid's TV show playing in the background. Also, the once organized space was littered with toys and mismatched shoes.

"I'll introduce Libby to the boys."

I followed Scott, dropping her change bag on the floor before I stepped into the sitting room. The two boys were parked in front of the TV, where some loud and brash show was playing. The younger of the two was on his feet doing a dance, while the eldest's attention drifted between the screen and the cars.

"Toby, Hunter." Scott's voice was light, and I was certain there was a smile on his face. His nephews turned to face him. "This here is Libby." He sank to his knees and placed Libby down. Immediately, she reached for a car and started to bang it on the ground.

Toby's mouth twisted a little when he looked at Libby, his toy, then at Scott.

"This is Davis's daughter."

He looked in my direction, and I watched Toby follow his gaze as he took me in. His eyes narrowed a little, and he tilted his head as he said, "You're Uncle Scottie's boyfriend, Mommy said, and we have to use our manners and be kind to Libby."

"Err—"

My glance flicked to Scott and my mouth split wide. "That's right, I am. And if you can use your manners, I'll be impressed, but nudge me if I burp and forget to say excuse me."

Toby's eyes widened, and he giggled. Hunter seemed to take that as his cue to stop dancing, spin to face me, and burp. And holy shit, who knew a kid that little could not only belch on cue but so freakin' loud.

"Impressive," I said just as "Hunter Samuel, that had better have been real and you had better have remembered your manners," flowed into the room.

Hunter dropped to his ass, a look of panic flicking across his features. "Sorry, Mommy."

Scott snorted and ruffled his hair. "Good job, kiddo."

"Uncle Scottie's boyfriend…?"

I glanced over at Toby. "Yes, Toby?" I asked, stepping further into the room, super aware Scott was watching our whole exchange with a somewhat bemused expression.

"One of my friends, Jessie, has two mommies, and she's gay."

I clamped my mouth shut, trying my hardest not to laugh. "That's great." I had no idea what to do with that.

He nodded. "Jessie picks her nose and eats it." He wrinkled his nose. "Does Libby pick her nose and eat it?" His gaze shot to his car Libby had gripped in her hand.

I pressed my lips together, determined to ignore Scott's shaking shoulders and address Toby as seriously as his frown suggested the question was. "No, Toby. There's no nose picking as yet. She may suck and nibble at it though." He looked at me in horror, his focus returning to Libby just as she shoved half of his car into his mouth.

"That's not my bestest toy, so she can keep that." He scooted away from my slobbering child.

I laughed and took the car from Libby, fearing she'd end up swallowing one of its wheels. She looked at me hard, no doubt debating whether or not she would share the strength of her lungs with the house. Fortunately, Hunter's whooping as he stood and started dancing distracted her enough that she pushed herself up and ambled over to watch him intently.

"How about I get this car washed so it's saliva free?"

Toby nodded. "Okay." He then returned to his cars, his interest immediately elsewhere.

Scott stood and bumped shoulders with me. "You had a good day?"

I turned toward him and placed my palm on his lower back. He'd popped into the coffee shop not long after lunch, and we'd been rushed off our feet. He'd apologized so many times about leaving me high and dry while he was sorting out his return to the hospital. It was sweet, but I'd reminded him with a laugh that the replacement dishes we'd purchased appreciated him returning to his calling as a vet. His cheeks had immediately colored, and he'd rolled his eyes.

"Yeah, thanks. It settled down not much after you left."

Guilt once again flittered in his eyes.

I shook my head before he could even start. "I've already advertised, so don't worry yourself about it, boyfriend."

His narrowed eyes made me smile.

"What?" I laughed. "From the mouth of babes and all that."

"You're impossible." He shook his head, but humor lit his eyes. "Jenna told him that, not—"

My hand curled around his waist and I squeezed. "No getting away from it now. No take backs." I waggled my brows at him.

He snorted. "No take backs, huh?"

I pressed a light kiss on his lips. "That's correct," I said, pulling away.

His eyes had closed when my mouth had touched his. Every kiss, no matter how brief or passionate, had him responding similarly—his eyes would close, a soft sigh would escape as he breathed into me, and his shoulders would relax the slightest amount. I fucking loved it.

A throat clearing had Scott pulling back more fully and looking over my shoulder. A pink hue touched his cheeks, so light I was sure I wouldn't have seen it if I were a little further away. I stepped to his side. Jenna stood in the doorway, a small smile on her lips and her eyes wet. Her hand was at the bottom of her neck. After a moment, she blinked and stepped toward me. I reached out my hand only for her to sweep it aside and pull me into a tight hug. For a little woman, she was strong.

"Thank you," she whispered close to my ear, the words barely audible. I held her a little tighter. With one more squeeze, she stepped out of my arms, her mouth stretched wide, her eyes almost dry. "It's so good to meet you, Davis." She peered around me. "And this beautiful girl must be Libby." I turned in my daughter's direction. She was bouncing on her feet, her knees bending like crazy and her gaze still fixed on Hunter.

"Yes, ma'am. And it looks like she's besotted with Hunter. I've already started preparing speeches to warn off her wannabe dates."

Jenna laughed. "From what I've heard about her daddy, I can imagine you're not exaggerating." I wasn't. Tanner thought it was hilarious. "But I would imagine she's going to be a force to be reckoned with too."

I grinned with pride, having no doubt she would. "I wouldn't have it any other way."

"I'll stay here and keep an eye on the kids if you want to finish off, Scott." She cast a happy glance at her brother.

"Thanks, Jen." He turned in the direction of the kitchen, grabbing my hand and tugging me along.

"You cooked?" He'd told me he could cook, but I'd yet to eat at his place.

"Why d'you sound so surprised?"

I shrugged. "Not surprised as much as happy that you're cooking for me," I replied honestly.

His gray eyes met mine. "Hopefully that happy feeling will stay, as long as it's edible."

In the kitchen, I looked around. I was impressed with how tidy everything was. "So, what's on the menu?"

"Don't get too excited." He picked up the oven gloves. "I had to make sure the boys could eat, and Libby would manage too."

"I have some—"

"No, it's all good. I made sure she'd be well fed."

Heat bubbled up my body at Scott's ability to keep surprising me with his thoughtfulness. "Thank you." I stepped behind him when he'd placed the hot tray down safely, and pressed a kiss to his neck. His breath hitching was one of the sweetest damn sounds ever.

"My pleasure." His voice was whisper soft. He turned. With half-lidded eyes, he zeroed in on my mouth. The pinging of the microwave had him jumping, though. I huffed in amusement.

"I'll get that." Stepping away reluctantly, I collected the container and set it to the side. "What do you need me to do?"

"If you can sort everyone's drinks, that would be great."

"No problem. What would you like?"

He angled his head to look at me. "There's wine and beer, but I wasn't sure if you'd be having a drink."

He was already aware I rarely had anything beyond a single beer when I was driving, especially when I had Libby with me. "I'm good with water."

He nodded his understanding. "Then that's fine by me too. Jenna will probably want wine; the white in the fridge will be good."

I set about organizing drinks for us all, collecting Libby's sippy cup from her bag in the process. Placing the drinks on the table and Libby's on the high chair, which I recognized as hers from Tanner's place, a firm sense of rightness settled over me. Scott was making all the right moves, going above and beyond in ensuring Libby was considered in everything we did. I turned to watch him starting to dish up. He moved around the kitchen, seeming content in the space despite the busyness of his task.

"I was thinking." I stepped away from the table I'd finish setting. "Maybe after dinner, if Jenna and the boys can do without you, you could come back to mine, help me tuck Libby in for the night, and maybe then we can have something stronger." He paused, a spoon raised in the air as he threw me a look with such heat that my eyes flared and my pants tightened. "It'll still be early." I cocked a shoulder and offered him a smile that I hoped to hell was as seductive as I intended it to be.

"Yes." With a bob of his head, he threw me a wide grin. "I'd like that. A lot."

He'd been right. I liked it when he said yes to me. I mentally shook my head, aware we had to get through our early dinner, and I had to maintain a civil conversation with his sister. "Shall I rally the troops?" I indicated my head toward the sitting room.

"That'd be great. Thanks."

Turning on my heel, I took a deep breath, ready to put on my game face and win Jenna and his nephews over.

My nerves had proved to be unnecessary. By the end of dinner, which had been simple yet tasty, I'd managed to offer Jenna a job as Scott's replacement, but on a trial run, which Jenna had insisted on. Not only that, but I'd achieved the killer of belches after dinner. Both boys had been so impressed they'd demanded to show me their new bedroom.

Jenna was great. It was obvious with how she steered away from trickier conversations regarding her husband and her move that the next few weeks or maybe months were going to be a challenge, no doubt not just for her but also the boys, but she was assertive and together. It didn't fully connect with the picture Scott had painted about her marriage. This version had a glimmer of hope in her eyes and excitement in her voice. I liked her, and her boys were fun.

"Righto, boys." I stretched my legs out before me, readying to stand. "I imagine it's your bath time." I'd heard the tub filling in the bathroom.

"It certainly is."

I angled and looked at Jenna, who stood in the open doorway to the boys' shared bedroom. I offered her a smile, then turned back to the boys. "Let's get these cars quickly put away first; then it's time to get moving." They groaned in sync but put away their toys without any second request. I was impressed. "Is Libby downstairs?" I glanced at Jenna as I stood.

"Scott has her." She took a step out of the room, which I read was her invitation for me to follow. In the hallway, she studied me for the briefest of moments. "I hate that I haven't been around for him through all this." She hugged her sides, a tremor in her voice.

I tilted my head and said softly, "I think he feels the same way about not being there for you."

A single tear spilled down her cheek. She wiped it away quickly, her gaze flicking to the boys' room and then back to me. "We make a pair, right?" She laughed humorlessly.

I fought hard not to fidget, uncomfortable with her tears. "I think we all have heavy baggage to drag around with us at times, you know? All we can ever do is learn from whatever has happened, what we've lived through, and grow. Make sure the same shit doesn't hit us."

Jenna looked a little calmer when she spoke. "Thank you."

"What for?"

"For Scott, for seeing how special he is. He could be an arrogant prick growing up." I snorted and she laughed. "It's true."

"Oh, I believe you."

Her laughter sobered. "I now understand why he was that way though, why he felt he had to protect himself—"

"By being an asshole."

Her smile was watery when she nodded. "Yeah.

But I haven't seen that in him since being here, and I think you have a lot to do with that, so thank you."

I shook my head. "I can't take credit for anything. Well, maybe for making him a bit happier." He'd definitely brought me that. "But the rest of it, Scott accepting who he is, coming out, making this new choice for him, are *all* him. We haven't known each other all that long, but I'm proud as hell of him."

"You care about him." There was no question intended.

"I do, a great deal."

Her smile was blinding. "So thank you for that." She stepped over to me, placed a small kiss on my cheek, and squeezed my bicep. When she leaned away, she said, "Scott seems eager to head back to your place. Best not keep him waiting." She stepped around me to collect her boys.

Satisfaction rushed through me. I was just as eager.

WHEN I STEPPED BACK INTO THE ROOM AFTER settling Libby down, Scott's eyes immediately held mine. I didn't miss the slight shake in his hand when he brought his beer to his lips, nor did I miss when he downed the entire contents. I somehow contained my self-satisfied smirk that he was so wound up, only managing to do so because of the ball of nerves in my own gut.

We both knew that him being here meant we'd be progressing from the hot kisses we'd shared. While it was unspoken, the heated glances and touches were all an agreement to something more. He still wasn't ready for sex, and I wasn't sure when he would be, and that was okay. I could wait until he was certain.

Foreplay could be a hell of a thing, and I was eager to reach that point.

With a determined stride, I headed toward him, my focus on his every movement. His chest rose and fell quickly, his hand trembling when he placed the empty bottle on the table.

"Did Libby go down okay?"

Silently, I nodded and stopped before him. My hand found its way to his cheek, and he expelled a shaky breath. A smile formed on his mouth. After moving my hand to his nape, I let my eyes roam his face, landing on his lips—the only warning before I pulled his mouth to mine.

The kiss was bruising and perfect. Heat whipped through me, fueling my need to speed this up and get a taste of the man I'd been dreaming about. I couldn't wait to get him under me, have him at my mercy so I could show him exactly what he could look forward to.

I tugged at his shirt, managing to pull it off him with the slightest of breaks, my lips returning to his with a ferocity that had me scrambling for more. My shirt quickly followed, and his jeans were next. I hesitated the barest of moments over my fly.

"What?" Concern filled his breathless voice.

Our eyes connected and my tongue traced my bottom lip, his gaze following it.

"I want to see you too." He'd read my hesitancy correctly. This could all be too much, too soon for him, which seemed crazy in my head since his cock was bare and hard between us.

I stripped, my grin unapologetic, my need obvious with my straining cock that bounced free. His wide eyes took me in, his breathing picking up as he closed the fraction of an inch between us. We brushed against each other, hardness and heat, the contact making us both gasp.

"Sit down." I edged him toward the sofa, caressing his chest, enjoying the softness of his skin and the ridges of his pecs. His stomach was blissfully not a hard slab of muscles. Instead, his flesh was supple and warm, perfect for the kisses I started to trail down there.

Finally, he sat, and I shifted between his opened legs. Trailing my hands up his calves, then his thighs, I deliberately kept my gaze on his face. Pleasure warred with a sweet nervousness that was so fucking endearing, my dick twitched. "I've got you." My whispered words had his eyes connecting with mine, and he exhaled audibly. Scott's lips ticked up slightly, his fingers reaching out and touching my cheek.

"I know."

It was all the permission I needed as I lowered my mouth to between his legs.

Admittedly it had been a while, but it was so much better than I remembered. Having Scott needy, groaning, desperate before me as I darted out my tongue and encircled the tip was a heady thing. I knew this was only the second BJ he'd ever received from a man, but that first time would soon become insignificant and be buried under the memory I was going to give him. I was on a mission to blow his fucking mind. Lapping at the bead of moisture, I gave his balls a gentle squeeze, careful not to be too heavy handed. I sucked and licked, and then flicked my tongue over the tip, knowing it would feel unbelievably sensitive and be driving him to distraction.

"God," he hissed, and I averted my eyes up to look at his face. Sweat beaded his brow, and his face was contorted in glorious agony.

"Does that feel good?" I asked, coming up for air and letting my hand glide over him while I spoke. "Do you want to feel what it's like when I suck you so damn deep you hit the back of my throat?" He jerked in my hand, his body convulsing. Half-lidded eyes peered down at me. I raised my brows while still stroking him, waiting for a response. He nodded and I grinned, satisfied he was on his way to having his mind and his dick blown.

I moaned around him as I took him in, stretching to take in his girth. He was wider but slightly shorter than me, and I couldn't wait for the time he would take me. I sucked slowly at first, with a few well-placed licks on the underside of his length, enjoying every shudder and groan I teased out of him. Before I took him down as far as his length could go, I lightly scraped my teeth over his sensitive skin.

His words were incoherent, and I was glad I had him sitting down as I was sure his legs would have buckled by now.

I bobbed my head, sucking hard and then gripped

him with firm lips from base to tip. The moment he hit my throat, I worked hard to control my gag reflex and my own cock. I hadn't come without touching myself since I was a teenager and had watched my first porno. But with Scott's jerky movements, his garbled pleas, and the fact I wanted him so fiercely, I hoped today would not be the day I shot my load without any action. I continued to suck and work him over until I was sure neither of us could see straight. Meanwhile, I throbbed with my own need, ready to explode.

"Holy shit." They were the first clear words he'd said since I'd started. "I'm going to—" He cut himself off with a groan as I sucked harder and edged my finger toward his ass. I tapped gently, and his mouth opened. I then placed just the tip of my finger in, not quite sure how ready he was, or if he'd ever been penetrated before. The move pushed him over the edge.

With a cry, a grunt, and a groan that had my own balls tightening, his seed hit my tongue and the back of my throat. I pulled back and he shuddered as I continued to suck up and down, coaxing out a few more spurts. He sagged, his half-lidded gaze settling on me. A dreamy smile lifted his mouth, and he sucked in a breath, his stomach contracting as I finally pulled away.

I leaned back, my ass on my feet, hand still on his thighs as I grinned up at him. "You okay?"

He nodded, his face full of wonder and something like awe, and I swallowed hard, loving that expression and the fact I'd put it there. Pride fluttered in my chest. He opened his mouth to speak, closed it, then tried again, this time with success. "I've never…. Not like that…. Fuck."

My eyes widened as he darted forward, placed his hands under my arms, and dragged me on top of him. His lips found mind immediately. His warm tongue traced the seam of my lips and then entered my mouth. In sync, we both groaned, but rather than it speeding the kiss up, our lips touched slowly, languorously. Hands down it was the best kiss I'd ever had.

He tilted his head a little, so I pulled back. I felt him shift, the only notice I had before I jerked at the contact of his hand touching my cock. "Fuck," I mumbled.

"This okay?" There was no uncertainty in his question. He actually looked pretty damn pleased with himself.

I laughed, then groaned when his touch turned into a grip. "Hell yes." He kissed me again, but I needed more. I needed to come so badly I was sure my balls were going to explode. I dragged my mouth from his and leaned back, allowing him easier access to me. He switched hands a moment to allow his right hand to come to his mouth. He licked it. Biting back a groan, I closed my eyes as his wet hand wrapped around me.

The friction was perfect. The speed just right. His left hand scooped my balls and stroked lightly, one finger every now and then brushing my taint, which was so sensitive every touch sent a fresh shiver through my body.

I was almost there, almost ready to empty my load in his hand, and I hoped to God some spilled on his stomach too. It was that thought that sent me over the edge. I looked at Scott, whose gaze was fixed to my cock. Satisfaction rolled through me as my semen painted his soft flesh. Seeing my hot cum on the guy I desperately wanted to claim was a fucking turn-on, but seeing the same man dip his finger to taste my seed for himself… hell, I toppled over the edge of need and desire. This man could easily have half of my heart.

CHAPTER SIXTEEN

SCOTT

IT WAS NO USE. THERE WAS NO OTHER OPTION. Shoving one hand in my jeans pocket, I knocked on Carter's door, probably a little too hard, but I couldn't help it. Nerves had slammed into me one too many times, and I was driving myself to distraction. I had to talk this out. And that meant Carter was going to be the poor sucker to have to deal with my shit.

I considered hammering again, the few seconds feeling more like minutes as I tapped my foot, unable to keep still. Before I had the chance to lift my hand to do so, Carter opened the door. Relief poured through me.

He smiled in greeting, but then it dropped, slowly slipping off his face when he got a good look at me.

He opened his mouth to speak, his brow dipping into a frown, but I cut him off with a shake of my head and stepped inside and past him. I spun back to face him as he pushed the front door closed, then the onslaught began before I could rethink my decision.

"If I watch another goddamn porno, I think my eyes and my ears are going to bleed. I've worn my keypad out from hitting Pause, and if I watch in slow motion again focusing on angles…. I just can't." I shook my head vehemently, choosing to ignore Carter's wide-eyed expression. "I'm so fucking terrified but simultaneously can't wait. What's that even about? Did you know it hurts like a… like I don't know, like shoving something up your ass, I suppose?" For real, it did. "But then it feels so fucking good, and when I imagine it being Davis…." My eyes all but rolled into the back of my head.

"Sco—"

"I have seven, *seven* goddamn dildos now, trying to get ready, trying to make sure I don't make a fool out of myself when we finally, you know." I paused, my stomach tightening. Davis and I had mastered foreplay over the past couple of weeks. I even gave myself a damn gold star when it came to giving head. "What if I'm crap? What if I can't take it? What if I hurt—"

"Scott." He tried again, this time his eyes impossibly wide. He even threw in a head shake for good measure. But I couldn't stop the words from coming.

"—him? What did you do, you know, your first time?" His face actually paled at that. "Shit, it's not okay for me to ask that, right? Yeah, sorry, but what if—"

"Scott, for the love of God, please stop. Just stop." He shook his head, horror written on his face.

That worked. I stopped short, and sickness churned in my gut. I was going to hurl.

"My mom and dad arrived late last night for a surprise visit."

I swallowed. Hard. I needed to remember how to breathe and had to figure out how I could both disappear and eradicate memories at the same time. I couldn't speak in fear I'd vomit. It was a very real possibility.

"They're in the kitchen."

I closed my eyes, humiliation rushing through me. It clawed at my skin, threatening to do permanent damage.

Carter's sigh was both resigned and somehow filled with sympathy. "Come on. Let's just get this out of the way."

Rooted. I was rooted to the spot. There was no

way in hell I was going to meet his parents. I'd been in the kitchen plenty of times. I'd sat on those kitchen stools regularly enough to know you could hear everything that took place in the hallway. And I was hardly quiet during my breakdown. What the hell had I been thinking?

I tried to shake my head, but I couldn't even seem to be able to manage that.

"Come on," Carter tried again. This time he took my arm and pulled me toward the kitchen.

Reluctantly, I allowed him to do so. *Best I get it over with.* I attempted to put on my game face, not quite sure exactly what that would look like yet. This wasn't a situation I ever expected to be in, *ever*. It rated high on the list of nightmare situations.

"Mom, Dad, this is Scott. Scott, these are my parents, Jack and Marcy."

With a deep breath, I stepped further into the room. My face fixed in a painful half smile. I could do nothing about the small dip of my brows or the sweat breaking out on my skin though. "Erm, hi, Mr. and Mrs. Falon." I stretched out my hand as I moved toward them. "Pleased to meet you both." I swallowed the bile threatening to crawl up my throat.

Carter's dad stood and took my hand in his, giving it a firm squeeze. He gave me a sympathetic nod, though I didn't miss the amusement dancing in his eyes. "Scott."

I turned to Carter's mom. Her eyes narrowed a fraction as she studied me, doing a long sweep of my body. I held my hand out, not quite sure what I'd do if she refused. Probably turn tail and run, but I stayed as strong as I could manage considering the circumstances.

Her gaze dropped to my hand. "It's not going to be a limp-lettuce handshake after all that porn watching, is it?"

"Mom!"

"Marcy!"

I blanched and shook my head furiously. "No, ma'am." I breathed hard through my nose, willing my stomach to settle. Me vomiting all over her would take this meeting to a whole other level of humiliating.

She appraised me a moment longer. "Good." Her hand took mine, her grip strong. When she released it, she smiled, and air rushed out of my lungs. And just in time too. Vomit and me blacking out from holding my breath would have been the icing on the cake. "So, you're the enig-matic Scott." There was no question in her statement.

"Mom, really? Leave him alone and drink your tea."

An arched brow lifted ever so slowly, and she shot Carter a look a lesser man would have withered under. "And you"—she shook her head—"have been holding out on me."

A mumbled, "Here we go," left Carter as he stepped to my side. "It's not too late to run," he said in my direction.

I laughed. It was small and nervous. I wasn't quite sure if he was joking or not, and I seriously wanted to do just that.

"No chance. Sit your heinie on this here stool, Scott. It seems like my dearest son has not been keeping me in the loop, and it sounds as though you need some advice."

"Oh boy." Jack shook his head. "Son," he called out to Carter, who had since fully stepped into the kitchen. "Scott here will need something stronger. Coffee is not going to get him through this." A small smile sat on his lips, and I lifted mine in return. He reminded me a lot of Carter. "No chance of escaping now, Scott. Best get comfortable and ride this one out."

I took a seat on the offered stool, my back straight, as far from comfortable as could be.

Carter's family were insane, but in that quirky, awesome way. They were so unlike my own family, and I'd never experienced parents quite like them before. That was obvious in just the three minutes in their presence. Not to say I hadn't heard stories. Saying that, I didn't think anything could have prepared me for the Falons.

Facing straight ahead, I watched Carter grab a beer. He removed the cap and shook his head with a smile, passing it to me. I didn't even comment that it was only ten in the morning. He pressed his lips together. The bastard was enjoying this, his sympathy long gone. Before I had the chance to shoot him a dirty look, it began.

"You and Davis are an item now?" Marcy turned toward me, her gaze unflinching though not necessarily disapproving.

I cleared my throat. "Well, we haven't exactly put a label on what we are, but we've been spending time together." I willed the flush from my cheeks when I thought about where our tongues had been. We'd been exploring a lot recently.

She nodded. "Obviously enough time that you're thinking about the next step."

I clamped my mouth shut, heat creeping to my face. I did not want to talk about this. Shit, I didn't have to talk about this, and wouldn't. "Well, ma'am, that would be between Davis and mys—"

"I think it's between everyone in this room, considering your overabundance of questions earlier." Her gaze softened. "I'm not really going to ask all of the details, but it's clear you need to be reassured that everything you're worried about is normal." She reached out and squeezed my arm. I wasn't quite sure whether it was emotion at being spoken to so softly, with such understanding, that caught in my throat, or abject horror.

"When Jack and I first started even considering anal sex—"

"Mom, holy shit, for the love of God, no. Absolutely not."

Horror. Abject horror. Who was this woman? I was a grown-ass man, yet felt like I was being dragged up and expected to explain myself like a teenager, and while nothing about that sat comfortably, it was obvious enough that she cared about Davis, and for some reason was being kind to me too. I could not get my head around the bizarreness of the moment.

"Well," she huffed almost indignantly, but seeming a little too amused for that to be true, considering the twinkle in her eyes and the smirk on her husband's face, "I'm only trying to be supportive and offer my pearls of wisdom." She rolled her eyes at her son and then fixed her unwavering gaze on me, her expression becoming somber. "Scott." I honest to God gulped hard when she said my name. There was no reprimand in her tone, but something about this moment put me on edge. "I know who you are and what you did." And there it was. The not-so-invisible elephant in the room. "But," she emphasized that one word, "I also know that Carter likes you, has forgiven you, and has reassured me you're a good man."

I would not fucking cry. Holy shit. I forced my eyes to stay wide and willed away the emotion clawing at me. This was so far beyond what I was anticipating when I'd banged on Carter's door in a moment of desperation.

"Based on what you said and what I know, if you're so anxious about doing the right thing by Davis and are planning for the next step, I also know for myself that you're a good man and are ready."

I blinked. Thank God the initial emotion was gone. Instead, I was trying to get to grips with the fact that this sixtysomething-year-old woman was giving me sex advice, and I didn't know if it was worse or not, but hell, she made sense.

She reached out and cupped my hands with her own, giving a reassuring squeeze. "It's good to be prepared, important, but not to the point where you're stressing yourself out and panicking." There was no attempt to argue as she spoke the truth. I'd panicked big time, to the extreme of finding myself in one of the strangest situations in my life.

"You're an intelligent man. So use that brain of yours and those big words I *know* you know and have a conversation with Davis." Her smile was kind, and I found myself smiling back. "And I'd also really consider using a butt plug on the big day"—Carter groaned, I laughed, Jack coughed, but Marcy remained undeterred—"as it really will help, dear." With that, she released my hands, picked up her cup, threw me a wink, and took a dainty sip.

Speechless. Truly, the woman had rendered me speechless. After a moment of looking at the other two occupants in the room, I grasped my beer and mumbled a barely audible, "Erm, thanks," before draining the whole bottle.

For once, the front door opening, no doubt signaling Tanner, was a welcome relief. I released an audible sigh, only to freeze when not only Tanner entered, but Davis too. This could not be happening. I almost got whiplash when I looked at Marcy, my eyes pleading. She patted my hand and threw me another wink. I had no idea if that was meant to be reassuring, but it didn't work. What the hell did it mean? I just hoped to all that was holy that it meant she'd keep quiet.

The room remained silent, tense, and it was so bizarre that my gaze flicked to Carter in panic and then to Davis. Despite amusement dancing in his eyes, he tilted his head to the side as if studying me.

"Everything all right in here?" Davis asked, his question directed at me. I nodded. I didn't even have the chance to organize a response before Marcy was talking.

"We're all perfect, and you, Davis, are going to adore me even more."

Good God, no.

"Mom."

Marcy threw Carter an annoyed glance. "Hush." She then refocused on Davis, who stepped further into the room. His expression remained uncertain. Tanner placed his keys down and walked up to Carter, but my attention was solely on the exit. "Jack and I have offered to babysit your beautiful Libby. We're here for a few nights, so thought tomorrow would be perfect. It would give you and your new beau here an opportunity to go out and have a date and follow the night on to wherever it may lead you. She can sleep here the night."

Carter barely held back his smirk.

I pressed my lips together as her words sank in and I realized she hadn't ratted me out. It was actually amazingly generous of her to offer to look after Libby. I ignored the fact that it was her way of helping me get it on with Davis. Returning my gaze to the man who already held a piece of me, I found his questioning gaze on me. I shrugged, pleading none the wiser. I had no idea if he bought it, but I couldn't back down now.

"That's really great of you, Marcy. Thanks." He stepped up to me and stood to my side. His hand found its place at the back of my neck, and he squeezed lightly, offering comfort. There was no doubt he was aware something bigger was going on, and I appreciated that he was allowing it to play out. A gentle finger brushed against me, and I relaxed a little more. When he reached out for the bottle of beer, shook it, and then placed it down, I glanced at him, aware his attention was on me.

I shrugged again and grimaced, but still, my lips twitched. It was then I realized not only how quiet the room was, but also that Libby wasn't with him. "Where's Libby?"

He grinned. "With your sister and the boys." My eyes widened, and he laughed. "She was heading to the park and wanted to take Libby so called up and offered. I tried to stick around, but she all but shoved me back in the car. Something about finally being able to have some girl time or something." He lifted a shoulder. "I just went with it. Your sister can really be a force of nature when she chooses to be."

I agreed wholeheartedly. She could. It made her marriage and her putting up with Stan's BS for so long bizarre. But then I supposed marriage could be a pig to get out of; add in a mortgage and of course the boys, and she'd felt trapped. "That was kind of her. How long ago did you drop Libby off?"

He looked at his watch. "An hour, so it's time to collect her."

I nodded. "I'll come too if you want?"

"Always." He threw me a wink, and my heart fluttered. Tanner gave an exaggerated groan, Marcy sighed happily, and I was certain Jack was now on the scotch and ignoring everyone. Davis didn't pay any attention to any of it as he stole a kiss, took my hand, and pulled me to my feet. His gaze finally left mine. "Thanks for the run, Tanner."

My eyes zeroed in on his damp shirt, and I took what I hoped was a subtle sniff. It was probably creepy that I liked when Davis was sweaty. His scent was all kinds of a turn-on. It was a good thing I hadn't noticed he'd been out for a run until now.

Davis cleared his throat, and my gaze shot to his. Busted. His eyes flared. There was no doubt he knew exactly what I was thinking and doing. He gripped my hand a little tighter, before loosening and running his thumb over my wrist. I closed my eyes, relieved my back was to everyone else. This man's ability to turn me inside out was impressive, and maybe just a bit terrifying.

"What time shall I bring Libby by tomorrow?" Davis's voice took me by surprise, and my eyes sprung open.

"Whenever you're ready, dear. We'll be here."

He smiled. "Thanks, will do."

We headed toward the exit, and I turned before I left, clearing my throat. "Lovely meeting you both," I directed at Marcy and Jack. Jack raised his half-full glass in my direction.

"You too, Scott. Don't forget what I said." She gave me a pointed look, and I was sure I blanched. Carter groaned, and I saw him shaking his head at Tanner's questioning look.

"Erm, sure, thanks." I nodded and gave one last wide-eyed stare in Carter's direction. His smile was soft, and I relaxed a little. It was enough to remind me that so much had changed and that I'd handle this new path I'd led myself on.

My sister was home when we walked back. I doggedly ignored Davis's questions about what he'd walked into, brushing it off and offering him noncommittal responses in the process. The reality was, there was no way Carter wouldn't be telling Tanner, which meant Davis would know eventually. I just hoped it would be after tomorrow night.

The thought gave me pause.

"You okay?" Davis whispered.

I nodded. "Yeah." My voice was equally low so we wouldn't wake Libby.

Davis didn't look convinced by my response as he led me out of the spare room where Libby was sprawled out on the double bed, pillows surrounding her to buffer any fall. He pulled the door not quite shut and led me to my bedroom.

"Are you worried about something?"

I swallowed hard and looked at the man before me. "Nope." I was doing enough overthinking as it was. I did not want to talk this to death. Instead, I'd leave it to play out. And if tomorrow night led to hot and heavy and ended up with us sealing the deal, then I had faith in Davis he'd support me with that and take care of me. My shoulders sagged a little in relief at the thought, and a real smile touched my lips. "So tomorrow, what do you want to do?"

With a lazy roam of my face, he didn't rush with his response. But I wouldn't budge and speak any more about the bizarre encounter at Carter's, allowing him to read whatever expression he found on my face. After another few beats, he took my hand in his, a lopsided grin forming on his mouth. "How about I surprise you?"

I mirrored his expression and nodded. "I'm down with that."

My phone chimed with a text alert the next morning when I was in bed on my laptop, filling out the never-ending paperwork that went with the purchase of the clinic. It was early, and my nephews were still asleep, the house unusually silent. When I'd woken early, too antsy to sleep properly, I'd switched on my laptop, needing the distraction.

Davis: I'll pick you up at 6. Dress smart-casual, pack a toothbrush.

My eyes widened, and heat rushed to my face. This was happening, and at six. How in the hell was I going to get through the day?

Me: Okay. Do I need anything else?

Davis: An overnight bag. And just yourself.

Alrighty then. I glanced at the time, and it was barely past six thirty. No doubt he was up with Libby. With another look at my laptop, I angled my neck from side to side until I heard a satisfying click. Work. It was the only option I had to get through my day, and it wasn't like I didn't have a heap I needed to achieve.

With my new plan, I got out of bed to make coffee and breakfast for Jenna and the boys. It didn't take much movement in the kitchen for the stampede of feet to trample down the staircase, followed quickly by chattering.

"Who wants pancakes?" I asked the boys when they entered the kitchen, hair messy and both pairs of eyes springing open in delight at the word.

"Me!" Toby and Hunter answered in unison.

I nudged my head toward the utensil drawer. "Set the table for me, please. We also need juice, Toby, if you can get that from the fridge for me, please?"

The boys sprang into action, liking it when I gave them tasks. I expected when they got older that would change, but for the time being, they like to be treated like big boys.

"Hey." Jenna's voice carried over the din of cutlery being dropped on the table.

My gaze flicked to her. "Morning." She looked

refreshed despite the early start and the noise. She was also looking a damn sight happier and more like herself from before marrying her shithead of a husband.

"Morning." She stepped fully into the room. "Coffee?"

I indicated the pot. "Already done. I'd love a fresh cup."

Jenna placed a kiss on my cheek, then hugged her boys close and dotted kisses over their heads, causing a riot of giggles before she collected two mugs and poured our coffees. "What's this for?" She sidled next to me as I flipped a pancake.

I shrugged. "Do I need an excuse to have breakfast with my family?" I side-eyed her and saw her studying me. "What?"

She tilted her head to the side. "Nothing." She threw me a smile and then made her way to the table when I switched off the stove.

With the pancakes stacked high, the boys' eyes were as big as saucers. It didn't take us long to dive in and the boys to be sticky with maple syrup.

"What are your plans for the day?" Jenna asked before taking a sip of her coffee.

"I'm going to be neck deep in paperwork with the sale of the clinic. Everything with the house is pretty much taken care of. I just need to sort through the additional legalities." It was a tiresome task, and I loved every moment of it since it would mean taking full control of my life and truly starting afresh.

Jenna nodded. "I'm so proud of you."

Tightness squeezed my chest, the feeling foreign. I took a moment to deal with the surge of emotion threatening to spill forth. This whole process, this journey of finally beginning my life in a way I'd never allowed myself to dream it could be, had been a roller coaster of trials, and my sister being proud of me helped unravel some of the fear clutching my weary heart.

"Thank you." I reached out and squeezed her free hand lightly. "I'm proud of you too." I raked my eyes over her sons. "They're amazing." I returned my attention to her. "You're amazing."

Her eyes were watery when she sniffed and smiled. After clearing her throat, she waved in front of her face and sighed. "What are your plans tonight? Are you seeing Davis?"

My heart rate spiked at the mention of his name and the thought of our evening. With a nod, I cast my gaze away from her and turned it to my coffee cup.

"Right." That one word was all-knowing and light. It was also filled with humor.

I met her amused gaze, and rolled my eyes when her lips curved into a grin. "We're heading out and I plan to stay over."

Wide-eyed, Jenna stared back at me and remained silent for a beat. "Boys," she said, her eyes fixed on mine.

"Yes," Hunter said.

"If you've finished, please take your plates to the sink, then head to the bathroom and rinse your hands. Toby, please help your brother."

A scrape of chairs, the clatter of plates and knives and forks followed closely by the patter of feet filled the space between us. A moment later, the boys raced upstairs.

"Do you want to talk about to—"

"Nope." I leaned back in my chair and picked up my coffee. "Make that a hell no."

Jenna pursed her lips together. "Okay, I get that. I'm probably the last person you want to talk to about this."

I held back a snort. Actually, Carter's parents had been the last people I'd wanted to discuss my sex life with, but apparently, shit happened.

"But know that I'm here and can talk about hot

men whenever you wish." A smirk crossed her lips and she waggled her brows at me.

This time I did snort. "And while I appreciate that, I'm good, thanks." The words were out there, and my nerves took but a moment to settle. I grinned. I really was good, better than good in fact. A quiet calm descended over me, one lit with an undercurrent of excitement and formed with certainty that spending the night—and I hoped many more after—with Davis was the right choice. I wanted it fiercely, wanted *him* fiercely.

I stood with renewed lightness. After pressing a kiss to Jenna's head, I picked up our empty plates. "I've got this. You go and shower. I'll keep an eye on the boys." And with that, I turned and busied myself in the tasks of the day while eagerly counting down the hours until six o'clock.

Surprisingly, the day sped by, but that didn't mean I wasn't relieved to close my laptop and give my eyes and brain a break. After quickly showering, I dressed and headed downstairs. Jenna was making dinner for her and the boys, while they banged around in the small play area we'd set up for them in a section of the dining room. It was the perfect positioning to be able to keep an eye on them while in the kitchen.

"You look handsome."

I smiled over at her, kind of relieved she noticed the extra effort I'd put in. I'd been on dates over the years of course, all admittedly with women, and none had I made an effort for. I'd seen no point. While I'd made sure the woman on my arm had a good time, usually with a nice meal and an expensive bottle of wine, that had been as far as I'd gone to impress. It had also been enough to placate my father and to stop any possible gossip about me from forming.

"Thank you." I brushed down my crisp light blue shirt, pleased I'd selected it. When Davis had said smart-casual, I hadn't realized how hard that was. I'd decided on a good quality shirt and a pair of dark jeans. Clean shaven, I'd also put on one of my favorite colognes. It was one Davis had previously mentioned liking.

I glanced at the time. It was almost six. "Need a hand with anything before I head out?"

She was already shaking her head by the time I'd finished speaking. "Nope." She walked over to me and pressed a kiss on my cheek and squeezed my forearm. "Just concentrate on having an amazing time." When she pulled back fully, she quirked a brow at me. "And stay safe!"

I rolled my eyes at her, hoping it would keep away the heat threatening to hit my cheeks. It didn't work. She walked away giggling, and called over her shoulder, "Do you have everything you need?" She eyed the bag I'd already left near the door over an hour ago, amusement crossing her features.

Admittedly, I'd been eager packing my overnight bag, and in the past hour there'd been a buzz of energy sweeping through me and following me around. "Yes, thanks."

Just then there was a knock on the front door, and I jumped. Jenna snorted. I stuck up my middle finger at her and then darted my eyes to my nephews. They were too focused on the blocks to see me flipping their mom off.

Taking a calming breath in an attempt to quiet my pounding heart, I reached out and opened the door. Davis's bright eyes were the first thing I connected with, and I immediately saw him smile. I followed suit and waved him in. "Hey." I was impressed my voice appeared clear and normal.

"Hey, back." He stepped through the open doorway and his lips grazed mine.

While the thumping of my heart eased off at the now familiar contact, a rush of blood traveled quickly south. Only a little of my reaction to this evening was about nerves. Mainly, anticipation swept through me with the force of a tidal wave. I considered prompting him to skip whatever dinner plans he'd arranged and instead for us to make our way straight to his bedroom. I then considered how rare a night sans child was for him, so figured he was looking forward to an adult night away from home.

When he leaned back, his eyes roamed my face, a similar anticipation swirling in his eyes. "That your bag?" He tilted his head to the right but didn't break eye contact.

Silently, I nodded. Only then did he look away to call out to my sister and my nephews, and a moment later, after kissing Hunter and Toby goodbye, I was swept up in the whirlwind that was Davis. I'd never seen him like this before. A man on a mission, he'd gone through the most basic of pleasantries with impressive speed while remaining polite. Then with his searing hand on my back, he shepherded me out to his car, opened the door for me, planted a firm kiss on my mouth, and then all but raced around to the driver side.

When he finally yanked the door open and jumped into the seat, pulling the door firmly shut, I was angled toward him, wide-eyed and amused as hell. Laughter bubbled in my chest, along with concern that he was acting kind of crazy. "You want to take a breath?"

His eyes flared before he opened his mouth and then snapped it shut. With both hands on the steering wheel, he exhaled loudly.

What the hell was going on? I'd never seen Davis so out of it before.

"I've changed my mind."

My tongue stuck to the roof of my mouth when he rushed out those words, and I struggled to breathe for a moment before I remembered what to do. I froze, an amazing feat considering my heart galloped in my chest at such a pace I figured it vibrated my whole body.

"I had this whole corny meal planned at a cool restaurant in the city and had a hotel room booked." He finally looked at me and concern lit his eyes. I was sure I looked a hell of a sight, sitting, struggling for proper breath, but I wasn't quite sure if I was beet red or as pale as a ghost. I was too numb to tell as fear vibrated through me. "Hey." Davis reached out and took my hand in his. He leaned forward and kissed my mouth, a few short pecks, and whispered, "Not about you or us. Never about that."

Far too wound up to speak and too afraid the vomit that had attempted to crawl up my esophagus would make an appearance, my silence continued, but feeling slowly returned, first in my fingers and then in my tingling lips.

Despite edging back into his seat, his hand gripped mine. I needed the tether while I listened to him and hopefully quickly understood what he was talking about.

"I'm sorry if I made you think I was canceling tonight. That's the furthest thing from the truth. I just have a shit way of explaining myself; I'm too worked up." Davis swept his thumb against the skin on my hand. "Let's go and grab a drink, and we'll start the night again without me screwing shit up. Okay?"

"Okay." I managed a nod and a relieved smile, though I was still clueless about what he'd been talking about.

With drinks in front of us a short time later, I debated whether or not to let him clarify himself, ignore his words in the car altogether and do as he said and start again, or simply go ahead and clear this mess up myself. I stared at my untouched drink, needing a clear head and not liquid courage, and made my decision.

"You didn't want to take me out to dinner or stay in a hotel overnight with me?" I controlled my face as best as I could. He'd already told me he wanted the two of us to work out, but that didn't explain why he'd changed our plans. The thought of a good meal and night in a hotel room sounded amazing, so I remained clueless.

A chagrined expression took over his handsome features. His usually bright, wide eyes dipped a little, but a small smile played on his lips, though it wasn't as full or as natural as usual. "I'm sorry." He brushed a hand through his hair and his shoulders dropped. "Perhaps we should head there now. We'd only be a little late—"

I shook my head. "No, honestly it's fine. I suppose I'm just trying to figure out what's going on."

With his eyes fixed to mine, he said, "You never have to figure things out with me. It's just my shit-show of explaining was pretty impressive." Davis reached out and took my hand, and while there was the smallest of urges to glance around to see if anyone was looking, I stood my ground and focused on the man I was happy to give my whole attention to. "Would you forgive me if I said I was thinking with my cock?"

A loud snort rushed out of me, scratching my throat and all but echoing around the bar. I laughed loud and long, managing to say, "Okay, so not what I was expecting you to say." I shook my head. "Care to elaborate?"

His shit-eating grin was back, stirring a thrill of happiness in me. Tension fled from my shoulders at that one natural gesture. "The plan was all set, to wine and dine before the night in the hotel, which was five stars by the way." He raised his brows, and I pressed my lips together, controlling my laughter. "But then you opened the door." He shrugged and trailed off as though that was answer enough.

"Huh?"

He angled even more toward me and shook his head. "You don't see it, Scott, and it's as endearing as hell, but when you opened your door almost bouncing in excitement, there was no way I'd be able to handle the hour and a half journey into the city, let alone sit through a meal having to be all civilized and shit. Christ, it took all my willpower to bring you here when my house is empty, and you're not lying naked in my bed already."

Surprise had my eyes opening wide, and lust rushed through me at the speed of lightning. Me naked in his bed... that was an idea I could get on board with. "Oh." It was all I could manage to get out as the visual and possibility cemented themselves in my brain.

Davis groaned and squeezed my hand. "That look right there." His needy gaze roamed my face, and a moment later, he pressed his mouth to my parted lips.

From sheer willpower that I managed to somehow drag out of myself, I held back the strangled moan threatening to burst free when his tongue lightly brushed against mine. I pulled back quickly. "I'm good with that." The words spilled out, eager and desperate. I didn't care. I needed Davis to know I was as ready for this night as he was. "I'm not thirsty anyway."

His eyes zeroed in on my mouth before flicking up to my own. "You sure?"

I nodded so quickly, whiplash threatened. "Definitely."

With that, he stood and pulled me up with him, and I was only half aware of him calling out to Ted, the owner, as he ushered me out the bar's door.

———

THE FIVE-MINUTE JOURNEY TO DAVIS'S ONLY TOOK three minutes, despite it seeming to take fifteen.

Almost at hyperspeed, we were both naked and in Davis's bedroom, and that's when reality caught up and I held my breath. We were both naked. As in legit, bare-assed, bobbing dicks, and every inch of skin on show. While we had admittedly been in this position before, it felt different, more raw and real, knowing there'd be no holding back. I struggled to take it all in. I didn't want to miss anything.

Fingers brushed across my skin, the contact making me jump despite the fact I'd watched Davis's every move. My gaze shot to his and then traveled to his mouth. His smirk was gone. Once our eyes reconnected, the heat greeting me slammed hard into my chest. I caught my breath and then groaned. Us finally being together, having sex had been all I'd been thinking about over the past few weeks, but that didn't mean I wasn't wound up with antic-ipation.

Everything about his movements was fire, gentle pauses, and tension coiled so tightly I was sure something was going to snap. I just hoped to God it wouldn't be my heart. The moment that errant thought entered my mind, I brushed it aside. One of many things I could be certain of with Davis was his care and his honesty.

My attention moved to his fingers. They stroked

mine a moment longer before tightening and clasping my hand. A teasing sweep of this thumb over my skin had me swallowing hard—all of this from a simple touch. But it was so much more than that. I knew it. He knew it. This moment was everything.

Davis didn't speak as his fingers squeezed mine, but his lips quirked into a reassuring smile. He then stepped into my space, our chests practically touching. I couldn't help but think my plan to seduce him had fallen apart, as there was no doubt about it: Davis was fully in control, leading the way.

Warm breath fanned across my face. When his tongue dipped out and gave the smallest of passes over his bottom lip, my gaze homed in and my stomach tightened. There was a pause, but not a hesitation as Davis's lips descended to mine. It wasn't about going so slowly so I could stop it—we were beyond that point—instead, it was appreciating the buildup, the moment.

And I was going to memorize every last second of it.

CHAPTER SEVENTEEN

DAVIS

Sunlight filtered in through the closed curtains, but rather than open my eyes, I luxuriated in the feel of heat and supple flesh against mine. Easing closer, I dropped my head to Scott's back and inhaled before pressing a kiss against his skin. He wriggled in response, his ass pushing back and rubbing perfectly against my groin. If my cock hadn't already been awake, the soft sigh and the rub would have been enough to get me started. Instead, I'd been rock-hard seemingly all night.

I ached deliciously. It had been so long since I'd been with a man, and I was happy I'd waited for Scott to be the one to remind me how good it felt to be filled to the edge of pain with just the perfect amount of friction. Pleasure had consumed me last night, and from the way Scott had filled me up, I knew he'd been right there with me. Orgasm by P-spot didn't get enough headline recognition as far as I was concerned. And last night, with impressive precision from Scott, he'd found my holy grail and had taken me to the brink of blowing my mind just a second before I'd come so hard I struggled to see straight for a good hour.

And I couldn't wait to do the same for him.

"Morning." I dotted kisses along his spine, traveling down and then back up again until he groaned and turned onto his back. Scott peeked his eyes open at the same time he smiled at me.

"Morning."

I pecked his lips and then went immediately to his nipples and took a bud in my mouth. He grunted, his hand appearing in my hair.

"A guy could get used to this," he said breathily.

I grinned around a nipple before I nibbled it and pulled away. "Sounds good." I winked and maneuvered on top of him. Face-to-face, I rubbed my nose against his. "You okay?"

He nodded, his hands coming down on my ass cheeks. He tugged me against him, and we both groaned as we rubbed against each other.

"More than okay." He angled his head for a kiss,

and I didn't keep him hanging as my mouth slid against his. Scott pulled back and resettled his head on the pillow. His brows creased. "Are you okay?" He caressed my ass cheeks as he spoke, so I knew exactly what he was referring too.

"I'm fucking perfect. Sore." His frown deepened, but I shook my head at his expression. "I wouldn't want it any other way. It reminds me of how perfect you felt balls deep inside me last night." My cock pulsated not only at the memory but at the crimson lighting his cheeks and the hardness of his swallow.

"So it feels… good?"

I nodded, my heart tripping over itself at the need and vulnerability in his question. "The best." I kissed him gently, then said, "But that doesn't mean you have—"

"No." Heat punctuated the word. "I want to." He closed his eyes and the force of his heartbeat pushed against my chest. "God, I really want you inside me." When he opened his eyes, his pupils were dilated, and if I hadn't believed his words or his body, then everything I needed to know could be read in that one look.

He was ready.

The need for breath seemed to disappear as I slammed my mouth to his, taking, tasting, and trying my hardest not to come while rubbing against him. As my lips slid against his, my tongue making gentle caresses, I angled to lean on my forearm, freeing my left hand to dance over his skin, loving the goose-flesh the touch left behind. When my fingers traced across his hip, he bucked, squirmed, and tore his mouth away as he grinned. Bright eyes took their fill, and my heart stuttered. He was gorgeous like this, happy and quite possibly the most at ease I'd ever seen him, despite being as coiled tightly as he was.

Scott's eyelids dipped to half-mast when my touch traveled to his balls, then sprung open when I angled my hips completely off him so I could get full access. With a swipe of his precum, I traced the liquid over his silky skin and gave gentle strokes. His whole body vibrated, small grunts spilling out of his mouth when I picked up the pace. After I placed a small kiss to his mouth, I kissed my way down his body, my focus on tasting him. Just the thought of sucking him in made my mouth water. I sped up my descent and reached my goal with a triumphant lick of his long length and a smirk when Scott bucked so hard I had to clamp him down.

"No," he gargled.

Wide-eyed, I stared at him, confused. "No?" Shit,

what had happened in the last few minutes? He was all but wriggling his ass, begging me to take him.

"Lube," he said with a needy gasp. "I just need you inside me, your fingers, your cock." My own sprung to renewed life with vigor. God, I wanted inside him so badly. "Davis."

My name spurred me into action.

Lube and condom at the ready, I caressed his hole and eased a finger in slowly. I knew he'd used his own fingers, just like I knew he'd used toys, but this was a hell of a lot different. He had a virgin ass, as none of those things counted when it came down to it. His channel gripped my finger, and I closed my eyes, breathing slowly and begging for control. When he moaned, my eyes connected with his. "You okay?"

"Yeah." He managed a small smile. "I need more though." Heat crept up his cheeks.

I leaned over and slid a second finger inside him, and pulled at his bottom lip, pressing a small kiss there. "I'll give you everything."

Soft eyes gazed back at me, and he nodded, drawing his swollen bottom lip into his mouth.

"This"—I entered a third finger slowly and gently stroked and probed—"once I'm in there." I took a stilling breath, willing myself to keep going, keep talking, get everything out on the table. "I want to be the only one." My pulse skyrocketed. "I only ever want to be the one who's had this piece of you. That okay?"

His nod was slow, somehow sensual. Scott parted his lips and bucked again as I found that perfect spot of his. His yes came out on a growl, swiftly followed by, "Fuck yes."

"And that means," I added for clarity, "only you will ride me, only you will take my fine ass." I quirked a brow and gave a half grin, but fuck if I didn't mean every word and feel the promise soul deep.

His frantic eyes refocused, and he cupped my cheek, sweeping his thumb over my lips. I was impressed as hell by his control, since I had three fingers buried inside him. His voice was low and steady. "I want that, with you."

And with those words, there was no going back. I was going to make him scream and never regret his promise. After a bruising kiss, my fingers working him over while I deliberately left his cock alone, not wanting to distract him from the epic pleasure of the P-spot, I moved fully to my knees before him. "Hands and knees or back?"

He hesitated a moment. "Hands and knees."

Heat curled inside me as he turned and offered me his ass. I leaned over him and kissed against his spine, then his ass cheeks before pressing my thumb inside him while I added more lube to my latex-covered cock and directly to his opening. It wouldn't take me long before I exploded inside the rubber, but I needed to make this so good for him that he'd never regret his promise to give me his world.

"Tell me if it's too much or you need to slow or stop."

With a glance over his shoulder and his body vibrating before me, he said, "And what if it's not enough and I need you to go harder?"

I laughed loudly, warmth spreading through me. "That," I said, grinning widely and pressing myself against his hole, "you can say as loud as you want." With the last word, I eased into him. Scott's head dropped forward, his ass high in the air and a strangled moan ripping from his lips. I paused before continuing, certain he would tell me what he needed. After edging out slightly, this time I entered fully, balls deep. I angled my head back and gasped for breath as he gripped me so tightly, so perfectly I was convinced my cock would die happily and go to cock heaven.

Waiting a few moments, I tested his reaction by

easing back. When a breathy moan escaped him, I edged back in, only to receive the perfect movement from his hips as he pushed against me. "Fuck yeah," I grunted. I throbbed inside him, almost in time with the increasing movements as I pushed then pounded into him.

With both hands, I eased his cheeks open a little more, taking in the view. Groaning, I kept my eyes fixed on how he ate up my cock. We fit so perfectly. I had to fight the build of my orgasm. I did not want to come yet.

I shifted my angle slightly, and Scott cried out. I knew that sound so well. He'd managed to tear the same sound out of me last night. He twisted his head around to peer at me. "Holy shit," he grunted. I didn't have the ability to throw him the smirk I intended. Instead, I focused on brushing against his prostate, wanting him to go cross-eyed. I watched his reaction through the blur of building desire. With every broken, gasping breath he took, each ripple of his body, the flush of heat across his skin, I was lost in it all. In him. Scott clamped around me, and I repositioned my hands on his hips, needing the stability as I pressed into him deeper, faster.

As I ground my hips, I managed to say, "Touch yourself." I needed him to see stars before I did. On a shaking cry, he did so. My fingers bit into his hips when he tightened impossibly around me, almost strangling my cock. The intensity of the action had me bucking harder.

Gentle was a distant memory as I pounded deeper. He matched my rhythm, his ass slamming back and softly mumbled words slipping out of his mouth incoherently.

A loud groan followed by his body jerking and coiling tightly meant I no longer had to fight the inevitable. Thank fuck. It was a battle I would have lost if he'd milked my cock a second longer. A deep, guttural groan left me when I gave a final thrust, spilling my release into the latex. Scott dropped onto his forearms, and I pressed heavily against him before bracing my arms on the bed.

Blissfully spent, I inhaled and exhaled a shuddery breath. He still held me firmly, so when his body jerked, he gripped my cock, and I groaned. His matching groan quickly followed. Tension eased out of me, and I pressed my lips to his neck, seeking his face. Scott angled his head and lifted slightly so my lips found his, soft, warm, and perfect. My lips pressed against his, our mouths working softly against each other's.

"You are fucking incredible, and I am so fucked."

His grinning mouth against mine was his initial answer. He then murmured, "I think you'll find I am the one who's thoroughly fucked."

I leaned my face away to make sure I could see his eyes and his face for a reaction. "I wasn't talking about my impressive cock in your ass." Despite the humor of my words, my voice was steady, serious.

I was expecting surprise, perhaps denial; instead, with Scott's unwavering gaze on me, he said, "I know exactly what you meant, and my words still stand."

Happiness chased my relief. Against his lips, I whispered, "We can both be fucked together."

AFTER FINALLY GETTING A MOUTHFUL OF COCK AND cum in the shower, I sat and watched Scott in my kitchen as he made coffee. He looked relaxed and at home in my space. "You look good in my kitchen."

He paused what he was doing and cocked his brow. "You know I'm not the barefoot and pregnant kind of guy, right?"

I snorted as he handed me a mug of coffee. "Maybe a barefoot and naked any chance I can make it happen kind of guy?" I grinned at him as I blew at my steaming drink.

He rolled his eyes at me before finishing his own drink and sitting next to me.

"Plus I already have Libby."

Scott angled toward me. "You don't want more kids?"

Surprise flitted through me at the question. Before I'd met his sister and nephews, I hadn't imagined Scott to be the kind of guy who could handle kids, let alone like them. He'd been beyond amazing with Libby though, but then seeing him with the boys had opened my eyes even more to the kind of man he was. He'd make a good dad for sure. I placed my drink down and looked at him. "Honestly, I never thought beyond Libby. She's my world, you know?"

He nodded, his eyes fixed on mine.

"But hell, maybe her having a brother or sister would be a great thing. What about you?"

His eyes widened. "What about me what?"

"Kids."

Color rose in his cheeks and he shifted in his seat. He cleared his throat before he spoke. "Erm, I... hell, I don't know. I love my nephews. They're amazing. To be honest, kids were never on my radar, I suppose because of the whole confused-as-fuck thing I had going on. My world exploded not long ago." He offered a small shrug.

I understood his concerns, the confusion involved, but there was also a huge *but* and not of the nice, tight ass variety. "You know Libby and I come as a pac—"

"Don't even." Anger dipped his brows. "I know what this is, know Libby is your life, so please don't insult me by—"

"Hey." I reached out and cupped his cheek, effectively shutting him up. His venom surprised me, but fuck if my jeans weren't struggling to keep my hard-on contained. Rather than responding to him verbally, I kissed him. There was nothing soft or gentle about this kiss. It was hard, demanding, possessive, and he welcomed every stroke, every brush, until I was the one who was a needy mess and somehow he'd taken control of the kiss. "What the fuck…," I said, pulling away with a gasp.

The intensity in his eyes made me groan. "I love Libby, okay." He stared at me pointedly, once again with the intensity that was quickly becoming the hottest thing I'd seen. I mutely nodded. "And if we're fucked together"—I raised my brows at that, humor and lust coiling deep in my stomach, but I didn't dare smirk—"then we start thinking of doing this together."

I understood what he was saying, even if he was having a difficult time ensuring his words made sense. I nodded again, but he wasn't finished yet.

"So I was hoping that means I get to spend more time with not only you, but with Libby as well." I heard the strain of emotion in his voice, understood the courage it took for him to put himself on the line like this. I felt it, lived it, breathed it.

"I'd like that, a lot." I didn't conceal the emotion from my voice. He deserved it all. With a light grip on the back of his neck, I tugged his forehead toward mine. "You good?"

He blinked before he answered. "Yeah."

"Good." After pressing my lips to his, I pulled back. "What do you want to do today? Carter's mom said she'd have Libby till later this afternoon if we want to take advantage." I wagged my brows at him, wanting to ease his frown.

Scott's grin was both sweet and sexy, especially when combined with the slow creep of color traveling up his neck. "I… erm…."

"Is your ass sore?"

Even though he squinted at me in annoyance, he

nodded, and the pink turned to red as it crawled up his cheeks.

"Have I told you how hot you are when you blush like that?"

He rolled his eyes at me and nudged me away, but I grabbed on to his arms, laughing. His voice was a pitiful attempt at indignant when he said, "I was going to offer to suck you off, but if you're going to—"

"Don't finish that sentence. I can totally get on board with your mouth around my cock." Said cock jumped for joy in my pants, and lust unfurled in my stomach.

"Here?" His gaze moved to my groin, his brows high.

My lips curved. "I was thinking bed and 69."

Scott shot up so fast he spilled his undrunk coffee on the table. I saw him eye it and hesitate.

"Leave it and stick with the enthusiasm." I stood with a teasing grin, and we raced to my bedroom, though I wasn't quite sure who dragged who.

Mouths, saliva, and blow-my-load induced gagging… the combination of the three had us soon spiraling out of control and grunting aloud. While it had been a while since I'd had any, it had been a lot longer since I'd been involved with someone of significance. It made every touch, caress, and orgasm that much sweeter.

Relaxed and with my head on Scott's chest, I reached out and grabbed my phone to look at the time. "I need to go get Libby."

He nodded and pressed a kiss to my head. "I'll come with you."

I glanced up at him. "Will you then come back here?"

"Is that what you want?" When I bobbed my head, he smiled. "Okay. Let me stop by my place though to check on my sister and grab some fresh clothes."

Before long we were pulling up outside Scott's. I left him with a kiss and headed to Tanner's to pick up my girl. I let myself inside, although if Carter's parents hadn't been there, there was no chance in hell I would have done so unannounced. I'd made that mistake before and couldn't quite look at the staircase the same way.

"Hello, hello?" I called up. I heard Rex's bark coming from out back, quickly followed by Libby's squeals of delight. I followed the sound to the patio doors and stood and watched Libby sitting and throwing a ball. It barely went a couple of feet away from her, but Rex grabbing the ball and bringing it back to her was apparently enough to get her crazy excited. Carter sat beside her, grinning and encouraging both Libby and Rex.

"Hey." Tanner appeared beside me.

I cast him a glance and indicated the scene outside. "He'll make a great dad, you know." I saw Tanner nod in my periphery. "Have you thought about it?"

"I need to make an honest man of him first."

My head whipped to the side, my eyes wide, a grin already on my face. "Yeah?" He didn't remove his eyes from outside. "Is that going to be soon?"

Tanner's lips twitched. "Quite possibly."

I pushed against his shoulder, happiness filling me up. Tanner deserved it all. He was the best man I knew. "Let me know if there's anything you want help with."

"Thanks." He bobbed his head. "How was your night?" He angled toward me and immediately rolled his eyes at the shit-eating grin I wore. "I'll take that as good."

I scoffed. "Try fucking spectacular."

"No details," he said with a grin. "For the love of God, no damn details."

Clamping my hand on his shoulder, I laughed.

"No chance of me kissing and telling, Tanner, you know that."

His gaze raked my face. "You seem happy."

"I am."

"Good. Doesn't mean I won't kick his ass if he screws up."

It was my turn to roll my eyes. "I hardly need anyone kicking someone's ass for me." I sent him a challenging quirk of my eyebrow. "But I appreciate the thought." With my gaze returning to my daughter, I asked, "Everything okay last night?"

"Peachy. Carter's mom dotes on her and is actively encouraging the need for grandbabies. She keeps emailing adoption links."

My smile was broad. "They're great, right? Nut jobs, but it's great they're so supportive."

"Yeah, they are. You heading straight off?"

"Yeah. Just going to grab my girl, go and collect Scott, who's getting a change of clothes, and then heading back to my place."

I expected a dig, maybe another threat, maybe this time on Scott's manhood, but I didn't get one. Instead, Tanner smirked. "Best get your ass into gear… you know, if you can manage it while walking straight… without wincing. It's been a while."

"Ha fucking ha." I flipped him off as I stepped

outside and quickly swept my beautiful Libby into my arms.

Five minutes later, I was at Scott's door and ringing the bell. His voice called, "The door's open."

I opened up, Libby on my hip. I stumbled upon his nephews first as they sped on by, both wearing superhero costumes. Libby squealed and bounced in my arms, chanting "Dow, dow," in her desperation to get down and join them. "You'll get trampled on. You're not big enough yet." I tickled her tummy to try to distract her, but she batted my hand away, her eyes fixed on the empty doorway where the boys had disappeared. "As soon as you're old enough, I'll buy you a kick-ass superhero costume, okay?"

"Hey."

I glanced up at Scott's voice, my heart leaping as he strode toward me. He stopped and kissed me, no hesitation, no doubt, and my heart celebrated at the action. He'd come so far, changed so much from the man I'd first met and only known about by name.

"Cot." Libby lunged out of my arms toward him, and Scott reeled her in immediately, surprise and delight battling for position on his face.

"Do you just…. Did she just say my name?" Wide-eyed, he stared first at me and then at my daughter in wonder.

Gone. Fucked. Truly. I'd meant my words to him earlier, but seeing him with Libby, watching how they interacted, I was sure to God that he was going to be it. I mulled over the thought, not even surprised I relaxed a little at him being in my life, hopefully forever. While I'd dicked around when I was younger, I'd never given away my heart before, other than to Libby, but hell, she'd snatched the damn thing clean out of my chest the moment I'd laid eyes on her. I hadn't thought it was possible to share a piece of myself with anyone but her, but Scott remained the enigma I considered him to be and had snuck on inside my chest when I hadn't been paying attention, cementing a piece of himself in there too.

Still speechless, my eyes softened and I stood back and admired them both. I only dragged my eyes away when Jenna entered the large entrance room. With a glance in her direction, I returned her tender smile. She saw what I saw, that much was obvious.

"Are you staying for dinner or are you heading straight out?"

Turning my focus on Scott, I said, "We can stay."

His smile was full of appreciation. I knew he worried about his sister and all she'd been through and was going through. I was more than happy to spend time with her, not only because I liked her, but if it eased the frown lines from Scott's brow, I'd make it happen.

"Great," she said. "I've Libby-proofed the dining area, so you can come on back and let her play."

"Thanks, Jenna." I threw her a grateful smile and followed her to the split dining/kitchen area. "Something smells good."

"Just lasagna. It'll be a while yet, but I do tend to eat early because of the boys." She busied herself with the stove while Scott settled Libby on the floor near a tub of toys. Sitting on a stool, I pressed my lips together when I realized they were all baby toys, much more suited to Libby than her sons. When I looked back at her, she was watching me and offered a shy smile. "We just thought it would be good for her to have something to play with when she was here."

"It's amazing of you. Thank you." I was touched she'd thought of such a thing.

"It was Scott's idea. I was just the shopper."

My heart thumped wildly in my chest as I angled once more to look at Scott. He was on the floor with all three kids. They had blocks out, and the boys seemed to be building them as high as possible before Libby punched out with a giggle to smack them over. "He's something else."

"He is."

Jenna's voice made me jump. I hadn't intended to speak aloud.

Looking at her brother, then at me, she smiled. "I'm so pleased he's going back to the clinic and has this opportunity to purchase it. For a while there, he started to resent practicing."

"Because of your dad?"

"Yeah. He's a piece of work. I think we both love him because it seemed like we had to, but there was a lot of unhealthy fear instilled in us from the time we could walk."

I hated that for the two of them. "But now you're here, it's better, right?"

She smiled, the movement lighting up her eyes. "Definitely. And thank you."

"For?"

"Giving me the chance at work, making my brother so happy."

"I'm pleased I could help, and truth be told, I'm relieved you're there to take some of the pressure off. Plus, your brother can't make a coffee for shit and was sure to make me bankrupt with the number of breakages."

"I was not that bad." Scott nudged me with his shoulder as he sat beside me.

"He's right about the coffee though. Your ability to destroy coffee beans is incredible. Impressive even," Jenna said.

I laughed as the banter continued and Jenna continued preparing the meal while the kids played happily in the background.

CHAPTER EIGHTEEN

SCOTT

IT WAS DONE. FINALLY. THE *i*'s HAD BEEN DOTTED, the *t*'s had been crossed, and I was the official owner not only of an incredible house but of a clinic I loved. The past couple of weeks had been tied up in contracts and reassuring the staff that their jobs were safe and I wasn't an asshole—well, only occasionally. I was lucky that only a limited number of staff knew the real reason behind my initial resignation, and Carter had gone above and beyond to tell anyone who listened that while I could be a grumpy dick without coffee in the morning, I was a good guy.

I was a lucky son of a bitch and kept reminding myself of that every morning I rolled up to work, and every night I spent around Davis's and got to give Libby a kiss goodnight before wrapping myself up in Davis's arms.

I switched off my computer and stretched out, surprised when Lauren called my name from the door. By far she'd been the hardest to convince, but despite her uncertainty, I was grateful that she remained professional at work and around the staff.

"I just received a call from Tanner, as Carter's wrapped up in something apparently. He told me to, and I quote, 'get Dickwad's ass to the bar within the next ten minutes,' and if we're late, he's going to make me buy the first round." She looked unimpressed and snorted at the latter.

I held back a snort as all thoughts of her professionalism flew out the window. I grinned at her, my brows dipping in confusion. "Why are we going to the bar? I have to collect Libby."

She shrugged. "Something about Carter or Sandy or someone is doing that, and you now have one minute to get your ass into gear."

My brows dipped even further as I pulled out my cell. The bar I could handle; letting Davis down by not picking up Libby, however, was not happening. I pressed his name, and he answered after a couple of rings. "Hey," I greeted as I grabbed my laptop bag and keys.

"Hey, handsome."

I grinned. "Lauren said something about Libby—"

"Yep. All sorted. Carter's already picked her up for us"—my chest expanded every time he said something about *us*—"and Sandy's now looking after her for a few hours."

"Okay." Confusion lit my words, and I wasn't paying attention to my surroundings, so jumped when Lauren clamped her hand on my forearm and tugged me out of my office, grumbling about me being slow and how I'd be buying drinks, and she'd be having an expensive-ass cocktail.

"Just let Lauren get you here."

"You're at the bar?"

"Just hurry your ass up."

The line went dead and I was still none the wiser. It did look like we were heading to the bar though. I followed Lauren out. She led me to my car and waited at the passenger side door.

After eyeballing me while I unlocked the car, she got in. "You doing okay?"

I raised my brows at her while starting the engine.

"You look like you may pass out or something." Her brows dipped into a concerned frown.

Releasing a sigh, I shook my head, pulling myself together. Of course I had nothing to worry about since Davis was involved, but that didn't stop unease pulling at my gut. "It's just weird this has been sprung on me, is all." And it was. Nobody had done anything like this to me... for me before. My hands were clammy and my body heated.

She remained quiet for a moment, but I felt her eyes on me. "You're an onion." It didn't sound like an insult necessarily, but it had me raising my brows high.

"I'm a what now?"

"Onion. Or maybe a chameleon, maybe a combination of both."

"I'm a stinky lizard." I cast a brief glance her way and caught the assessing amusement on her face.

She laughed. "Quite possibly. I was thinking more about you being this confident, arrogant asshole who's hot and got everyone talking and swooning when you started. You won a lot of people over, but then there was all of the BS with Carter"—my stomach dipped, which it always did when I thought of my behavior. Both Carter and Davis had told me I had to forgive myself. I wanted to, but it took time—"which you know elevated your assholery status, but then I get it. I understand the whys of it all. And then there's this… you. You've come back and played the confident boss card to perfection. You can still be an asshat before you get at least a couple of coffees down your neck in the morning, but I've also seen you laugh, and smile, and be really kind."

My eyes danced between dipping and lifting high as she blurted out her assessment of me. I remained quiet throughout, equally mortified and impressed that she seemed to understand me well.

"And now here you are freaking out because the guy who loves your sexy ass is doing something sweet for you. Onions and chameleons."

I didn't fidget, I didn't challenge, and I even ignored the awkward reference to me being sexy. What I couldn't move on from was her saying Davis loved me.

"You can breathe, you know. There are no clowns." She laughed, and the sound and her words broke me out of my spell and reminded me I needed air.

"Would I get fired if you found out I did beg Carter to organize a clown for tonight?" She snorted as she spoke, and I shook my head.

"You'd be so fired." I rolled my eyes. In Carter's wisdom, he'd organized a clown for Libby's birthday party, which had come and gone in the blink of an eye. When Libby had burst into tears, petrified of the sadist clown, I'd been the first to spring into action, welcoming the ability to get the hell away from the creepy-ass clown. I may have yelled and tripped, something about killer clowns and voodoo. It hadn't made sense to me either, but clowns were the devil. A reoccurring dream at the age of seven had told me as such.

Lauren was still chuckling as we found a parking space, and before I opened the bar door, I paused in anticipation. Love. Davis and I hadn't skirted around the issue, per se. We both cared for each other a lot, we spent most nights together, and I'd happily taken on some caring duties for Libby. A few times I'd made a slip about *our* Libby or *our* girl, and rather than correcting me, Davis had pressed his sweet kisses to my neck.

"You have one minute, boss man." She waited by my side though, rather than forcing me through the doors.

I nodded before stepping into the bar.

A Congratulations banner greeted me, along with a roomful of bodies and cheers. Apart from the banner though, I only had eyes for one person, who stood front and center before he marched on over to me. I grinned, my heart beating furiously in my chest and forcing emotion into my throat. Overwhelmed by what Davis had organized, I couldn't move, but still, my grin stayed, the happiness genuine.

Stopping before me, he immediately cupped my face with both of his palms. He swept his thumbs across my cheeks. "Congratulations, baby, on your big day."

I swallowed thickly, and Davis's eyes softened. I had no doubt he understood my difficulty to deal with the moment. This was the kindest thing anyone had ever done for me, which he was fully aware of. When I'd graduated high school, my father had grabbed me by the collar and told me to get to work on my reading list ready for college. That no son of his would be a failure. This was after I received a 4.8 GPA. And when I'd graduated from college at the top of my class, he'd told me he'd set me up with a job and in no uncertain terms was I to screw up else he'd cut me off and make sure I never worked in veterinary medicine again. So this, all Davis, and I was assuming my friends—which amounted to Carter and tentatively Tanner—had done was a big fucking deal.

Davis pressed his lips to my mouth, and after a

few caresses of his lips against mine, he whispered, "I'm so proud of you."

There went that damn emotion again clambering up my throat.

He pulled away, his gaze examining my reaction. Seemingly reassured by what he saw, he leaned in once more, but this time his mouth grazed my cheek as he said close to my ear, "Later I'll show you exactly how proud of you I am when I let you take me up the ass." I almost swallowed my tongue when I laughed. He pulled away so we were eye to eye. "I'll even go down on you before I tell you how much I love you."

My breath caught and my heart stilled before it let loose and threatened to gallop out of my chest. I struggled to speak, to react, to do anything but gaze at this beautiful man before me. While his shit-eating grin was back, the one I thought was all levels of sexy, his eyes were warm and filled with truth.

"Come on," he said, "you have people waiting to congratulate you." He took my hand and stepped away, turning from me.

I gripped his hand and remained rooted. "Wait."

He spun back with raised brows.

"I love you too." My heart tripped over itself as I

spoke, wishing we were already home so we could carry out his plans.

With one step, his lips reconnected to mine. It was all too brief, but the few catcalls brought me out of love- and lust-fueled haze enough to remind me we had an audience. He grinned against my mouth, my hand still in his. "Later," he promised.

Stepping more fully into the bar, I was accosted by Carter, who pulled me into a hug. I should have been weirded out, considering our past and possibly by the fact I was now his boss, but I happily hugged him back and warmed at his excited congratulations. It took five minutes before Ted passed me a drink.

"Congrats, Scott. It's quite an achievement."

I felt heat creep to my cheeks, overwhelmed by all of the support. "Thank you." I reached out and shook his hand.

"I finally met your sister." I followed his line of sight and saw Jenna with a drink in hand, chatting to Lauren. Her laughter lifted into the air, and I relaxed at the sight. It was good to see her looking so care-free. "She's great."

I turned back to Ted. "She really is and is an amazing mom."

He nodded. "Do you have any other family here?"

I shook my head, refusing to let my stomach

bottom out. As far as I was concerned, my sister and nephews were it.

"He does." A hand clamped on my shoulder, and I startled, eyes wide. "Congratulations, kiddo."

I turned, my smile immediate as Denver tugged me close, patting my back. "You're here?"

He grinned at me. "I would say Carter can be tenacious when he wants to be, but it didn't take much convincing. I wanted to be here to celebrate with you."

I fought the tears as I clasped his hand. "Thank you. It means a lot." It was a wonder how Denver was close to my dad. They were like oil and water. Denver had always been warm and kind, but their friendship didn't make a lick of sense to me.

Davis appeared by my side, and I immediately reached for him, my arm moving around his waist. In another time, another world, I would have only dreamed of having the courage to do such a thing. Fear, I decided, could go screw itself, especially when it attempted to mess with Davis. I then looked at Denver, who was observing me closely.

"Denver, have you got a drink?" Davis asked, his voice carefree, his strong fingers gripping my waist.

With a smile, Denver nodded. "I do, thanks, Davis."

I glanced back and forth between their exchange. "You know each other?"

Davis's lips curved upwards. "As of about thirty minutes ago officially, but we've chatted a couple of times on the phone making arrangements."

I closed my gaping mouth. "Aren't you just full of surprises?"

He shrugged good-naturedly. "I have my moments."

Heat flared between us, which I had to force down, a mammoth task since those whispered words had been ringing around my head for the past fifteen minutes. Hell, was that all it had been? How was I meant to survive the night?

Widening his eyes a little, Davis cleared his throat. "I'll leave you to catch up. Let me know if you need me."

I'd always need him. I pushed that thought into the tender look I gave him and the squeeze of his fingers before he released me. He threw me a wink, and I watched his ass leave, only to drag my gaze away when Denver chuckled beside me.

"I can see why you finally opened yourself up, with a man like Davis in your life. He has a daughter too?"

Despite my embarrassment at being caught

checking out my boyfriend's ass by my godfather, a grin stretched my cheeks. "Libby's not long turned one. She's amazing and keeps us both happy and exhausted."

"I'm glad. I'd love to meet her while I'm here. Perhaps I can stop by tomorrow?"

"I'd love that. Did Davis sort out a bed for you?"

He nodded. "He did. He offered to put me up, but I was more than happy at a hotel. It means I don't have to clean up after myself." Denver chuckled.

"Are you staying long?"

"Just a couple of days before the next jaunt."

I took him in. He looked good, happy. "Retirement suits you."

"I think I suit it too," he said, beaming at me. "Let's go and see your sister. She seems to have a few admirers."

My gaze jerked up. Jenna was now in a conversation with a couple of guys I recognized but didn't know. My eyes narrowed. I didn't think so.

Denver slapped my back and laughed loudly. "Oh boy."

"I'll go," Davis mumbled. I groaned and turned to my side, burying my head under the covers. Davis's footsteps moved across the landing, and I heard him open Libby's door and her rambling get louder.

"Da Da," she squealed, and I imagined that was in response to Davis lifting her out of her crib.

"Geez, you stink, little lady."

I snorted and pushed the cover off me. Bathroom, then coffee. Davis would need a hit of caffeine quickly if he was dealing with a monster poop. Before long, I had the coffee maker on, eggs boiling, and bread out ready to toast. Libby's new favorite breakfast was egg and soldiers, something I'd never heard of before, but apparently it was a thing.

"Cot, Cot." I looked at the doorway and a fully dressed Libby wobbled in. She was sure-footed, but as soon as she put any aspect of speed into her movements, she was hilariously wobbly, something akin to a drunken sailor.

"Hey, baby girl." I scooped her up and gave her a cuddle, then dotted kisses over her face. "You ready for soldiers?"

She clapped enthusiastically as I took her to her high chair and strapped her in. A moment later, I placed buttered toast down for her and her sippy cup of water.

"You're up." Surprise lifted Davis's voice as he entered the room and immediately stepped over to me and planted a solid kiss on my mouth. "Morning."

I eyed him up and down, appreciating how well he filled his jeans. "Morning. The coffee should be good to pour. I'm just sorting the eggs."

"Thank God. I think I need a double hit this morning, even if it's coffee you've made."

"Hey." I shot him the evil eye and snorted. "And you were surprised I'm up? I wasn't the one drinking random cocktails Ted was concocting last night." I quirked my brows at him.

"Never again." He looked a little peaky, but still sexy as hell despite his tired eyes. He sipped his coffee and sat next to Libby while I dished out the eggs. "This looks great. Thank you."

"It's the least I could do after last night."

Davis leaned back and eyed me, his gaze trailing from my face to my groin and back up again. "That good, huh?" He looked pleased with himself, if not a little unsure.

I scoffed. "Erm, no, stud. I had to pour you into bed last night. I made sure Sandy got home safely, and Jenna took the boys home, despite my protests." I shrugged.

Placing down his toast, Davis ran his tongue over his top teeth and quirked his brow at me. "So my promise—"

"You owe me." I grinned salaciously. "I figured you could make good on it tonight."

He sat forward, angling closer to me and picked up his toast. "I can make that happen, but only because I love you."

My heart stuttered and threatened to burst out of my chest when it picked up speed. While I knew he hadn't been drunk when he'd said those words to me yesterday, there was a trickle of anxiety that came with the light of day—maybe he wouldn't be willing to repeat them. Insecurities sucked ass, and not in a good way.

"Well, it's a good job I'll hold you to it, as I love you." I angled forward and snatched the toast from his hand, and leaned back laughing. While Davis looked unimpressed, Libby thought I was hilarious, so I took it as a win. "Denver is going to stop by later."

Davis nodded, buttering another piece of toast. "Sounds good."

"Thank you for contacting him. It meant a lot that he was here."

"You're welcome."

Before I had a chance to dip into my yolk, my phone rang. I stood and collected it off the sideboard. It was Jenna. "Morning, sis, you—"

"Dad's here."

My gut clenched and I pursed my lips. "Why?"

"He's being Dad. He also has my unsigned divorce papers that he keeps wafting around."

"What the hell?"

"Yeah. I need—"

"Give me ten and just do your best to ignore him."

"Okay. Thanks."

"You'll be fine. Ten."

I was already out of the door and halfway up the stairs when I called back to Davis, "My dad's arrived, causing shit for Jenna. I have to—"

"Hey."

I made it to the top, my breath ragged, my heart working overtime as my anxiety ratcheted. I turned and looked at him. He was already fully dressed, unlike me, but he also had Libby in his arms and his car keys in his hand.

"Deep breaths, get a shirt and shoes on, and I'll

get Libby strapped in her seat. I'll meet you in the car."

I did as he said and inhaled and exhaled. I even managed a small smile. "Thank you."

He winked and turned, heading to the front door while I tore away to dress and prepare to confront my father.

I vibrated with tension as Davis drove us back to my place. I hated that Jenna had dealt with him by herself. Dad was a stubborn, manipulative bastard, but to go this far and intercept the divorce papers took his interference to a whole new level. There was not a chance I'd let him hurt Jenna any more than she already had been—or the boys, for that matter.

When we pulled up, Davis placed a firm hand on my forearm. "You need to be calm and strong for Jenna."

I nodded, undid my belt, and made for the door handle, but he didn't release his grip. With a quick glance at him, I dipped my brow in question.

"How do you want to play this?" No doubt reading the confusion still creasing my brow, he clarified, "Me, us."

My heart settled rather than sped up. So concerned with my needs, he was willing to do whatever I asked. I turned fully toward him, and after a smiling glance at Libby strapped safely in her chair, I pressed my lips to his. "We do this together. It's going to be a shitshow, but I need you with me." My gaze turned wary. "I'm just worried about Libby."

He nodded his understanding and pulled out his cell. His eyes remained locked to mine as he spoke, "Hey, can you come and collect Libby? ... I'm at Scott's. His dad's shown up." He seemed to listen a moment before he ended the call. "You lead and I'll follow."

I closed my eyes and pressed my head against his, allowing myself five seconds to inhale his scent and absorb his strength. "Okay." We got out of the car and unstrapped Libby. Just as we made toward my house, Tanner and Carter showed up, and my chest constricted. They'd both arrived; even Tanner, who regularly called me a dickwad, was here to support me.

Carter took Libby from Davis. "I've got her. Do you want me to take her home or...?"

"Home would be great, please." Davis pressed a small kiss to his daughter's head.

"On it." Carter leaned over and kissed Tanner, who seemed set to stay.

"I'll just hover." Tanner grinned at me.

I laughed, an impressive feat considering the nerves pulsing through me. "My dad may be a fifty-nine-year-old bully, but his bark is worse—"

"Thanks," Davis interrupted, and stared me down. I knew that look. I also knew he was thinking about the time I'd spent in the hospital at the hands of the man I called Father. It was one of the moments I'd admitted to him over the weeks.

I nodded and released a breath. "I need to get in there and get him away from Jenna." I reached out my hand, and Davis immediately took it and gave me a small squeeze. "Actually, Tanner?" He looked over at me. "Can you come in and collect the boys and take them to your place too, please?"

He bobbed his head. "Of course. Whatever you need." He smiled, quite possibly the first genuine one he'd sent my way. I would have commented on it if it wasn't for my shaky legs as I headed toward my house.

Once inside, I called out, "Hey, Jenna, where are the boys?"

"We're here," Hunter called out, and two pairs of racing footsteps quickly followed. Just as the boys appeared, Jenna stepped into the hallway. She was pale, shaken, and most definitely relieved when she saw the three of us. There was also determination brewing in her eyes. I grinned when I spotted it.

"Tanner's going to take the boys."

She closed her eyes briefly and sighed a loud exhale. "That would be great, thank you."

"Come on, Trouble One and Trouble Two. Let's go and pay Rex a visit." Tanner held out both hands for the boys to take. They rushed over to him cheering, only seeming to remember a second later to race back to Jenna and hug her legs before they were off again shouting goodbye.

"You okay?" I asked.

"I will be. Thanks for getting back so quickly."

"What happened? How'd he get the papers?"

"Stan happened." Her cheeks heated with anger. Good, I was glad she was pissed off. "He went bitching to Dad, and now apparently he's here to talk sense into me and take me and the boys back home." An impressive snarl lifted her lips, making her look fierce.

"Shall we just get this over with?" I wanted him out of my house, out of town, and as far away from all of us as possible.

She nodded and then glanced at my and Davis's hands. A smirk broke her frown. "Is it bad that I'm kind of hoping for a heart attack? Just a mild one, of course."

A laugh burst free, easing the tension a little more. "It should be interesting, that's for sure." I exhaled and tightened my grip. "Let's go."

I wished to God I had home surveillance, the internal kind with mics and high res recording capabilities. If I had, I was sure to have hit Repeat on the moment my father's eyes bulged and his face turned ashen before then becoming the brightest red I'd ever seen on a human being. To top it off, he was legitimately lost for words for at least twenty seconds. Twenty seconds was a crazy long time in the standoff taking place in my kitchen, but it was twenty seconds I would have gladly watched over and over again. When his brain finally caught up with his eyes, his explosion was pretty damn remarkable. Even more so was the fact that as he reeled off abuse in my direction, all I wanted to do was laugh. I was sure Davis knew as he gripped my hand even tighter, probably in warning that laughing in the old man's face was quite possibly a step too far and would likely induce cardiac arrest.

So I let him shout, let the spittle fly forth, let his dyed-black brows practically touch and almost fly off his face when he lifted them so high. Approximately ten minutes into his tirade, he realized I hadn't spoken, wasn't defending myself. It was then he turned on Jenna.

"And you knew about this, you stupid girl. Allowing my grandchildren to stay in the same house as a faggot. Stan will be able to file for cu—"

"Enough." My voice was strong, loud, but not a shout. "Leave Jenna alone and stop with your point-less threats." I could handle every vile slur he threw my way, but by threatening Jenna, he'd taken it once again a step too far. "Rather than the usual divorce proceedings that have been started, Jenna is more than prepared to state the real reasons for the marriage dissolving." I stepped further into the room, wanting to be closer to Jenna. Davis remained by my side the whole time, a silent support. "You saw the stitches, right? Brushed it aside? Pretty much allowed it to continue to happen. Hid the affairs." Disgust swept through me, and I pushed every ounce of that emotion in his direction. "You facilitated this, helped make this happen."

"And where the hell were you?" he sneered. "Out here being a pansy fag taking it up the—"

"Watch your mouth." Davis's voice was low, threatening, and I swallowed thickly at the sound.

"I warned you what would happen if this continued. Well, it has. It's over. You think you can stay here in fantasy land living this disgusting life, disgracing me and our family name? You'll be cut off, fired, kicked out—"

My sharp burst of laughter interrupted his tirade.

"You think this is funny, think I can't—"

I was already shaking my head at him, my eyes wide, anger and amusement at war in my chest. "You're standing in *my* house. The clinic I work at is mine, *my* practice. I own it all. I don't need shit from you, I never have. And honestly, if you don't cut me out of your will, let me tell you now that if I receive a single cent from you, every penny will go to gay-friendly charities." I wanted to fist pump as the idea came to me, but instead, I fought hard to control my need to vomit. I was exhausted, and scared, and my body started to tremble with repressed rage and emotion, all of the pain inflicted on me by this worthless human in front of me.

"Now you need to get out of my home, off my property. Take those papers back with you, and tell Stan unless he wants Jenna to share with the courts the abuse he rolled out, and I'm assuming at some point he'd like to see his children again, then he has forty-eight hours to get them signed and returned." I paused and looked at my sister. We'd previously discussed how she would handle Stan if he chose to be difficult, thank Christ. "Anything else?"

Her eyes stayed on our father. "I'm not coming back. The boys and I have started a great life here. I want you and Mom to know them, see them grow up, but not like this, not if all you can bring to them is hatred. That's up to you, Dad."

My dad gritted his teeth and pulled a face as if he'd smelled something bad. "You've made your choices. You'll live with the consequences."

Jenna grinned. "Happily so."

He narrowed his gaze at her and then picked up the envelope that I assumed contained the divorce papers. He didn't even look in my direction as he walked past me and left the house.

CHAPTER NINETEEN

DAVIS

BARELY RESTRAINED ANGER MADE MY HEAD THROB. I had no idea how Scott had done it, kept his cool like that. He'd owned every single word. I gave him space to comfort Jenna, who was crying. I was certain Scott cried right alongside her. Once outside, I made my way over to Tanner.

"Everything okay?"

I shoved a hand in my pocket and rubbed my head with my other hand. "Yeah, but fuck, that was intense."

"I saw the asshole storm out here. He looked pissed."

I grunted, my jaw clenching. "He was lucky he came out in one piece." I shook my head, disgusted that human beings could be such pieces of shit.

There were not enough cuss words in the world to even begin to describe what I thought of Scott's dad. All I could do was shake out my anger and marvel at how Scott, despite the bullshit upbringing he'd experienced, had ended up intact. Yeah, he'd had what I imagined was all the material crap any kid could ever want, went to the best schools, and never once had to ever worry about money, but I firmly believed it meant nothing in comparison to love, respect, and support.

But he had that now. I'd make sure he knew how important he was for the rest of our days together.

Tanner eyeballed me. "That bad?"

My lips turned up in a sneer. "I know you have your reservations about Scott, but fuck, if you'd heard the bullcrap spewing out of the guy's mouth, his fucking *dad's* mouth, knew everything he'd been through…." I shook my head, not able to carry on as my fury resurfaced. I really had to get myself together. Above all else, I had to be strong for Scott, and that meant being able to think straight.

Tanner's jaw ticked. "I hate that for him. I do." He sighed, blowing out a breath. "I do think he's a good guy. He's taken all of my surly-ass comments, is great with Libby." He shrugged. "I think he's good for you. You're happy."

I nodded. "He makes me happy, yeah. I love him."

Tanner snorted and groaned. "Okay, I don't need to hear any mushy shit. Just know I'll get off his case. I think he's proven himself." He grinned. "Doesn't mean I won't kick his ass if he hurts you or Libby though." I narrowed my eyes at him. "Yeah, yeah, you can take care of yourself, but the truth remains." He looked toward the door and gave a nod. I followed his line of sight. Scott. "I'll leave you to it. We've got the kids as long as you all need."

"Thanks."

Tanner squeezed my shoulder and headed back home while I turned my full attention to Scott. Despite his red-rimmed eyes, he managed a small smile as he stepped over to me. He looked exhausted, but there was also something else evident in his eyes. I searched them, trying to figure it out.

"Hey." He stepped into my open arms, and I held him close. Scott's nose pressed against my skin and he inhaled, causing goose bumps to travel up my arms. "What do you need?" I whispered the question next to his ear.

He shook his head. "Just this."

I tightened my hold on him, pressed an open palm against the back of his head, and angled to press my lips on the first piece of exposed skin I could reach. Silent and still, our slowing breaths and the distant sound of traffic were the only sounds encroaching in our small bubble.

A short time later, he edged his head away so we stood face-to-face. While his eyes remained a little pink, he appeared more together. Emotion stared back at me through his expressive eyes, something akin to relief, maybe even peace.

"I'm glad it's done, you know?"

I nodded and swept a thumb over his cheek, cupping his face. He leaned into my touch, his lips twitching. With a tilt of his head, he pressed a kiss against my palm.

"Thank you for being by my side through it all. I'm not sure I could have—"

"I wouldn't have been anywhere else, but I also call bullshit."

Scott's eyes widened with humor and surprise. "Bullshit?"

"Yep. You're a hell of a lot stronger and braver than you give yourself credit for. You could have done this with or without me. I'm just pleased it was with me," I answered honestly. "How's Jenna?"

Before he answered, Scott's mouth pressed to mine. With his lips moving, he angled his head, taking the kiss deeper. I welcomed the contact, a thrill of desire bolting through me. Far too soon, he pulled back a hairsbreadth. "Whether you believe it or not, you've helped to make me strong and brave. Knowing you've got me means everything." His eyes were wide, his voice passionate.

My lips curved and I still felt the touch of his kiss on them. "I think we can safely say we've got each other." I dotted a kiss to the end of his nose, and his breathy sigh was a sound I'd never tire of hearing. "Jenna?"

"She's okay, *will* be okay. She's having a hot bath, and I talked her into having a glass of wine." He laughed. "It's noon somewhere in the world, right?"

I snorted. "It sure is. Do you want to get the kids and go back to my place or stay here at yours? Or Tanner said he and Carter will look after them for a while. It's up to you."

"I could really do with some cuddles from all three right about now, if that's okay?"

My heart squeezed and my gaze softened. "You never have to ask that." I took his hand in mine and led him toward my best friend's house to pick up our girl and his nephews. While I knew his lifetime of hiding, of being terrified would take time to recover from, my love for him, our love of Libby, of our family, both blood and those we chose as our own, would be enough to get us through it all. With my heart big enough for them all, I smiled.

This was just the beginning.

WANT TO KNOW WHAT HAPPENS NEXT FOR DAVIS AND Scott? Be sure to check out book 3, BECOMING US, for a jump 2 years into the future with this amazing couple.

If you're looking for more heat and sweetness, check out NOT USED TO CUTE. I think you'll love Elijah and Sebastian.

Don't miss out on new releases! Sign up to my NEWSLETTER today!

SNEAK PEEK - BECOMING US
CHAPTER ONE - DAVIS

A QUIET GROAN ESCAPED THE MAN AT MY SIDE. THE sound had me grinning. "Morning," I whispered. While the alarm had gone off, I didn't want to break the morning haze.

"Umm-mmm."

Not sure if Scott was giving a strangled, garbled message, purring, or simply not fully awake, I turned over to face him. His eyes were closed, but a soft smile splayed his lips.

I pressed my own to his mouth, gave him a quick peck, and pulled back. "You awake?" Humor lightened my words.

Scott was not a morning person. For the past six months of us living together, I'd quickly discovered that caffeine and a pastry, or even better, pancakes and bacon, made morning Scott a much nicer guy to be around.

And I had zero problem with that.

Just like I managed his morning woes, he not only wrangled my manic three-year-old, he also clamped his mouth shut when I dumped my dirty clothes on the floor just a few feet away from the laundry basket.

I knew it was a dick move, but after a long day at the coffee shop, spending exhausting, fun hours with Libby, and catching up with everything else that needed doing, that damn basket became my Achilles.

"Was that really the alarm?" He forced one eye open before closing it again.

I snorted. "Afraid so. You can stay in bed, but I have to get my ass up and ready. Jasper's opening for me, but I need to get on top of the weekend prep."

Business was good. While there'd been a turnover in staff due to college starting up, some moving away and such, the past eight months had been solid. Jenna, Scott's sister, was still with me full-time. It took a heap of stress and worry off my shoulders, having someone I trusted implicitly.

We managed to balance shifts fairly, so we were able to work just one weekend each a month as well as managing to be available for our kids.

Though having Scott, and sometimes Carter or Tanner, sorting the pickups and drop-offs too helped. Tanner and I had previously made a good team, but now, with Scott by my side and the addition of Jenna and her boys, we'd become a big extended family.

It worked.

Scott nodded, face still burrowed in the pillow. "I can happily stay in bed."

I pulled myself away from the warm sheets, the chill of the floorboards making me shiver. The holidays were fast approaching, and the weather seemed to be keeping up nicely. We hadn't had snow, but it was colder than a witch's tit some nights.

Once showered and dressed, I returned to our bedroom and leaned over Scott once more, my knee to the bed. He rolled into me and angled his face, knowing what I wanted.

"Love you," I said just as I kissed him. I made to pull away, but his hand clamped on the back of my head, and his mouth opened a little. His tongue swept against the seam of my lips, and I parted for him. I swore, every time this man laid one on me, I became putty in his hands.

The kiss slowed, and I lifted away. My eyes

searched his deep brown ones before roaming to his lips. "I wish I could stay."

Scott no longer looked as sleepy. Instead, heat swirled in his gaze. "I know. Later, your ass is mine." His hand brushed across my thigh and landed on one of my butt cheeks. He gave a light squeeze. "Love you. Have a good day."

"You too." One more brief kiss and I was able to tear myself away.

I crept past Libby's room, not wanting to wake her. Last night she'd woken a couple of times grumbling about something. Her temperature was okay, so whatever had made her wake, I hoped it wouldn't happen again.

Not bothering with a coffee since I'd grab one at work, I headed out. Before I knew it, I was in the kitchen, elbow-deep in pastry and bobbing my head to a dodgy beat Jasper had put on.

"Dare I ask what this song is called?" I asked when Jasper stepped into the kitchen to grab stock for the front counter.

He threw me a mischievous grin. "Too trendy and upbeat for you, old man?" He ducked when I threw a small ball of pastry at him.

"I'm not that damn old," I grumbled. "Just 'cause you're wet behind the ears and have hearing you're still yet to destroy doesn't mean I'm not down with the kids."

I winced, and he laughed. Yeah, saying such bull-shit meant I was getting past it. What the hell? I was barely in my midthirties, but since being a dad, and especially after too many sleepless nights, I felt a hell of a lot more ancient than that.

"You want me to ignore that?" Jasper asked, picking up the pastry I'd thrown and dumping it in the trash.

"Yeah, that'd be best."

"You and Scott should come to the city one weekend with me. I'm heading out in a couple of weekends, meeting some friends and hitting a club."

The look on my face made him snort, so I followed with "Maybe. I'll ask Scott."

"Ha! That means no, right?"

"No." *Yes.* "It just means I'll ask Scott." The thought of heading out for a night of drinks and dancing wasn't what put me off. Hell, getting my buzz on and grinding against Scott was almost enough to get me saying hell yes, but the potential hangover if I drank too much, let alone the late night, had me internally moaning at the thought.

Yes, I was seriously past it.

"I'm staying in a motel just a couple of miles from

the club. It's cheap and cheerful. It'll mean the Uber's cheap too."

I smiled at Jasper, thinking about our differences. He was twenty-three, a college grad who'd returned to town to support his mom after his dad's passing, and a genuinely nice kid. He was also so overqualified for the position that I kinda felt guilty he was still working for me and letting his teaching degree go to waste. The problem with such a small town as Kirkby was with only one high school close by and the next a good sixty miles away, it made teaching positions really difficult to get.

It also meant the poor guy was dealing with the wages from the coffeeshop alone. Yeah, I paid above minimum wage, but it wasn't that much in the grand scheme of things.

"Honestly, I'll think about it and chat to Scott." Admittedly, it had been a while since Scott and I had some alone time. Not that it was a hardship to spend our time with Libby and at home.

I grinned internally, still crazy happy that Scott had agreed to move in with me. It had all worked out. Especially since Jenna was able to take over his place.

"Sure thing," Jasper answered as he headed back out to finish setting up.

The day whizzed on by after that. Between the weekend prep, doing some paperwork, and saying hi to Carter, who stopped by on his lunch break, I considered more and more that a night out of town just may be a good thing.

When Scott came by, Libby holding his hand, I pulled them both into a hug and planted a kiss on both their cheeks. "Hey, you two. That time already?" I glanced at my watch, realizing I was due to wrap up and head on home.

"It sure is." Scott offered that sexy-as-hell smile he reserved solely for me. My gut tightened with the memory of this morning's kiss. The thought of a night away with zero interruptions so we could turn it into one of debauchery was looking even better when heat crept up his neck.

I rarely held back how much Scott affected me and meant to me. And after a couple of years together, all it took was a glance for him to know exactly what was on my mind.

Pulling my gaze away from Scott, I focused on Libby and crouched before her. "You had a great day?"

She nodded enthusiastically and almost socked me in the eye as she thrust out her arm to show me what she was wearing. "Made it with my Scott." A quick glance in Scott's direction showed me he melted at her words. It got the both of us every time.

"Wow. Pretty bracelet there, princess. You two did a great job."

"Yep." She looked thoroughly proud of herself. "And I made you one." She turned her gaze up to Scott. "Daddy's?"

"I've got it right here." Scott grinned down at her and pulled out a bright pink and green beaded bangle, with the odd bead having tinsel and some glitter attached. "I told you Daddy would love it. Here you go." He handed it over, a shit-eating grin on his face.

I had zero doubt my fixed smile was more of a grimace, but there was pretty much nothing I wouldn't do for my girl. She was spoiled rotten, and I had zero regrets about that. Plus, I'd wear whatever crazy stuff she created with absolute pride.

Just last week she'd discovered makeup, courtesy of Jenna. I'd managed to snap a photo of Scott complete with blue and green eyeshadow, something red and slimy on his cheeks with glitter on it, an orange lipstick that had made my sides hurt from laughing so much, and a black crayon or pen or something drawn all around his eyes.

While the same had been done to me, it was

Scott's hairclips and butterflies that had set his image off spectacularly.

We were both suckers.

We also had to pay Jenna back somehow for the makeup kit she'd provided.

With the elastic bracelet snapped into place on my wrist, I jiggled it.

"It's soooo pwety." Her pretty eyes were opened wide. "My Scott has one. Look, Daddy." She tugged at Scott's arm so he knelt, then snapped the grotesque necklace on his neck. Scott winced.

"Careful there, Libby. Don't destroy Scott's windpipe." I grinned widely at Scott, who, complete with bright and dodgy-looking necklace, was freakin' gorgeous. How could he not be when he wore the love he had for Libby so openly?

"Sorry." She spun to face Scott and threw her arms around his neck. After a big squeeze, she planted a loud kiss on his mouth. "You 'kay?"

Scott stood with her in his arm. "I sure am. I think this pretty necklace has magical powers, or maybe it's your kiss."

I stood and looked on as Libby nodded.

"I fink it's my kisses."

"Makes sense," he said.

After another bob of her head, she gave him one

more kiss. "Love you." She then wriggled her whole body to get down.

Scott's smile lit up his face. "Love you too, Libby." He set her on her feet, and she raced off to Jessie, one of my staff, who was clearing tables. His gaze on me, he asked, "You almost done?"

"Give me five and I'm all yours."

His eyes turned molten, urging me to get my ass into gear and spend the rest of the afternoon and evening with my favorite two people.

DOWNLOAD **BECOMING US (#3)** FOR FREE IN KINDLE Unlimited.

THANKS

Thanks for reading *I've Got You*. I do hope you enjoyed Scott and Davis's story. I appreciate your help in spreading the word, including telling a friend. Before you go, it would mean so much to me if you would take a few minutes to write a review and share how you feel about my story so others may find my work. Reviews really do help readers find books. Please leave a review on your favorite book site.

ACKNOWLEDGMENTS

I'm blessed with the level of support and love I receive every single day, not only by my direct family and friends, but also my chosen family in the book community. My Hot Tree Editing crew always have my back. Of course I'm biased, but my editors, final-eyes readers, betas, and my kickarse admin really are the best. Gorgeous HTE women, you keep me sane and grounded. I wouldn't have the head-space to achieve everything I do without your unwavering kindness and backing. I adore you all.

My bestie at BookSmith Design has once again rocked my cover, capturing the beauty of being a dad in her design. You know me so damn well, lady. Thank you.

RM Gilmore from RMGraphX, we've been working together for years. I appreciate your sass, your vision, and your mad formatting skills… all I count as a blessing. Thank you for being in my life.

Justine. I adore you, wench. Thanks for being

such a badass, and for your e-book formatting expertise.

Thanks to my lovely readers who've taken the time out to read my words. I hope they offered you escapism.

ABOUT THE AUTHOR

I live and breathe all things book related. Usually with at least three books being read and two WiPs being written at the same time, life is merrily hectic. I tend to do nothing by halves, so I happily seek the craziness and busyness life offers.

Living on my small property in Queensland with my human family as well as my animal family of cows, chooks, and dogs, I really do appreciate the beauty of the world around me and am a believer that love truly is love.

To check for updates head to my website:

HTTPS://BECCASEYMOUR.COM
HTTPS://LANDING.MAILERLITE.COM/WEBFORMS/LANDING/R9F0I4
Plus, join my Facebook group.
HTTPS://WWW.FACEBOOK.COM/GROUPS/ROMMANCEWITHBECCALOUISA/
On TikTok, follow me here: HTTPS://WWW.TIKTOK.COM/@BECCASEYMOURWRITES

facebook.com/beccaseymourauthor

twitter.com/beccaseymour_

instagram.com/authorbeccaseymour

bookbub.com/authors/becca-seymour

amazon.com/Becca-Seymour/e/B07NYXX6JP

ALSO BY BECCA SEYMOUR

Zone Defense

No Take Backs | No More Secrets | No Wrong Moves

Fast Break

Rules, Schmules! | Facts, Smacts!

True-Blue

Let Me Show You | I've Got You | Becoming Us | Thinking It Over| Always For You | It's Not You | Our First & Last

Outback Boys

Stumble | Bounce | Wobble

Stand-Alone Contemporary

Not Used To Cute | High Alert | Realigned | Amalgamated

Urban Fantasy Romance

Thicker Than Water